LICCLE BIT

LICCLE BIT

Alex Wheatle

www.atombooks.net

For Clement, Peter and Dorothy

ATOM

First published in Great Britain in 2015 by Atom

7 9 10 8

Copyright © 2015 by Alex Wheatle

The moral right of the author has been asserted.

A CIP catalogue record for this book is available from the British Library.

ISBN 978-0-349-00199-9

Printed and bound in Great Britain by Clays Ltd, Elcograf S.p.A.

Papers used by Atom are from well-managed forests
and other responsible sources.

Atom
An imprint of
Little, Brown Book Group
Carmelite House
50 Victoria Embankment
London EC4Y 0DZ

An Hachette UK Company
www.hachette.co.uk

www.atombooks.co.uk

1

Beauty and the Beast

It all started two months ago. A normal day at school, if you can call going to my school normal. The buzzer signalled the end of the last lesson of the day. It was Wednesday. And after school on Wednesdays, the girls in my year practise their street-dancing in the gym. So Jonah Hani, McKay Tambo and I ran through the corridors, bumping into other kids and teachers, to try and get the best view through the gym door window.

When we arrived, there were two kids from our year already in our space. They saw us coming, looked at the size of McKay and decided to go missing. As usual, McKay hogged the window.

'Get your fat head out of the way, man!' complained Jonah.

'Give us room, man!' I moaned.

Although I was looking at the back of McKay's head, I

could tell he was grinning. 'Rest your toes, bredren,' McKay said. 'Sweetness is staring at me. Venetia's looking *ripe*, I'm telling you. Man! Her legs are seriously fit. Believe it!'

Using our combined strength, Jonah and I managed to shove McKay aside and take a peep for ourselves. McKay wasn't wrong. Venetia, dressed in a pink vest and white shorts, was rocking it. The other girls were all looking at her, trying to keep up with her movements, and man, Venetia could rock. Ms Lane, the street-dancing tutor, was nodding and tapping her feet. Too right she was nodding! Venetia could dance better than her!

'Man! If I had ten minutes with Venetia,' Jonah remarked.

'If you had ten minutes with her you wouldn't know what to do, bruv,' laughed McKay.

'Ten minutes?' I said. 'All I need is half of that and she'll be my girl! Believe it!'

McKay and Jonah collapsed, laughing, and fell to the floor holding their stomachs. 'You, Bit?' McKay said.

I wasn't the tallest guy in our year. In fact I was about the second shortest. Some girl called me Liccle Bit in Year 7 and it stuck.

'With your Oompa-Loompa height and your slavery days' haircut?' McKay teased. 'There's more chance of Lionel Messi playing for Crongton Wanderers.'

'OK,' said Jonah, climbing to his feet. 'If you think you're a G, chat to Venetia when she finishes her dance session.'

'Yeah,' said McKay, pushing me out of the way so he could look through the window. 'I dare you to ask her to link you up.'

'Not with you two around,' I said.

'Man! I can feel the chicken wings flapping over my head,' joked Jonah.

'For a girl like Venetia you have to have the goods, bruv,' reasoned McKay. 'You have to have an iPhone, Dr Dre headphones, the latest Adidas trainers, a decent Mohican head-trim and be tall enough so her head can fit under your chin. Fit girls like to look up at a brother.'

'And, Bit, you ain't got none of that,' said Jonah. 'So just step off and forget about chatting to a piece of fitness like Venetia.'

I began to walk away, knowing that even if I did have Dr Dre headphones and the rest of it, I still wouldn't have the nerve to talk to Venetia. Jonah and McKay caught up with me and we bounced out of the school.

We all lived on the South Crongton estate, a ten-minute step from the school. Jonah Hani lived on the second floor of my block and I was on the fifth. McKay Tambo lived with his dad and his older brother in the block opposite. God knows what they sank in his flat cos they were all pay-per-view wrestler size.

'Believe me, man,' McKay boasted. 'In five years' time I'm gonna be riding in a sick car and have two girls sitting on my lap that'll make Venetia look like an elephant danced on her face.'

'And where you gonna get money for your sick car?' asked Jonah.

'I'm gonna be a businessman!' said McKay. 'You think I'm joking? I'm gonna open up a world of hot wings restaurants with my special recipe. If that bruv from Ashburton ends can do it with the sauce then why not me? Trust me! My wings are gonna be hotter and tastier than any rubbish that Kentucky or Alabama sell. Believe it! I'll have chicks serving, dressed in little aprons and nothing underneath. They'll be wearing six-inch stilettos and sunglasses. And there'll be music playing in all of my takeaways.'

'But you have to go to uni to learn how to run a business,' I said. 'And your maths? Your maths is just . . . *wrong*! How you gonna count the money good? You'll need a degree . . .'

'And that takes three years,' added Jonah.

'Three years *after* you done your A levels,' I said. 'And going uni costs a mad bag of money these days.'

'Man!' McKay exclaimed. 'You brothers know how to pop a man's flow.'

'And you won't make any money anyway,' laughed Jonah. 'Cos you'll get your munch on and sink all the profits. If you're in the takeaway, customers ain't seeing no wings. Believe it!'

'Bomb you.'

McKay chased Jonah all the way to our estate but by the time we got there, McKay was breathing and walking all funny.

'Jonah, I'm gonna mess you up tomorrow,' McKay threatened. 'Your little round head is gonna say hello to my big fist. And after that I'm gonna drop you in the boys' toilet!'

'And you're gonna say hello to my frisbee that I'm gonna put in your mouth so you can't eat any more hot wings,' retaliated Jonah.

McKay, now breathing like a white guy in an Olympic

4

10,000-metre final, didn't have the energy to chase any more so he wearily stepped his way to his block. Jonah and I headed to our own concrete slab. 'So what homework you gonna do tonight?' he asked.

'Art,' I answered. 'Gonna sketch my gran. You know I love to get my portraits on rather than draw a sad apple or someting.'

'What about maths?'

'Never gonna be good at it so what's the point?'

I watched Jonah run along the second-floor balcony to his front door. I was hoping that his sixteen-year-old sister, Heather, would open the door. She had it going on but I'd never tell Jonah that.

She didn't appear.

Deciding to remain on the concrete staircase instead of taking the lift, I trudged my way to the fourth floor. I heard loud voices and kept still. It was my sister, Elaine, and her ex, Manjaro.

'What's wrong with you!' Manjaro yelled. I remembered that he had this mad vein in his neck that always bulged whenever he raised his voice. I always imagined it was a sleeping baby snake. 'Take the money! Buy some garms for the baby, innit. Buy some nappies and toys or something.'

'I ain't taking your dirty money,' Elaine shouted back. 'Why can't you leave me alone? Mum's gonna be back soon. Don't you get it? We're over! Your account has expired! The machine has rejected your card and spat it out. I ain't taking your shit any more so stop coming around and blocking my doormat!'

'So I can't be a dad to my son? Is that what you're telling me, Elaine? Don't you know me? You *know* I can't let that happen. At least take the money.'

'*Piss* your money! Leave me alone!'

'You're gonna wish you didn't say that.'

'You don't even realise what you've done to me!' yelled Elaine. 'You just *don't* get it. You're so messed up you don't even think you've done me wrong. Trust me! You need help. So why don't you remove your sad self off my slab and leave me alone.'

I heard my sister's footsteps stomping up the concrete steps and then my front door being slammed. At that moment my mobile phone rang. I answered it as I started to climb the stairs again. It was Gran. 'Where are you, Lemar?'

'Just coming, Gran. I'll be home in a sec.'

I looked up. Manjaro was coming down the stairs. He looked at my cheap phone and smiled. 'Let me have a look,' he said.

I didn't want to look him in the eye. He had a don't-mess-with-me build, a slim moustache like my granddad had had and a goatee beard. I think the stud in his left ear was a diamond and his hair was always well trimmed. His clothes weren't name-brand though. He was wearing a plain blue T-shirt, an anorak, black jeans and cool Reeboks. Every time I saw him my heart Usain Bolted; McKay reckoned he had deleted two brothers. He was rumoured to be the grandson of some legendary G called Herbman Blue. Why did my sister have a baby with him?

'Didn't you hear me, Liccle Bit?' he said. 'Let me have a look at your phone. Stop fretting. Ain't gonna do anything to you. Cool your foot.'

I hated him calling me Liccle Bit. But what could I do? Manjaro was about ten years older than me and he was the king G of our estate. Reluctantly, I gave him my phone. He scanned it like those forensic feds in the white shell suits studying a murder scene – they'd been to South Crongton a few times. 'You know,' he said. 'If you did a liccle something for me I might be able to set you up for an upgrade.'

I said nothing. He looked at me and laughed. He ruffled my hair with his right hand. 'Could do with a trim,' he said. 'If you do a liccle something for me I might trim your head myself. I look after the brothers who work for me, you know it.'

He gave me my phone back, then he bounced down five steps. I breathed out a long sigh. He stopped and turned around. My heart sprinted again. 'Tell your sister she should have taken the money. I know your fam is struggling. Your mum can't make too much at her DIY store.'

I tried damn hard not to show my vexness with him chatting about my mum – she tried her best. He offered me one final look and was gone.

2

The Home Front

I turned my key in my front door and entered my flat. Gran was cooking. Elaine was trying to feed Jerome with something out of a jar but my baby nephew wasn't having it. Screaming down the flat he was. Mind you, if I had to sink what Jerome was served I would bawl murder too.

'You were going to walk right past me,' Gran said, spotting me in the hallway. 'Come here, Lemar! Let me see you.'

I went over to Gran, peeped into the pan and saw bolognese bubbling sweetly. The spaghetti was waiting to be boiled in another pot. Gran hugged me like I was a money tree – her forearms were thick like the two-litre Coke bottles Mum liked to buy. She gave me a long kiss on my forehead and embraced me again. 'Don't walk past like you don't know me!' she warned.

I tried not to walk on the street with Gran because she could get embarrassing.

After nodding a quick hi to Elaine I went to my bedroom to fetch my sketch pad. I returned to the kitchen, pencils in hand. 'So, Gran, you ready?'

'Can't you see I'm cooking? When we've eaten I'll sit down for you then. Now go off and do whatever other homework you have.'

'And let me check it when you've finished,' Elaine added.

Jerome was still kicking up a fuss and refusing his food.

We had three bedrooms in our flat. Gran had one, Elaine and Jerome had another and I had the smallest. Mum slept on the couch during the week but at weekends she swapped with Gran. Elaine and Jerome were waiting for a council place and a world of people from the council housing department and social services had been to visit them. But Jerome was now eleven months old and still no flat.

Entering my room, I threw my rucksack on to my single bed and thought about doing my maths homework. Mum had set up a little desk-sized table in the corner of my room with a second-hand swivel chair she had carried home from work. I sat on that chair, opened my maths book and looked at all the questions to do with circles, radiuses and something called pi. I couldn't make any sense out of it so I closed my book and got my snooze on.

Dinner was served an hour later. It was just Gran and me at the table. Mum hadn't arrived home from work yet and Elaine was trying to rock Jerome asleep.

'Have you spoken to that girl you're sweet on?' Gran asked with a twinkle. She had these caramel eyes surrounded by untold tiny moles – I would have to draw them in when I got my sketch on.

Before I had a chance to reply, we heard the key turning in the front door. Mum entered the flat looking all weary and preoccupied. She dumped a couple of shopping bags in the kitchen, kissed Gran on the cheek, ruffled my hair and took a can of beer from the fridge.

'Hi, Mum,' I said. 'Good day at work?'

'Not really. Damn customers are so feisty sometimes.'

'What did they do to you today?'

'Not now, Lemar,' Mum replied. 'I can't sit down and eat. There's a bag of dirty clothes in the front room and they're not gonna wash themselves. Did you ring the washing machine people, Mum?'

Staring at her food, Gran twirled some spaghetti bolognese on her fork and fed herself. She didn't answer until she stuck it in her mouth. 'You told me late last night, Yvonne,' Gran explained. 'I was half-sleeping! I'm sorry ... I forgot.'

'*Mum!* I *need* our washing machine to be working again. The drum is out of shape. Call them now. I have to go to the launderette.'

'Do you want a hand, Mum?' I offered.

'Haven't you got homework to do?'

'Yes, but ...'

'But do your homework, Lemar!'

An hour and a half later I was sketching Gran in the lounge. Every other second she was making it difficult for me by smiling and turning her head. I just about got the outline of her face and I had started on the eyes. It was hard to get her double chin right and she had two wavy lines that roller-coasted her forehead. I guessed Gran was in her late sixties but she never told me her age. Mum once told me not to ask. Elaine had finally managed to get Jerome asleep and she was watching some music video station on the TV.

'You never answered my question,' Gran said. 'Did you talk to that girl who tickles your fancy?'

My hard drive tried to think of a response while my face was warming up like someone had connected me to the kettle. My sister answered for me. 'Venetia is the girl he likes,' she revealed. 'Lemar has got more chance of winning *The X Factor* than linking with her. All the brothers in her year and Year 11 want her. Even a couple of girls I know fancy her.'

'It's *not* Venetia,' I protested. 'What do you know? You don't even go to my school any more.'

'I've still got friends in the sixth form,' Elaine argued.

'That's enough,' said Gran.

Just then we all heard the front door opening. Mum appeared with two trolleyfulls of washing. I ran to give her a hand and helped her hang the garms on a clothes horse in the bathroom. When I returned to the lounge Gran had got up to make herself a cup of coffee.

'Gran!'

'I soon come, Lemar. Don't fret.'

Picking up my sketch pad, Mum looked at my quarter-sketched portrait of Gran. 'This is really good,' she remarked. 'Keep it up.'

'He hasn't done his maths yet though,' Elaine put in.

'I'll do it later, Mum.'

Mum was still nodding, appreciating my artwork. It was nice to see. Mum hardly ever stopped to take a look at my schoolwork. 'Mum, can you take me to get a haircut on the weekend?'

Placing her hands on her hips, Mum gave me one of her looks. Then the right hand came off and started pointing at me. 'Lemar, you know the washing machine isn't working. You know how much that gonna cost me if I need a new drum? Them cable people are ringing me up at work complaining that I haven't paid their bill, the catalogue people are ringing off my phone every day asking for their money and you're asking about a blasted haircut!'

'He wants a Mohican, Mum,' Elaine jumped in. 'That's the latest lick for kids of his age.'

'The latest lick is gonna have to wait,' said Mum. 'Or if he wants he can have a lick in his friggin head!'

Storming off to the kitchen, Mum warmed up her dinner in the microwave. Gran returned with her coffee and I worked on my portrait for the next twenty minutes before Gran got tired and wanted to lie down.

I went to my bed that night feeling cheated. *I didn't tell Elaine to go out and have a baby,* I thought. *It's not my fault that Gran is living with us and no one can blame me for the money Mum owes to the catalogue people; most of what she ordered was spent on buggies and stuff for Jerome. She can't even give me ten pounds to get my hair trimmed. What's ten pounds? And I'll go to school tomorrow and the day after and Jonah and McKay will keep taking the living piss out of my head.*

3

A Job for Manjaro

Next day, there wasn't time to dwell on what Manjaro had said. Some kid in my year was caught selling skunk in the library. Tavari Wilkins was his name. He didn't exactly have all the letters on his keypad. I mean, what was he thinking selling weed in the library with the Google Map eyes of Mrs Parfitt on everyone? He lived in the North Crongton estate, where they put all the single mothers, asylum people and the refugees; my sister said that if they offered her a flat there, she wasn't taking it.

As McKay, Jonah and I bounced out of school, Jonah asked, 'So what's gonna happen to Tavari?'

'The feds are gonna interrogate him,' said McKay. 'He'll be taken down the fed station, beat up by ten feds and told to sink his own shit and theirs too.'

'The feds do that?' Jonah wondered.

'Trust me, they would do worse than that if he was over sixteen. They would rape him with a mallet, give him a serious injection, take out his kidney and then say to him, "If you don't spill who gave you the drugs, you ain't getting your kidney back."'

'I think that's a bit Hollywood,' I said.

'What did you say, Bit?' McKay challenged. 'What do you know? The feds get away with anything. Look how they blasted that brother on the northside with a rocket-propelled grenade the other day . . .'

'It was a gun,' I argued.

'*That's* what they told you on the news,' insisted McKay. 'It was a grenade that killed the brother. The same ones they use in Afghanistan. He had bits of road, car-metal, engine and wheel-rubber in his face. There's a crater in the street. The feds can get away with any shit.'

'It's true,' Jonah said. 'My sister told me that her boyfriend got stopped and searched in a charity shop.'

'Your sister got a boyfriend?' I asked.

'Yeah,' confirmed Jonah. 'He goes to Crongton College, plays basketball. He's got some serious detail in his arm muscles and a crazy bald head.'

My heart sank and I had this weird feeling in my stomach. Why I'd thought I would ever stand a chance with Heather, I didn't know.

We stepped into the corner shop near the entrance of the estate. As usual there was a queue of people waiting to charge their electric keys and gas meters. McKay bought a Twix, a Mars bar and a Coke, Jonah bought a packet of custard creams and I found enough change to buy a Twirl. We came out of the shop getting our munch on. I sank my teeth into my Twirl, looked up and spotted Manjaro and his crew cycling towards us. *Damn!* I said in my head. I'd never thought I'd see Manjaro on a bike. He was wearing the same blue T-shirt. The other two guys were wearing blue baseball caps. The sleeping baby snake in his neck looked skinnier today. I tried to casually turn around but he had spotted me.

Before I knew it, Jonah took off and sprinted towards our block like a Jamaican who couldn't hold his piss, McKay returned to the shop and I was left to face Manjaro on my own. He knew I'd seen him so I couldn't just pretend I hadn't. His mountain bike screeched to a halt right in front of me. 'Liccle Bit!' he greeted.

'What's going on, Manjaro?' I tried to sound cool and older than my years but my heart was pumping like a poodle about to be mauled by a tiger.

'So you just finished school?' he said.

'Yeah.' *It's a quarter to four and I'm wearing my school uniform. Dumb question*, I thought.

'A waste of time, bredren,' Manjaro dismissed. He climbed off his bike and stepped towards me. 'You're doing what they want you to do.'

'Huh?'

'So you can survive in this world,' Manjaro reasoned. 'They want you to go school, then to uni, then have a job so they can collect your taxes. They don't really give a shit about you unless you *don't* pay their taxes.'

I didn't respond.

'Do me a favour, Liccle Bit,' Manjaro asked.

'What favour?' I asked.

'Go into that shop and buy me three of those choc-nut lollies.'

I thought about it as Manjaro plucked a fat wallet from his back jeans pocket. It didn't seem real – the top G of our estate wanted to suck on a lolly? He peeled out a twenty-pound note and handed it over. The note was crisp and brand new. I could almost smell it.

'Three choc-nut lollies,' Manjaro repeated. 'And if you want get one for yourself.'

Manjaro's two friends looked at each other and laughed. I went into the shop. McKay was still in there, flicking through a football magazine. 'I'm listening and watching, bruv,' he whispered.

'Yeah, thanks for having my back!' I said.

'Just buy the lollies and go missing.'

'That was my plan.'

'If you buy a choc-nut lolly for yourself can you give me half?'

'*No!* Why don't you read more about Cristiano Ronaldo!'

I went back outside and handed over the choc-nut lollies to Manjaro. His two bredrens were still chuckling. They made me feel smaller than I was. If I was bigger and older I would have banged them up. Or I would've hoped that I could've banged them up. I went to hand over the ten-pound note plus change.

'Keep it,' said Manjaro.

'What?'

'I said keep it. And you don't have to pay any tax on it. Me *gone!*'

Manjaro and his bredrens zigzagged down the road with one hand on their handlebars as they sucked on their lollies. I hoped they would lose their balance and drop their cold treats.

I stared at the tenner in my hand like it was a gold nugget in silent film days. *Could get a wicked hair-trim with this,* I thought. *Or maybe I should buy a new baseball hat? Might be better if I put it towards a new pair of trainers?* Before I could think of any other way I could spend my money, I felt McKay's big right hand on my shoulder. 'You can buy me a choc-nut lolly.' He smiled. 'And don't go on tight. You know I would do the same for you.'

'No, you wouldn't,' I said.

'Bit, bredren!' McKay protested. 'How can you slander me like that? If my granny was dying of thirst on a summer's day in her flat on the ninety-ninth floor, I would *still* buy you a choc-nut ice lolly first before I checked on her. You know that!'

McKay's granny lived on the third floor in a block the other side of our estate. I bought McKay his ice lolly just to shut him up and I pocketed the change. As I made my way to my slab McKay was telling me I was his best bredren, but I'd heard him say similar stuff when Jonah bought him something.

I was walking up the steps to my gates when I heard a familiar voice. It was my dad. But it was Wednesday. I couldn't remember the last time I saw my dad on a Wednesday, the day Mum had an afternoon off during the week. I waited on the concrete landing in the stairwell below my parents.

'So what is your worthless backside doing at my door?' snapped Mum.

'I wanted to see my kids,' replied Dad. 'I wanted to see my grandson. I haven't seen him for a while.'

'Take your miserable self from my door, man!' Mum raised her voice. 'I don't want you messing up their heads when you promise to come but don't reach and all of a sudden you're planting your dirty foot on my doormat. You've let them down too many times.'

'But I explained,' Dad pleaded. 'Stefanie was sick. We had to take her to the hospital ...'

'Before you screwed *that* woman you had kids here. You still have kids here who you always let down so why don't you remove your worthless self from my door and go back to your dirty crotches ...'

'She has a name.'

'Yes she does, and I just called her it! Do you have some child support to give me?'

There was a long pause. 'No. It's been very difficult with Shirley not being able to work. She has to care for Stefanie, you know ...' Another pause. 'I just wanna see Elaine or Lemar if they're home. Chat to them for a few minutes, see my grandson and explain to them what happened ...'

'Elaine and Lemar ain't here!'

'I'm here, Mum,' I said, climbing the stairs again. I wasn't going to let her fling my dad away before I'd had the chance to see him.

Dad looked at me in surprise and sort of half-smiled. He was wearing his denim jacket over his catalogue-delivery-man sweater. I could see from the look on Mum's face that she wasn't happy about my timing. Not happy at all. 'Lemar, get your late self in the yard and I'm sure you've got some homework to deal with.'

I shot Dad a glance as I passed him and gave him a touch of a smile. 'Hi, Dad,' I greeted. I wanted to ask how Stefanie was doing but I didn't want to annoy Mum. Not with her I'm-going-to-war face on.

Dad looked stressed around the eyes. 'What's gwarnin', Lemar?'

'Same old,' I replied. 'Just—'

'Get your backside in the yard!' Mum ordered me. She folded her arms and I knew she was remove-my-TV-from-my-room serious. I felt the wind as she slammed the door behind me. Raised voices soon followed.

A smell of macaroni cheese niced up my nostrils and I found Gran in the kitchen checking on the oven. 'Looks good.' She smiled at me, straightening up. 'Don't worry your liccle self about your mother and father arguing. Them only arguing because them care for you.'

'Where's Elaine?' I asked.

'Oh, she and Jerome are visiting a friend.'

Gran couldn't make me feel better. She never could when Mum and Dad were arguing. She started to sing her favourite Bob Marley song. 'Don't worry, about a thing, cos every liccle thing, is gonna be all right!' She gave me a hopeful smile and I forced a smile back. I wish I could say that Gran's song made me feel better, but I'd heard it too many times and I was too old for that now.

I went to my room and threw my rucksack on my bed. I looked at my copy of an L. S. Lowry painting of men and women going about their business, backdropped by tall chimneys and factories. Dad had bought it for me for my last birthday and now it was hanging over my bed. Stefanie was my five-year-old half-sister and she'd been visiting the doctor's since she was born. Dad never fully explained what was wrong with her but it was something to do with her having bad blood or something.

Dad walked out on my mum when I was seven years old. Mum's never forgiven him for leaving her and moving in with Shirley, Stefanie's mum. They used to be long-time friends, went to school together. I didn't see Dad for the longest time, until I started secondary school; I think he was too scared to visit but Elaine used to sneak out and see him at Shirley's flat. If Mum ever found out about that she would probably fling Elaine over the balcony with a buggy and a high chair tied to her ankle. Dad started to visit just over a year ago, around about the same time Stefanie went into hospital for the first time. Mum was cussing bad-word at first but then she agreed to let Dad take me out every other Saturday. If he brought me home late then Mum would cuss him till Dad got back in his van. Mum gave me two instructions I had to keep to whenever Dad took me out for the day. One, never, ever call Shirley 'Mum', and two, never mention Stefanie's name when I returned. Over time, I'd grown closer to Dad, but he hadn't taken me out for months. He did send me the painting for my last birthday though. Yep, my family had the goods for any Jeremy Kyle show and I was kinda surprised that the producers hadn't offered us any money to roll on to the programme.

As I lay on my bed, I heard the front door slam and voices start up in the kitchen. I scrambled to my bedroom window and leaned out to peer down at the car park below the flats. I watched my dad get into his van and drive off, alone. I couldn't help wondering if he felt as bad as I did right then.

4

The Top G Always Asks Twice

The next Saturday, Jonah and I had been playing God of War on McKay's PlayStation 3. As usual I lost but I had a good vibe cos McKay's dad bought us a bucket of Tennessee Fried Chicken and fries for our lunch. We chased that down with two bottles of chilled Coke so we all had a trailer-load of energy to get rid of. We headed to the park between North and South Crongton just to chill out and watch the older brothers play football. Sometimes a few chicks would hang out there, so I got my strut on and walked like I owned half of New York. McKay and Jonah were laughing at me but I didn't care.

It was a nice day, warm enough to get away with just wearing a T-shirt, and when we reached the park most of the brothers who were balling were wearing blue tops and blue sweatbands – standard South Crong garms. At the other end of the park, the North Crong brothers, who were also playing some ball, wore black. The tall oak trees of Gully Wood towered behind them. This was an area where only a brave or a mad South Crong bruv of my age would tread. Too dangerous. Bisecting the wood, twisting this way and that was the Crongton stream, the location of the last shanking and murder in the area. I wanted to draw a sketch of this no-man's-land but what would those North Crong brothers make of me with my pencils and A3 sketch paper?

It was a North Crong bruv who had been deleted. The feds found him face-down in the water with half of his nose missing. McKay reckoned it was Manjaro who gave him the ratchet surgery. The whole thing was messed up. If my gran wanted to step to North Crong on one of her afternoon walks, she'd be much safer there than me. God! If Manjaro had to ask any more favours from me I hoped he kept it to buying lollies from a corner store.

Circling us at our end of the park were a few guys performing wheelies on bikes. Others were chilling, listening to rap, grime and R & B blasting out from boom boxes. Everybody else was playing with their mobile phones. There were a number of B-class girls showing off their tattooed necks and calves, cheap weaves and kiss-curls. You could've made some serious garden rakes from their false eyelashes. I did a quick scan of the place but got no sight of Venetia. A-class girls like her didn't come to the park. As we searched for a place to sit our asses down we overheard a couple of brothers saying that some beef had taken place earlier between a blue-topped South Crong brother and a black-vested North Crong guy.

Threats were promised and curses were spat. Nothing usually kicked off following these park beefs, not with everybody looking and their mobile phones primed to film it, so the brothers and sisters still had their chill on.

We found a spot just behind one of the goals.

'Should've bought another Coke with us,' said McKay. 'Jonah, man! Why did you have to kill off the last bottle?'

'I didn't kill off the last bottle,' protested Jonah. 'It was Bit.'

'I deny that to the fullest, man! Go away with that!'

'As you two deleted the last bottle then you two have to put forward your cents and pences to a next one,' demanded McKay. 'Can't believe it, bruv! Come to watch the game and I can't get my gulp on ... and I have the need for peanuts.'

Just then someone in a blue top scored a goal. The ball rolled to McKay and he picked it up. 'Hey, Nine Months, gimme the ball, man,' the goalkeeper jibed.

'Who are you calling Nine Months, you skinny piece of renkin' shit!' McKay retaliated.

Jonah and I swapped knowing glances and shook our heads.

'You come to the park to do some exercise, fat boy?' the goalkeeper taunted, turning around to the players to see if any of them were laughing. 'You need a football team of personal trainers, bruv, and mind you don't dent the turf when you're sitting on it!'

'I'm denting the turf cos I'm grinding your girl underneath me, skinny boy!'

I could not hold back my laughter any more and Jonah and other onlookers did likewise. I stopped laughing when I detected something mad going on with the goalkeeper's eyes.

'Come step up to me, fat boy, and say that again and we'll see who'll step out of the park on legs or a stretcher!'

McKay stood up and kicked the ball away. The goalkeeper ignored it and stepped towards McKay. Everybody tensed up. We heard another voice. It was calm but it had authority.

'Leave the boy alone, bruv.'

We all looked behind. It was Manjaro. Every time I saw him I got this feeling in my whole body like an ice cube sitting on a painful, wonky tooth. He had a blue vest on with a small white towel draped over his left shoulder. His arms were thick like an Olympic weightlifter's and he looked like he had just got his gym on. He was walking with three of his bredrens. One was white, one was mixed-race and the other black. They were all wearing blue baseball caps.

The goalkeeper smiled an uneasy smile. 'Respect, Manjaro, just bantering with the yout' dem, you know.'

McKay sat down and when I glanced at Jonah I noticed that he had crawled ten metres away.

'Man don't appreciate a bigger man troubling a smaller man,' said Manjaro. 'The biggest man was once a baby so leave the yout' them alone. You never know what size the baby might grow.'

'No worries, Manjaro.' The goalkeeper retreated. 'As I said, it was just banter. That's all.'

'That's all right then,' Manjaro said. 'Man doesn't like to see a South Crong yout' troubling another South Crong yout'. Are you receiving?'

'I'm receiving, Manjaro.' The goalkeeper tried a laugh to ease his nerves. 'Of course I'm receiving.'

Collecting the ball, the goalkeeper kicked it upfield and took his position in the goal. He didn't glance behind. I was edging closer to Jonah when Manjaro turned around and seized me with his eyes. *Shit!*

'Liccle Bit!' he greeted. The snake in his neck did a little dance. He swaggered over to me and wiped his forehead with his towel. Out of the corner of my eye I saw Jonah slide further away.

'What's going on, Manjaro?' I replied.

'Are you getting your chill on in the park for the next hour?'

I wasn't sure how to answer. I glanced at Jonah and he was nodding his head. I looked at McKay and he was shaking his. 'Er, yeah, just watching the football,' I finally answered.

'That's good,' Manjaro said. 'I have a shopping mission to go on but I'll check you back here, right?'

'Yeah, that's all good.' I nodded.

I spotted McKay still shaking his head.

'So wait till I return, right,' Manjaro said.

I nodded, despite McKay closing his eyes in despair.

Manjaro and his crew left. Jonah crawled back, warily glancing over his shoulder as he did so. He waited until Manjaro was out of earshot before he spoke. 'Wise move, Bit,' he said. 'You can't say no to man like that. I wonder what he wants to check you for?'

'You should've said no,' interrupted McKay. 'He might want you to do all kinds of shit. What you gonna do if he asks you to be his mule and fly to Thailand carrying a sack-load of drugs in your belly?'

'I don't think he's gonna ask me to do that, McKay.' *But*

what will he ask me to do? I fretted. Maybe McKay wasn't far wrong.

'How do you know?' said McKay. 'Don't be a mule, bruv! You'll have the runs for the rest of your days. Ain't no fun stepping everywhere with untold toilet rolls. And you know that in countries like Thailand if they find drugs on you they give you seven hundred years' prison with no parole. And their prisons are the worst in the world, bredren. They make you choose whether you want an arm or a leg chopped off. It's all part of the sentence, believe it! Then they strip you down to your boxers and drop you in a big hole two miles deep. Once a day they fling in stale bread, rat's liver and baboon soup for the prisoners to fight over. Believe it, bredren. You'll end up wishing they executed you and sliced off your head.'

'I'm not going to Thailand,' I protested. God! I wished he wouldn't make jokes about it. I tried not to let on how proper scared I was. 'Mum would kill me if I just thought about it,' I said. 'I haven't even got a passport.'

'If he offered me a million pounds I might do it,' Jonah said. His eyes lit up with thoughts of nice cars, houses with swimming pools and maybe Venetia in a bikini.

'Jonah, your crap makes more sense of tings than your mouth sometimes.' McKay laughed. 'Bit, you should've told Manjaro some kinda mum excuse. You should always have a mum excuse, bruv. If it was me I woulda told him my mum wants me to go to the market with her or something. Or I had to cook cos Mum is looking after Granny after she had a bitch of a stroke or something. Be creative, bredren.'

'I couldn't think of a lie when Manjaro was looking at me hard.'

'Don't say I didn't warn you,' said McKay.

I shook my head and tried to concentrate on the football.

In the next couple of hours brothers came and went. Girls posed and cussed. For a while I joined in the soccer game but the bigger guys always pushed me off the ball or didn't even pass to me. I sat down again and watched the ballers fouling and cursing.

McKay was telling us some scare stories about how the feds were setting up missile sites trained on North and South Crongton to finally deal with the gang problem in our ends. 'I ain't joking, bredren,' McKay said, getting his outrage on. 'The missiles are under the concrete in front of the fed station. Believe me, if the shankings and the killings don't stop they're gonna bomb the Mohicans and Afros out of us. Then they'll go on TV and tell the nation a brother stole a bomb from the army and was doing someting on it when it blew up. You can't trust the ...'

McKay paused his flow. He looked to his left and Manjaro and three of his crew were approaching us. Another ice-on-bones moment. *Damn!* They were carrying shopping bags. It was a messed-up thing to see – you didn't normally catch the bad men of South Crong carrying shopping.

'Liccle Bit,' Manjaro hailed me. 'Thanks and respect for waiting for me.'

I couldn't believe I'd heard him say that. Bad man Manjaro saying thanks to me! Jonah had an oh-my-god look going on; McKay shook his head. Manjaro and his crew stepped up and placed the shopping bags in front of me. Jonah crawled closer to get his peep on. The bags were full of little designer clothes, name-brand footwear and toys.

'For Jerome,' Manjaro explained. 'Make sure he gets them. You receive?'

I nodded. I couldn't see any harm in taking home some new garms for Jerome. *Man! He'll be the best-dressed baby in the whole of Crongton! Including Crongton Village where they park four-wheel drives and Audi convertibles in their driveways. And the toys might stop Jerome crying all the time.* McKay was still shaking his head but Jonah was nodding.

'Step with me,' Manjaro insisted.

I stood up. Manjaro placed a hand on my shoulder and smiled. Something cold Voldemorted through every artery in my body. We started walking. Brothers were looking at us all weird. I have to admit, I felt important stepping with Manjaro. Yeah, I was a somebody instead of a short-ass nobody who ballers wouldn't even pass to.

'It's kinda messed up that things didn't work out with your sister,' Manjaro began, once we were nuff steps away from the others. 'But being a dad is important to me, you receiving?'

Being a dad is important to him? It was a lot for my hard drive to take but I thought I'd better nod.

'I wanna be a part of Jerome's life,' Manjaro continued. His voice was calm and convincing. 'You miss your dad being part of your life, right?'

'Yeah I do,' I admitted after a while. 'I wish he was still living with us.'

'Jerome's part of me, you receive? Me and Elaine can't work

it out but I think it's kinda unfair that I can't be a good dad to him. My dad wasn't a good ...' I dared a glance up at him. There was a sheen of sweat on his face and that snake on his neck twitched as he strained back his shoulders. 'I'm telling you this, Liccle Bit, cos I trust you. You seem like you're on the level, not like most brothers around here. Believe it.' He stopped and stared me straight in the face. I forced myself to keep looking back. 'So I'd be grateful if you took these tings back home for Jerome.'

'Cool, bruv,' I replied. 'I'll do it.'

Manjaro smiled again. 'Glad you're receiving what I'm trying to say.' He took out his wallet, licked his right thumb and index finger and pinched two ten-pound notes. He passed on the cash to me. 'For your inconvenience.'

'What inconvenience?' I asked.

'You might come across a liccle hassle from your sister.'

He reassured me again by patting me on the shoulder and then he was gone, his three bredrens walking with him on to the football pitch. The game stopped, the players hanging their heads respectfully as they waited for them to pass. *Man! They wouldn't even think of doing that for the mayor of this crazy town.*

Jonah and McKay sidled up to me. 'You can buy the Coke,' Jonah insisted.

'And the peanuts,' McKay added.

'Not unless you help me carry this lot home.'

McKay and Jonah, carrying a bag each, followed me to the grocery store in our estate where I bought a two-litre bottle of Coke and two bags of peanuts. We got our gulp and our nibble on sitting on a low wall in front of the shop. We watched people come and go. It felt good to be able to buy whatever snacks we wanted, but then I sank so much Coke I began to feel queasy. I had to put up serious resistance to my two bredrens wanting me to buy choc bars, choc lollies and credit for their mobile phones. McKay argued a strong case, saying that his dad bought me fried chicken breasts and fries for lunch but I kept my money on lock in my pocket.

I drained the last of the Coke before I made my way back to my slab. Jonah helped me carry the bags back home as McKay headed in the opposite direction. I turned the key in my front door, trying not to think about what Manjaro had said about hassle from my sister. *It will be cool*, I told myself. *Jerome needs some new clothes, after all.* 'Elaine!' I called ahead, as I entered the flat. 'I've got something for you!'

5

The Dog House

'Stop shouting up the place, Lemar.' Gran came into the corridor, whispering to me. She jabbed a finger in the direction of Elaine's room. 'Knock on her door. You want to wake up Jerome?'

'Where's Mum?' I asked quietly.

'Your brain working today, Lemar? Don't you know it's Saturday? She's at work. She should be on her way home now.'

I was hoping Mum would be there. I wanted to show her that I had brought home something for Jerome. I know I wasn't the one who'd bought the garms but at least I'd delivered them. *Who knows?* I thought. *After this Manjaro and Elaine might get their diplomacy on and sort out their beef. Manjaro's right. Dads need to play a part in their kids' lives. Elaine should be on point with that.*

I knocked on Elaine's door, feeling a good vibe.

'Come in,' Elaine answered.

She was sitting on her bed, rocking Jerome to sleep. Her Jamaican headscarf niced up her forehead and her Afro seemed to grow out of it. The dimples in her cheeks deepened as she smiled. Tasha's World's 'New Me Dawning' was playing softly from Elaine's boom box – she reckoned laidback grooves helped Jerome sleep. She touched Jerome's lips with her right index finger. It felt good that I was his uncle. 'I've got something for him,' I said.

'What's that?' she asked, still gazing at Jerome.

'It's out in the hallway.'

'Can't you tell me what it is?'

'Come and find out, innit.' I smiled.

'You better not be wasting my time, Lemar. I've got to wash out Jerome's bottles, wash his clothes and then fix up my hair.'

'I'm not wasting your time, sis.'

Leaving the door ajar, she followed me to the hallway.

'All for Jerome,' I said proudly, pointing to the bags.

Elaine placed her hands on her hips and leaned her weight on one leg. Her eyes blazed. 'Where'd you get the money for all this, Lemar?'

My good vibe started to fade. 'I ... I bumped into Manjaro at the park. He wanted to get some tings for Jerome ...'

Elaine froze. 'What's a matter with you, Lemar? I can't take any shit from that man! You *know* the score.'

'Elaine! Why are you cussing bad-word inna de place?' Gran scolded as she emerged from the kitchen.

'I was ... I was just trying to help,' I explained.

'You're not helping!' Elaine spat. 'You know I want *nothing* to do with him and yet you're carrying tings home for Jerome? What's a matter with you? Do you have piss in your brain or ...'

'That's enough!' Gran said. 'And please stop the bad-word before you see me lose me temper! Lemar was only trying to help.' She went to the bags and started going through them.

'Well, tell this damn idiot boy that I don't want *nothing* from my ex. You *don't* know what that psycho put me through.'

'But I—'

Before I could finish my sentence, Elaine punched me in the shoulder. 'Sometimes you haven't got any sense, Lemar! You can take the bags back to him and tell him I don't want them! Tell him he can shove them up where the sun can't reach! You hear me? Now step off out of my face!'

Just then the front door opened and Mum walked in, looking from face to face. 'What is going on in my house? Elaine! I can hear your voice way down the stairs ...'

'Tell your idiot son to stop bringing tings from my ex into the yard! Can't believe what he's done!'

'You better drop your tone, Elaine, before I box it out of you,' warned Mum, slipping off her coat.

'Everybody calm down,' said Gran, holding up her palms. 'And *drop* the language.' There were too many of us ram-jammed in the hallway. I felt a sudden urge to escape to my bedroom.

We all heard Jerome starting to wail. 'You see what you cause, Lemar?' Elaine yelled at me. 'Sometimes I think I have a dumb prick of a brother!'

'Carry on talking like that and you can take yourself out of my flat!' Mum exploded.

'I can't wait! You think I wanna be here? Maybe I'll bring up Jerome better than you brought us up!'

Elaine stormed off to see to Jerome. Mum stood in the hallway, shaking her head. Her eyes drilled into me. Gran disappeared into the kitchen. 'Why did you have to get yourself involved with Manjaro?' Mum interrogated. From the way she was looking at me it didn't matter how I replied. She blamed me for all this.

'Elaine's always bitching about how she ain't got any money to buy Jerome all the garms he needs so when Manjaro stepped up—'

'We don't *need* his money,' Mum interrupted me.

'But—'

'But nothing, Lemar! You've upset your sister, Jerome's bawling the place down and I can't get any peace in my own yard after me done work! You know how tired I am?'

'I just wanted to do something—'

'Just get out of my eyesight, Lemar! Go to your room and do one of your drawings or something! I've had a long day, my legs are aching me and I don't need this!'

I went to my room, slammed my door behind me and collapsed on to my bed.

'If you break my door then I'll break your bones!' Mum shouted from the hallway.

What the hell is wrong with my family? I thought. *Why do I get the blame for everything? Why can't my mum or my sister realise that I was just trying to do something nice for Jerome? I'm fourteen years of age, for god's sake! Why do they talk to me like I'm a little piece of crap? If Elaine didn't want the stuff then she can take it back to Manjaro herself. I ain't doing it!*

I didn't move for over an hour, ignoring the smells of baking and the tip-tapping of cutlery, even though my belly was getting its rumble on. I just stared at my ceiling thinking what a messed-up life I was living. All fingers pointed at me as the cause of any family beef. If I hadn't been here, who would they have blamed then?

Eventually, there was a knock on my door and I climbed off my bed to answer it. I knew it was Gran because Elaine or Mum wouldn't bother knocking. She was carrying a plate with a generous portion of carrot cake on it. 'We've all had our slices,' Gran said. 'Me just wanted to make sure you had yours.'

'Thanks, Gran.'

I took two bites of the carrot cake as Gran sat down beside me. 'Elaine don't really mean what she says,' she said. 'It's hard for her – bringing up Jerome on her own and trying to get a place from the council. Plus, she's a clever girl. She should have been going on to make something of herself, but since Jerome came along ... Well, it's not easy for her. You remember how we celebrated when Elaine got the results for her Sats?'

'Yeah, you and Mum took us out to that cheesecake place off Crongton High Street. But she don't have to take out her present crap on me. She and Mum always take stuff out on me! I didn't tell Elaine to get pregnant and mash up her brainy school life! Not my fault Dad walked out.'

'No, it's not,' agreed Gran. 'Everyone is under stress. Tings are not easy.'

'That's why I took the bags from Manjaro,' I said. 'I still don't think I did anything wrong, Gran. And what do I get for that? Elaine cusses me out and Mum takes her side. She *always* takes her side.'

'No she doesn't, Lemar.'

'Yes she *does*! Didn't you hear her swearing up the place? What does Mum do? *Nothing!* If that was me my head would've said hello to the rice pot!'

'Eat your carrot cake, Lemar. In the morning you won't feel so bad.'

Placing a hand on my cheek, Gran smiled and kissed me on the forehead. She left my room and I got my nibble on.

The carrot cake was good. When I finished it I put the money left over from the drink and the peanuts in my shoebox in the wardrobe. At least now I knew what Manjaro had meant about inconvenience.

6

Crongton Warfare

I woke up at 6.45 a.m. the next morning and I didn't feel any better. I was thinking that maybe I could ask Dad if I could stay with him for a while but Mum would have probably been like a tornado ripping up a row of clogged toilets if I brought that up. I slapped on my TV and spotted that my phone was blinking. I picked it up and saw a text from Jonah. *Why's he texting me so early?* I opened his message.

> South Crong bruv found deleted near the bins by Wareika
> Way. Feds are taping up the place. McKay's already on
> his way. Meet us there.

Shit! It's kicking off. Wareika Way was only a few steps from the park. Most of it was taken up by a long row of flats, four storeys high, and at either end there were fifteen-storey-high tower blocks. There wasn't much stabbings or beef going on there cos it was an area that Manjaro controlled. Most of the brothers who lived there were part of Manjaro's crew so I was shocked that a bruv got deleted there. I texted Jonah back.

On my way

I hurriedly got washed and changed and by the time I had reached Wareika Way the ambulance was moving away. It wasn't going that fast and its siren wasn't blaring. The feds had sealed off the whole of the street but crowds had built up at either end. There were people of my mum's age still in their dressing gowns. I could hear a woman crying but I couldn't see her. Others stared out from upstairs windows and a few brothers were standing on walls or hanging off lamp posts. They were all watching the forensic feds in their white jumpsuits that covered everything from their heads to their toes. Some of them had face masks on. If it wasn't for the shanking, somebody might've thought that some evil liver-eating plague had hit Crongton. The feds were examining every last bit of ground. They had small brushes and little polythene bags in their hands and I thought to myself I wouldn't inspect that ground too closely cos I'd seen a world of guys piss and spit there. It flashed through my mind that the scene would've made a good sketch or painting.

I spotted McKay and Jonah at the opposite end of Wareika Way so I had to take a detour around the estate to reach them. By the time I arrived the feds were pushing us back further.

'Can you *please* move back,' one them said, holding out his hands in front of him. 'This is now a crime scene.'

It was times like this I really hated being a short-ass. All I saw were shoulders and heads in front of me.

'It was Nightlife,' whispered McKay into my ear. 'Man got pierced like a javelin field. They even tore off a bit of his ear – it's a North Crong sign. Patricia Byrne who lives up on the fourth floor said the blood was flowing into the drain like a little stream.'

'The tall white guy who was always wearing American football tops?'

'That's the brother.' McKay nodded. 'He loved the Washington Redskins. His dad bought him a Redskins helmet for his birthday a few years ago and then he went missing.'

'He was one of Manjaro's closest bruvs,' said Jonah.

'Why did they call him Nightlife?' I asked.

'Cos he had to go out at night cos his mum didn't let him smoke rockets in the flat,' answered McKay.

'So that's how they knew they could get him?' I whispered.

'Yep,' replied McKay. 'North Crong soldiers might have been watching his movements. The shit's really gonna slap the windmill. Manjaro will have to take some serious stance. Think about it: for a North Crong bruv to step on to South Crong turf – *Wareika Way* – and then delete a South Crong bruv? They might as well have crapped on Manjaro's head from a helicopter.'

I looked around and spotted only one South Crong bruv in a blue baseball cap. He was busy with his phone.

'The feds will probably start their door-to-door shit,' said McKay. 'If they knock on your gates don't tell them *nothing*.'

'I don't know anything anyway,' Jonah replied.

We made our way back to our slabs, wondering what would happen next in this South Crong–North Crong war. We took a shortcut through an alleyway as McKay moaned about not sinking breakfast yet.

I don't know why but it felt like someone was following us. I checked and glanced over my shoulder three times, but no one was there.

'What's a matter with you, Bit?' McKay asked. 'You think the feds are after you?'

'No,' I replied. 'Just thought someone was behind us for a sec.'

Jonah circled on the spot, looking here and there. I still felt uneasy and I guessed that Jonah and McKay felt the same but were hiding it.

'I can't really blame you for getting para,' McKay said. 'Still can't believe Nightlife got punctured on prime South Crong turf. Manjaro must be packing his AKs and strapping his grenades to his chest as we speak. Wouldn't surprise me if he's got anti-aircraft weapons and shit. You know, like the ones them Arab brothers use on the back of pickup trucks.'

Jonah and I shook our heads and rolled our eyes.

We turned into another lane that ran behind a street of small houses. The back gardens were hardly big enough to swing a hobbit. There were lots of 'Beware of the Dog' signs on the gates even though I knew many of the residents didn't own any.

'I don't know about you but there're some thick sausages, bacon, beans and fried tomato with my molars on it,' said

McKay. 'Gonna sink that down with mango and pineapple juice. Walk safe and don't get deleted.'

McKay jogged away as Jonah and I turned the next corner. *Kaboom!* We almost walked straight into Manjaro. My spine turned into an icicle. He was standing with his back against the wall. Alone. For a second I thought he was the one following us. *Nah, why would he stalk my shadow?* He was wearing a black T-shirt and black sweatbands on his wrists. It was the first time I had ever seen him without a cap. The morning sun glinted off his shaven head. He was looking into the sky as if he was making up his mind about some evil, messed-up Old Testament revenge. I glanced at Jonah and for a moment he was frozen in fear but then he turned around and sprinted like he had just found out a Year 7 kid was liberating his favourite PS3 games.

'Why does your bredren always do that?' Manjaro enquired. 'I'm not gonna trouble him.'

'He's a bit nervous,' I said.

'Understandable.' Manjaro nodded. His eyes looked east and west, wary of anybody who noticed him. I felt my heart get a rumble on inside my throat. 'I saw you up Wareika Way.'

'We ... we heard the news,' I managed.

'Nightlife ... he was a loyal brother,' Manjaro said. His voice was thick with emotion. I was surprised by his tone. 'If a brother was in the shit he'd be the first to come running, you receiving? Yeah, he was never afraid to back the heathen against the wall.'

'The what? Yeah, I'm receiving ... I'm sorry, you know, just sorry.'

'I appreciate that, Liccle Bit, yeah, appreciate that. I'm gonna look after his family, you know, give them a decent touch. They need it cos his dad went missing a long time ago. I dunno how he could leave them like that.' There was a pause. 'I want you to do me a favour.'

'Me?'

I hoped it was something simple like fetching something from the shops. But somehow I knew it wouldn't be.

'Yes, you,' he said. 'I feel like I can trust you. You're on the level.'

I imagined Elaine and Mum cussing me and all sorts but I could make my own decisions, couldn't I? Besides, no matter what I did I'd get cursed and hated for it by those two anyway.

'What do you want me to do?' I blurted out.

'Just to go somewhere and pick up something,' Manjaro replied. 'It's not a big deal but I'll give you a touch if you do this favour for me.'

I wondered how much a touch was. *If I keep on doing favours for Manjaro maybe I could think about a new Adidas top as well as a new pair of trainers.* That wouldn't be so bad, would it? Just a liccle errand in order to get some new garms? Maybe Venetia would notice me then. 'Is it a serious trek where you want me to go?'

'No, about a twenty-minute walking mission to the other side of the old factories. Not too far from Crong Village.'

'You want me to do it today?'

'No, not today. We're all mourning Nightlife today and for the next few days. Give me your mobile number and some-body will call you when this ting needs to be picked up.'

Do I really have to give up my number? Say he dings me at home when Elaine's there? Better keep my mobile on silent from now on.

'What is it?' I wanted to know.

'It's not a big deal.' Manjaro shrugged. 'I would pick it up myself but if I step out of the ends the feds follow me everywhere. You know how it is with the stop and search shit, you receiving? It'll be even worse now Nightlife has gone – he knew what it meant to be a true brother. I just don't wanna tolerate the feds when I'm mourning Nightlife.'

'I hear that,' I replied.

'And you've never been in trouble with the feds before, have you? If you're carrying anything it's usually your school-bags and your drawings, right?'

'Me been in trouble? You would've heard my mum mauling my ears from the other side of Crongton.'

Manjaro smiled but his face soon returned to its usual hard-road self.

I gave Manjaro my mobile number. I thought it was strange that he wrote it down rather than punched it into his phone.

'You'll hear from one of us,' he said.

'OK,' I said.

He pushed his hands into his pockets, and loped off. I watched his back until he turned a corner, wondering if I had done the right thing by offering him my number. *No big deal,* I concluded. *He probably wants me to pick up a pair of trainers or something from a girlfriend's house – McKay reckons that Manjaro has about six ladies all over Crongton. That's probably why my sister sacked him in the first place.*

7

Post Service

The next five days went by without me hearing anything from Manjaro. I definitely heard something from Mum and Elaine. They picked on me for forgetting to mop the hallway and kitchen, they cussed me for not taking out the rubbish following Monday dinner and they both barked at me for sinking three glasses and killing off the Ribena. Mum took my TV away on Tuesday evening for answering back when she called me a 'grabilicious pickney who's always demanding money'. I only dared ask her for the cash for a haircut.

I started another drawing project. I recalled the scene when the feds were investigating Nightlife's murder and began to sketch the slabs on Wareika Way with people looking out of windows. Gran came into my room now and again and silently watched what I was drawing and when she got up to

leave she always said, 'Keep it up, Lemar. God gave you blessings of talent in those liccle fingers of yours.'

Mum and Elaine didn't even notice.

It was on Wednesday evening when I was sketching in the
crowds that I heard my phone bleep. It was just after seven
and I thought it was Jonah or McKay sending me a text –
Manjaro asking for a favour was fading from my mind. I
opened the message.

Pick up goods at 269 Crongton Lane – you're expected
at 8.

It didn't say who the text was from. Not sure what it was but
something inside me tingled with mad excitement. I checked
the time on my phone. 7.10 p.m. I read the message again. *Do
I ignore it? Maybe I could tell Manjaro I was sleeping? Nah, he
won't pay ten pence for that excuse. Why am I sweating? He's only
asked me to pick up something and he's gonna give me a touch for
that. Right! I'm gonna go. Crongton Lane isn't too far.*

I went into the front room. Gran was watching *The One
Show* and Mum was curled up on the sofa getting her snooze
on. 'I'm … I'm just going over to McKay's. I … I need his help
with this maths homework I'm doing.'

'Make sure you do the homework and don't waste time
playing dem foolish PlayStation games,' Gran said. 'Be careful
out there.'

'Nah, Gran, we're gonna get our study on.' I raised my
voice a bit, hoping Mum would hear me. 'Mum! I'll be around
McKay's. See you later!'

Post Service

'You think I'm on the tenth floor?' Mum replied, opening one sleepy eye. 'I heard you the first time. Now, let me sleep.'

I went back to my room, took a deep breath and pulled on my trainers. Who would be at this place? Would it be some-body I'd recognise? Maybe it'd be someone high up in Manjaro's crew. What would I be picking up? I had to admit that fear was getting it on in my stomach but I couldn't help getting excited. Manjaro asked *me* to do this favour and he's gonna give *me* a touch. I sat on my bed thinking about the pluses and minuses of the situation.

Stepping out of my slab a quarter of an hour later, I kept on looking behind me, thinking Mum or Gran was following me. I made my way out of the ends, passed the mashed-up youth-club building where my dad used to go and stepped by the old broken-down factories where the bomb-heads crash. I headed for central Crongton.

Crongton Lane was a left turning fifty metres before the High Street. The houses had concrete steps leading up to wide front doors and a number of basements had pool tables sitting in them. BMWs, Mercedes and other well-expensive cars filled the diagonal parking bays. I couldn't hear any crazy arguments from households like you did almost every evening walking around my ends.

I started to read the numbers. Two-five-one, two-five-three. I stopped. *I can turn around and step home*, I thought. *I don't have to do this. I'm sure Manjaro can find another bruv to pick up whatever he wants.* But, hey-ho, I needed a new pair of train-ers and I didn't want to sit in front of Miss Fitness herself, Venetia King, with my messed-up hair again. I needed a serious trim. Two-five-seven, two-five-nine. I took a deep breath and jogged the rest of the way. Two-six-nine. I slowly walked up the steps and read the address once more on my phone. I arrived. I studied the doorbell for ten seconds like it was a detonator. For some reason I was thinking of old-school cartoons with mad explosions. Wile E. Coyote accidentally blew up himself in his messed-up chase of the Road Runner. I think that was my dad's favourite. I closed my eyes and pressed.

Seconds later, a light was switched on inside. I went down a step. Something wet and cold ran down my back. I could make out a shadow approaching the door through the misted glass. The door opened, and standing before me was a white girl, about nineteen years old. She had her hair pulled back in a ponytail and she was wearing a baggy blue T-shirt and blue tracksuit bottoms. Black sweatbands covered her wrists. Nothing was on her feet. Her mashed-up toes looked like she had tried to walk barefoot in eggcups.

'Liccle Bit?' she asked.

I nodded.

'Give me your phone,' she demanded.

'Why?'

'Just give me your freaking phone!' she insisted.

I passed my mobile over. She grabbed it from me, high-lighted my texts and deleted them all. She handed back my phone and said, 'Wait here.'

Some ice-cold demon swam through my bloodstream. She closed the door and I watched her shadow disappear into the house. Two minutes later she emerged again carrying a brown parcel that had been sealed with brown masking tape. It was about the size of my shoebox but not as deep. She then passed me a folded slip of paper. I unravelled it and recognised an address on my estate. 'Nine Remington House?' I said.

The girl nodded. 'Your touch,' she said, handing me a crisp ten pound note from her trouser pocket.

'Thanks.'

'Take it there now,' she insisted. 'Don't stop off at home or anywhere else. You receiving?'

'I'm receiving.'

'Give me back the address,' she ordered.

I read it one more time before handing it over. She ripped it into tiny pieces and crushed it in her fist.

'Remember,' she said, holding her right forefinger in front of my face. 'Head there now and you'll get another touch when you get there. They know you're coming.'

I wondered who *they* were.

She closed the door before I could ask any more questions. I stood for a short while, studying the packet. It was taped very neatly and precisely as if there was something valuable inside. *Shit! What have I got my liccle self into? This package could be drugs, ammo or anything. Maybe I should return it and give back the money? Then again, I'm not sure what that sister would do to me or have someone else do to me. She's probably a major player in Manjaro's crew. But I'm just a short-ass kid*, I told myself. *They're not gonna trust me with anything too serious.*

The package was as heavy as a couple of textbooks, maybe three, so the only way to get through this was *not* to think about what was inside.

I turned around and bounced down the steps two at a time. Remington House was a block going behind McKay's slab. I guessed it was a ground-floor flat, being number nine. Maybe I'd stop by McKay's on the way home.

Half-jogging to my delivery address, I wondered who would be there. Maybe Manjaro himself? Or another one of his girls. Elaine hadn't revealed too much about where she visited Manjaro when she was going with him. Not to me anyhow.

I arrived at the ground-floor flat in fifteen minutes. Sweat was dripping down my temples. I waited until my breathing got back to normal before I knocked on the varnished wooden door. I looked around but nobody was about. I did hear a dog barking above and one of the neighbours with their TV turned up too loudly, but that was standard living in South Crongton. I waited for two minutes but nobody came. I checked the number on the door again. Number nine. I knocked once more, this time louder.

A minute later I heard the crunching of a mortise key turning in the lock. The door opened ten centimetres. I heard the sound of a toilet finishing its flush. The face of a mixed-race guy about twenty years old filled the gap. His chest was broader than my gran's old wardrobe and he had a heavy-weight's fists. He was wearing his blue cap backwards and a single gold tooth niced up his mouth. My heart drummed up a solo.

'You Liccle Bit?' he asked.

'Yeah,' I replied.

He turned his head. 'Liccle Bit reach,' he yelled.

'Let the brother in,' someone shouted back.

The heavyweight let me in. He ran his eyes over me like I was an unwanted fly. He pointed along the hallway. 'Turn right at the end,' he instructed.

I was walking on varnished wooden tiles. I started to get a fret on cos I didn't wipe my feet. Black and white portraits of movie stars hung from the walls. Some cleaning liquid or room fragrance was making my nostrils itch. I passed an empty kitchen. I turned right into a living room but nobody was there. A big-screen TV was fixed to the wall and a news presenter was broadcasting something about the Middle East on a low volume. A black leather three-piece suite filled the floor space, semicircling a long table that had a chess board marked into it. The pieces were made out of glass or see-through plastic or something and I remembered my dad once tried to teach me how to play it.

'Sit down,' said a female voice.

I turned around and saw a brown-skin girl of about twenty-one. She was dressed all in blue with big gold pyramid-shaped earrings. She was James-Bond-film pretty.

I did as I was told, still clutching the parcel with both hands.

'You want a drink?' the girl asked. She probably noticed my sweat-soaked forehead.

'Yeah, thanks.'

'I've got pineapple juice, orange juice and apple juice.'

'I don't mind,' I replied. 'Anything will do.'

I preferred orange juice but I didn't want to be any trouble. She went to fetch my drink and I could hear her opening the fridge in the kitchen. I guessed that the guy who let me in was still standing by the door.

The girl returned with my drink and placed it on a coaster on the chess table. Two ice cubes were spinning in it. She also took out a ten-pound note from inside her dress and placed it next to my juice. I picked up my glass and sank three-quarters of it. I banked the money in my pocket. The girl sat beside me. My heart drummed like a mad grime tune.

'The man says you're on the level,' she said. 'Now, go back to your flat and forget you ever came here.'

I nodded.

'*Don't* chat to any of your school bredrens and don't say anything to Elaine. You receiving?'

'Yeah ... how do you know Elaine?'

As soon as it left my mouth I knew it was a dumb question. The girl laughed. 'We all know Elaine,' she said.

I wondered what she meant. Was Elaine part of Manjaro's operation? *Nah, maybe this girl just sees my sis as one of Manjaro's women.* I finished my drink and stood up.

'The man said to give you a drink and some food if you want it. I have some chicken and rice I can fling in the microwave for you if you—'

'No, thanks,' I cut in. 'Got to make a move.'

'That's up to you.' She smiled. 'The man thanks you for the favour. You're one of us now.'

I walked along the hallway and the giant mixed-race guy opened the door for me. He had the sort of face that if a spaceship landed in the middle of Crongton he wouldn't blink or think it was any big deal.

The girl said I was one of them now but not if I could help it. I just wanted to earn some money to get myself a trim or put towards some trainers. I got my stride on and made it to McKay's flat ten minutes later.

McKay opened his front door while getting his munch on with a giant packet of cheese and onion crisps. He led me to his front room where he was watching a DVD of Ultimate Fighting – some tattooed white guy was beating the ribs out of this other tattooed white guy.

McKay's lounge had this five-seater L-shaped sofa with leg rests and I crashed on that. He was wearing a white vest and tracksuit bottoms and he was giving me a messed-up look. Crumbs circled his mouth. 'What are you doing at my castle after nine on a Wednesday? You didn't accidentally delete your baby nephew did you?'

'Is your dad here?' I asked.

'Nah, he just left for work.'

'What about your brother?'

'He's on some girl mission. I could tell cos he sprayed up the whole place with his deodorant. If I was a girl I would get suspicious if a man stepped to me with all that Lynx going on. Wait a minute! Why you asking me where my family is?'

'Checking if you're alone.'

'And why do you wanna know if I'm alone? Listen, bredren, I hope you're not coming to my castle at this time of night to tell me that you're gay or something and you just had to tell someone cos your parents don't understand. Don't do that to me, bruv! If that's the case then let me tell you that this slot is closed! *Permanently!*'

'McKay, even if I was gay and you was the last man on earth, I'd prefer doing it with a hedgehog rather than you. You hearing that?'

'That's cold, bredren. And you'd better keep your funky animal sex issues to yourself! You don't wanna release that tape on YouTube, bruv. So anyway, what are you doing here?'

'I'm not sure if I should spill.'

'If you're not sure if you wanna spill then why bang on my drawbridge?'

There was logic to McKay's question. I knew the girl from Remington House said I shouldn't spill to anyone but what was the point in doing something exciting if I couldn't tell anyone about it? I couldn't tell Jonah though cos his mouth was bigger than Broadway.

'Manjaro asked me to do him a favour,' I revealed.

'What? He asked you to buy a lolly from the shop again?' McKay replied, getting his munch on once more. 'Big deal! Isn't it a bit late for sucking lollies?'

'No, no … He asked me to pick up a parcel for him from Crongton Lane.'

McKay stopped his munching. He gave me a long look. He angled his head.

'And I got twenty notes for it,' I added.

'Crongton Lane?' McKay repeated.

'Yeah.'

'Bankers, lawyers, footballers' mistresses live on that road.'

'Tell me about it! Expensive cars sexed up the whole street.'

'So who lives at this place where you picked up something?'

'This white girl,' I answered. 'Don't know if she lives there but she came out of the gates. She didn't let me in but she gave me the parcel.'

McKay narrowed his eyes as he booted-up his thought process. He paused the DVD and edged up closer to me. 'This don't sound good, bredren,' he said. 'Where did you take the parcel?'

'Nine Remington House.'

'And you don't know what's inside the parcel?'

'No, they never told me. I got twenty pound out of it.'

'Lemar, you're a bredren, so don't get offended by what I say next, right?'

'What do you mean, don't get offended? Say what you wanna say.'

'The hard drive in your brain is malfunctioning! Don't you have any sense? What did I say to you in the park a few days ago? I shook my head, telling you not to do favours for Manjaro. But did you listen? Did I get your attention? *No!* All you saw was the money!'

I didn't want to admit it but McKay wasn't wrong. It didn't even occur to me to ask what was inside the parcel. Well, it did, but I wasn't brave enough to ask. I felt stupid but didn't wanna show it to McKay. 'I don't have any sense? At least I've got twenty notes nicing up my pocket. You haven't got shit ...'

'*Think*, bredren! What do you think was in that parcel?'

'I dunno ... don't care.'

'You don't care? Your hard drive is proper messed up. Hear me out. Nightlife, one of Manjaro's closest bruvs, gets deleted. What is it? Five days later, he asks you to pick up something from Crongton Lane. Are you getting the flow of this or do I have to slow down, take you back to nursery and take out the alphabet? Or do you want Sky News to put it on their yellow breaking-news ticker?'

Damn! It's like McKay can read my mind. I didn't want to think about what was inside the parcel but now I couldn't help it. *But Manjaro wouldn't trust me to get arms for him, would he? He hardly knows me. Nah, he would get one of his close bruvs to do it.* 'I know what you're thinking, McKay, but Manjaro wouldn't ask me to carry a piece for him. It don't make sense.'

I'm not sure if I was convincing. I could hardly convince myself.

'Wouldn't he? Who are the feds gonna be watching? They're not gonna be watching some short-ass like you!'

'Who're you calling short-ass, you fat salad-hater! You're just hating cos Manjaro didn't ask you.'

'Jealous? Lemar, reboot your brain, bredren. This ain't good. Manjaro's a toxic brother, believe it. And he's got one of the best hard drives around – he's well smart. He might be using you to pick up—'

'He *ain't* using me!' I shouted. 'Like I said, you're jealous cos twenty notes ain't nicing up your pocket.'

McKay shook his head, turned his attention to the TV and pressed play on the remote. I was kind of embarrassed by my yelling but I always hated it when McKay was in the right and I was so wrong.

There was an uncomfortable silence for the next few minutes until McKay broke it. 'Lemar, just download this, yeah? Don't do any more favours for Manjaro, right. Trust me, you don't wanna go down on that ride. There are nuff brothers of our age being used by Manjaro and Major Worries to do their shit for them. Believe it, bruv.'

He was on point again, but if I admitted it I'd look like an idiot. 'Manjaro ain't using me! I'm his baby's uncle.'

'You think he gives a shit about that? Just watch your steps, Bit.'

After a while I replied, 'You don't have to fret about me, bruv. I've made my cents and pence from Manjaro. I'm not gonna do any more favours for him. I'm *not* one of them. I can step away. It's just a one-off. Trust me on that.'

8

Dad

I woke up on Saturday morning feeling relieved cos the only text I received up to that point was from Jonah. I had been getting another fret on about being asked to do another favour for Manjaro. I was even worried about receiving a message from McKay telling me how right he was.

Lemar, are you still going to your dad's? If not I wanna check out this new fit girl who's working at the corner shop.

I replied back.

You're gonna have to check out this new piece of fitness on your lonesome. Still going to my dad's.

Dad

Jonah could never step to any girl on his own but today he would have to chirp to this chick on his Jack Jones if he wanted to get in the starting blocks with her. He texted me back.

> I'll check her out next week when you'll be back. Gonna play games at McKay's.

As I made my way to the bathroom I could smell sausages, toast, eggs and bacon. I stepped into the kitchen thinking Gran was making breakfast but it was Mum. She was wearing her Jamaican headscarf and this old burgundy dressing gown that should have been deleted ages ago.

'How's my beautiful boy this morning?' she said, smiling.

I had to shake my head a little and get my focus on. Mum in a good mood?

Dad turned up an hour later but as soon as he said hello to me, Mum, now in her work uniform, yanked him into her bedroom for a private chat. I could hear them arguing for about ten minutes but they both came out of the room getting their smiles on. I had to chuckle on the quiet cos it was obvious they had issues but were trying to hide it. They must have to be stupid if they thought I didn't notice.

Dad, Shirley and Steff lived in this little house near Crongton Green. You could hardly fit a double bed in any of the bedrooms and a broken-down wooden shed took up most of the space in the garden. I was hoping that I wouldn't have to answer Dad's and Shirley's recurring questions as Dad led me up a short pathway to the house. I spotted Steff at the front window. She had a big grin on.

Dad opened the door and Steff was all over me like a cute dog in a Disney film. 'Lemar's come to see me! My big brother! Lemar!'

She had this tube thing up her nose and she was so pale I wondered if a vampire had got his nibble on. Pink ribbons niced up her brown frizzy hair. She grabbed my hand and led me up the stairs to her bedroom. She had a world of medical stuff on her dressing table but the walls were full of her drawings and paintings. Many of them were of matchstick doctors and matchstick nurses with red crosses on their foreheads.

'What do you think of my drawings?' she asked.

I noticed she was breathing heavy from running up the stairs and for a moment I felt bad about wanting a head-trim and new garms to show off to Venetia King. Those things didn't seem important.

'They're ... they're brilliant, Steff,' I answered, knowing how much effort must have gone into her sketches.

'I want to be as good as you,' she said, pointing at a portrait of herself that was overlooking her bed that I had sketched over a year ago. 'Yeah, I want to be a what-you-call-it? What d'you call it?'

'An artist,' I replied.

I sat down on her bed. God knows what crap she'd had to deal with in her short life and I wondered why Mum hated the very mention of her name.

I drew with Steff for over an hour until she got tired. Dad put her to bed and kissed her on the forehead. He turned to me. 'Thanks, Lemar. It means a lot to her that you spend time with her. She could hardly sleep knowing you were coming today.

'So how's school?' Dad started. 'I hope you'll get back to paying attention and doing the work on your core subjects.'

'I'm doing good, Dad. Mum goes over the top. If she thinks I've missed one piece of homework she tells the whole world and starts launching missiles at me.'

'But your mum tells me you haven't been doing any of your homework.'

'How would she know?' I countered. 'She doesn't check what I'm doing.'

'I'm sure that's not true.'

'It is true. She doesn't have any time for me. If she wants to know what I'm doing she asks Gran.'

'She works hard though,' said Dad. 'She probably gets very tired in the evening.'

'She ain't too tired to chat with Elaine and Gran and play with Jerome. She only talks to me when I forget to do something or when she wants to pick on someone after she's had some beef at work. Just the other day some customer cussed her out at work about returning something and Mum comes home with her rage on and—'

'How is your bolognese?' asked Shirley, trying to change the subject.

'It's good,' I replied. And it was. But I didn't want to chat about the food. I wanted to offload the crap that had built in my chest.

'How's Elaine doing?' Dad asked.

'She's … she's Elaine. Sometimes loses her temper for no reason,' I revealed. 'She's hating me at the moment. I think she's always hated me! She called me a dumb prick of a brother the other day. Don't know what I've done to her. Oh yeah, I forgot! Being born is what I've done to her!'

'Think you're being a bit OTT, Lemar,' Dad said. 'You might've had a row or something but she loves you to the bone—'

'No she don't! She hates the air I breathe and any words that might come out of my mouth! I try to do nice things for her and she just cusses me down. I just stay in my room and don't get in their way. They like it like that.'

Following dinner, I went to the small basketball court at the end of the green with Dad. Weeds and shit were growing out of the cracks in the concrete but at least you could get your bounce on. There was no net hanging from the hoop and North Crong and South Crong soldiers had graffitied the ground and the hoop backboard in their own colours. Dad and I didn't care as we played a rough game of one-on-one. Dad could be very competitive when he wanted to be and we both got our sweat on. I let my anger out by elbowing and driving my shoulder into him whenever I got the chance. I took out all my Mum and Elaine frustration on him but he didn't complain or retaliate. Forty minutes later, he still beat me 32–18.

Sweat was pouring off him as he sat on the basketball on the court and put his serious face on. I sat there thinking, *Why didn't he pass on his height to me?*

'Being an artist is all good if you come from a family that

can support you, Lemar, but you have to work on your other subjects. You gotta have a back-up, and English and maths are important. I know you're hot at drawing but it'll be very hard to support yourself, trust me on that one. Don't you wanna move away from here one day, have a steady wage and buy a place with your dream girl?'

'I want that, but I'm not good at English, maths and all the other subjects, Dad. Can't see why I'm wasting my time with them ...'

'Because it's hard to just rely on your artwork. Look at me! When I was your age I wanted to be the number one rapper in the world. I thought a recording contract would drop from the sky and looked forward to trimming my hedges in my back garden where I was gonna have my pool and a barbecue big enough to grill a cow ...'

'You could spit bars, Dad?'

'Is that what you call it now? Yep, we used to have DJ clashes in the youth club – shame it's been closed now for what ... six years? But yeah, I was a decent rapper. I used to get my props from the main players in the estate. I wasn't afraid of anybody. But did I get a recording contract? Hell no! I used to give my teachers grief, but what's parked outside my house now? A catalogue delivery van! Not a Benz or a BMW. And the only pool I have in my backyard is in the far right corner when it rains cos it doesn't drain properly there. That's my reality. I had no plan B.'

'Mum told you to have a word with me, didn't she, Dad?'

Dad looked away. I knew I was right though. It was at times like this, just chatting after we shot some hoops, that I really missed him being around every day. He'd have probably stood up for me when Mum and Elaine were picking on me.

'It doesn't matter who told me to have a word with you, Lemar. What matters is that you'll put some serious effort into your other lessons, right? Work on a plan B.'

'Right.'

'Promise?'

'Promise.'

'OK, then. Now that's out of the way, I'm going back to see how Steff is. She'll be awake by now. Are you coming?'

'Nah, Dad. I'm gonna stay out here for a bit. The weather's all good and I'm gonna practise.'

'Ha ha! You're gonna need to practise if you wanna beat me!'

'If I was fifteen centimetres taller I'd beat you every time!'

'Stop dreaming, Lemar!'

I watched Dad roll away and for a moment hated him for living with Shirley and Steff. When he was out of sight I glanced in the opposite direction. Circling Crongton Green was a big roundabout and I walked towards a signpost that was located at one of the exits. I read the travel directions. Crongton South was to the left and Crongton North was to the right. I wasn't sure what it was, maybe the excitement the other day of picking up that package for Manjaro, but I left the green, crossed the road and started stepping towards North Crongton. I must have had my curiosity hat on. The brothers and sisters there couldn't be too different from the ones at my ends. And it wasn't like I was a known soldier wearing the South Crong symbols of a blue cap and blue top. Nobody had any reason to get their rage on with me.

Dad

I bounced down a terraced street. I could just about see the tops of the tower blocks in the distance about a mile away. A couple of kids were performing wheelies on their bikes. A fit-looking girl went by on her roller skates. My heart drum-rolled but it felt good, exciting. I bounced my ball as I went along. There was nothing to be scared of, just an ordinary street where someone was putting taxi cards through letter boxes and kids sat on dustbins playing their handheld games.

I got to the end of the road and the slabs of North Crongton came into view. They had more tower blocks but the brickwork seemed that bit newer than South Crongton. Their windows seemed more modern but there weren't as many satellite dishes sticking out of walls as there was in South Crongton. They had more pathways and greenery though. And a community centre. *Damn.* It seemed that someone had actually planned this place. Maybe they built South Crongton first, realised they messed up and tried again with North Crongton. I guessed that some of the parents who lived here worked at the same factory as McKay's dad. Their kids probably played the same computer games as me and Jonah. I wondered when the beef between North and South Crong first kicked off. Maybe Dad knew something about it.

I crossed a street and stepped slowly on to the main estate road. I stopped bouncing my basketball; there seemed to be more road ramps than actual flat road. North Crong soldier signs were everywhere. It was usually a small 'n' in a big 'C'. All the graffiti was daubed in black. My heart started stomping but something told me to trod on. They even had an estate shop like we had. Teenagers about my age in black tracksuit tops were draining small bottles of Magnum tonic wine – just like the South Crong soldiers did. Others were chomping on some cheap chicken takeaway. A couple of older girls, about sixteen, maybe seventeen, were smoking rockets and some young kid, dressed all in black, was playing keepy-up with a football.

I looked at the ground beneath me and rolled by. I was ignored. Sometimes it was a plus being a short-ass. No one thought I was important or of any danger.

Fifty metres later, I heard shouts. I looked up. There was this basketball court in the middle of the estate that was surrounded by a three-metre-high meshed fence. The surface was some sort of blue-greenish soft tarmac. Bare-backed and black-vested guys in their late teens and early twenties were getting their bounce on. Their jeans were almost falling below their knees. A world of different-coloured boxers was on show. Girls of all shades in half-sleeved black leather jackets, black crop tops and knee-length black cycling shorts posed and laughed. I knew I should have kept my distance but my nosiness beat the shit out of my common sense. I took another ten paces forward. Then another five. I was only three metres or so away from the high fence. *Why should I get my fret on? I'm hardly a threat.*

It was a serious game. Gran would have covered her ears at the amount of swearing. Most of the players were wearing black head-rags and black trainers. For five minutes I wasn't even thinking I was in North Crong territory, I was just enjoying a hard-fought game. They were all better than my dad.

Dad

There was a break in the game as the ball slipped out of a player's hands and careered out of the court towards me. It eventually rested against the fence, close by to where I was standing. One of the younger guys ran over to fetch it. I looked down at my feet, then I slowly backed away three steps, not wanting anyone to know that my heart was pumping. This boy was maybe a year older than me and fifteen centimetres taller. He was wearing a plain black T-shirt and black tracksuit bottoms. One of his eyebrows was recovering from some gone-wrong trim. He picked up the ball and glanced at me. I looked away. Then I retreated another step and held on to my ball tighter. The boy went to return to his bredrens. But then he stopped, turned around and studied me again. My heart headbutted my kidneys and everything else inside my chest. Suddenly the inside of my head felt like my gran's beef-stew cooking pot. Sweat poured down my forehead. My back felt cold.

'Who are you?' the boy asked.

'I . . . I . . .'

I turned around, dropped my ball and got my sprint on. I nearly stumbled as I hurdled over a low brick wall but I regained my footing and blazed along the main estate road. I glanced behind and saw the boy who asked who I was hot-toeing after me. *Shit!* There were three more with him and they were all bigger than Broadway.

I wished I was as rapid as Jonah. I approached the shop but there were soldiers there so I busted a right turn into a maze of low-level slabs. I found a pathway but nearly ran into a mum pushing a buggy. Changing direction, I burned on to a green, jumped over a low hedge, sprinted across a road without even looking and zoomed down the first pathway I could find.

I found myself in an alleyway that ran between people's back gardens. It stank of piss and dog shit. Exhausted, I rested for a few seconds as my chest got its heave on. Boy! I thought I was gonna breathe out my lungs and my heart. Some dog was barking in the distance. I could hear the sound effects of a computer game somewhere above. I felt dizzy. For a second I thought I was having a heart attack, but I was only fourteen! *Hearts don't delete for fourteen-year-olds, do they?* Then I heard shouts.

'Did you see where the liccle yout' went?'

'Anyone recognise him?'

'Never seen him before!'

'He was well short.'

'Should we bother with him?'

'He might be spying on North Crong brothers. Manjaro ain't gonna step on our ends and check us out for himself, is he?'

'Yeah, it could've been a South Crong yout'.'

'If you find him, *fuck* him up! Give him ratchet surgery.'

'Yeah, teach the liccle yout' a lesson for stepping on North Crong ends.'

'Ratchet design his nose!'

'And send him back to South Crong in a box!'

'His mum won't recognise his short ass.'

My heart banged my ribcage. I dared not run to the end of the alleyway or go back to where I'd just come from so I climbed over the fence, praying that the 'Beware of the Dog' sign was a deterrent rather than the real fangs. I closed my eyes as I tried to control my breathing, praying I wouldn't hear any mad barking. The voices faded away.

Two minutes later I opened my eyes again. My T-shirt was sticking to my back. I was in a tiny back garden beside a kid's rusty bike that had lost a wheel. The back door was closed but there were two windows. Somebody was looking out from one of them. For a moment I thought of clambering back over the fence but I was too weary to do that. Besides, the North Crong soldiers might still be out and about looking to skin, scalp and redesign me. I remembered that deleted brother in the woods with half his nose missing.

The back door opened. I thought that if they sent for the feds and charged me with attempted burglary or some crap like that then it'd be better than three or four North Crong soldiers, all broader than Broadway, getting their Ultimate Fighter on my hide.

An Asian man stepped out of the house. He was wearing a simple white shirt and plain black trousers. He had this thin moustache like my granddad used to have. He looked like he taught physics or something. I felt a little better cos he was wearing these blue fluffy slippers. I thought that someone with blue fluffy slippers was not about to bang me up.

'Are you OK, young man? You look like you need some help?'

Pure relief flooded my hard drive and washed down to my chest.

'Are you in some sort of trouble, young man?'

I was still breathing heavy but I composed myself and thought of a response. 'I'm ... I'm lost.'

'Lost?' repeated the Asian man. 'Where do you need to go?'

'Crongton Green.'

'That's not far ... Would you like a drink of water?'

I nodded.

I followed the man into the house. He spoke in a language that I couldn't understand to his wife who was watching some Asian film in the front room. She smiled at me and I half-grinned back. I noticed a copy of what I think was the Koran on a glass coffee table. She ushered me to sit down as the man went to the kitchen. He came back with the water and I have never drunk so fast. Dribbles of water ran down my chin. I felt too embarrassed to wipe it away. I stood up when I finished and asked, 'Can I go out the front?'

'Wait a minute, young man,' the man said. 'I will see ... I will just go and see.'

As he went to the front door I swapped nervous glances with his wife. The man returned and advised, 'It's OK for you to go. Take care.'

'Thanks so much.'

He pointed in the direction I should take and as soon as his front door was closed I blazed across the road, burned to the right and hot-toed down the next left. Crongton Green was only half a mile away. Lungs bursting, I rested against a wall. *Shit!* My basketball. No way was I gonna go back and look for it so I had to let it go.

Before I set off again, I glanced behind, but no North Crong soldiers were about. I trod slowly back to Crongton Green wondering why I'd stepped to North Crong turf in the first place.

I reached Dad's and crashed on the sofa in the front room. Shirley and Dad were busy with Steff so they didn't realise I'd had a near-death experience or lost the basketball. I thought of texting McKay and Jonah about it but decided against it. They'd just take the living piss out of me.

One of the good things about staying with Dad was they went to bed quite early on the weekend, about eleven, and they had no probs me staying up and watching whatever I wanted to watch. There was nothing good on so I texted Jonah.

Did you step to the new girl in the shop?

Jonah took two minutes to reply.

No, spent the day at McKay's. His dad bought us a chicken bucket again.

I thought I'd wind him up.

You're a rodent, bredren! Too scared to chirps the chick.

Jonah's reply was rapid.

Look how long you know Venetia King and you can't even say shit to her!

9

Mum

When I got home, I could hear Elaine having a chat on her phone from her bedroom. I guessed Jerome must've been sleeping cos I didn't hear a squeak out of him. The running water from the kitchen sink sounded louder than it normally did. *Mum's in a good mood,* I convinced myself. *Nothing to get my fret on about. When's the last time she actually washed up my dinner plate? If I forget to wash up my stuff I usually get a conk in my head-top. Maybe she feels guilty about the way she's been treating me for the last two weeks or so. It'll be a nice break for me to spend a week at Dad's.*

Mum returned from the kitchen. She was drying her hands with a tea towel. Small bubbles were popping around her nose. 'What were you going to ask me, Lemar?'

'Er, the next time I stay at Dad's ...' I started.

Mum crossed her arms. 'Yes,' she said. 'Go on.'

'I ... I don't see Steff that often and me and her ... well, she's my little sister and we're really getting on. I'm helping her to sketch—'

'What is it you want to ask, Lemar?'

Mum's voice had gone up a touch. I could tell from her expression that her impatience levels were rising. I had to get this out very calmly. I thought of a chat I once had with the school counsellor. She was all calm and soft. I tried to talk like her.

'I thought it would be good if I can stay over for a week, you know – they said they wouldn't mind and would love to have me.'

Mum got her intense gaze on. It felt like her eyes were lasering into me. The dinner she had just served me felt like two hippos who'd woken up and were tag-wrestling with two elephants inside me. I couldn't move and held my breath. Mum stomped to the kitchen and I could hear her putting plates and cutlery away – she wasn't usually that loud. I breathed out a long sigh of relief and my heart stopped punching my ribs as the noise abated. I closed my eyes, thinking the shit could've really slapped the windmill, but it finally dropped into the hole.

Then Mum returned. I stole a rapid glance at her. *Uh oh.*

'First of all, he *walks* out on me after he's been banging that bitch for ten months behind my back,' Mum yelled. 'He used to tell me he was doing overtime, and he weren't lying! He was doing overtime on top of *her*! He leaves me, his two kids, he doesn't give me shit money for months and even years. He breeds that slut and we don't even see him for months on end. Then he breezes back into our lives crying that he "wants to be a proper daddy"! *Wants to see his kids grow up! Wants to be part of your lives!* Boo hoo! Forget about all the money he owes me! But don't worry about that, he wants to play Daddy! *He's a new man!* The forgotten birthdays, the Christmases when I worked all the *friggin* hours on God's good earth to get you and Elaine something. Remember your PlayStation 3? Forget all that!'

'But ... but I just wanna—'

'*No*, Lemar! You forget too easy! Who went out to work to put food on your table and pay the rent? Who scrimped and saved to put clothes on your back? Your computer? Your first football boots? Your Barcelona kit? Your phone? Your drawing stuff? It wasn't your daddy!'

Elaine came running out of her room and stood between me and Mum. 'Mum, that's enough,' she said. 'Lemar doesn't deserve this.'

Gran appeared. 'What's going on?' she asked.

Mum's voice only got louder. 'So after all that, Lemar, you want to live with him now? Play happy families with him now? Start calling that bitch your mum? Do you? Do ... She was one of my best friends! Have you forgotten that too?'

'I ... I ...'

I couldn't get the words out. I could feel the tears gathering behind my eyes.

Elaine somehow pulled Mum into her bedroom but couldn't stop her cursing some swear words I'd never heard before. I stared at the floor beneath me, wondering why I'd been so stupid to ask to spend a week with Dad. I found the strength two minutes later to walk to my room. I crashed out on my bed and I could still hear Mum ranting and cussing. I grabbed my pillow and pulled it over the back of my head and around my ears.

Eventually, there was a knock on the door and I got up to let Gran in. She cupped my face with her hands and kissed me on the cheek. She sat down on my bed and held my hands within hers. She looked at me for a long moment before she spoke. 'Don't be too angry with her, Lemar—'

'Why not? You heard what happened. Didn't you? They probably heard her in McKay's block. She just switched on me for no reason, no reason at all! What did I say wrong, Gran? I wasn't being feisty, I just asked her in a calm way. But she just went for me. You heard it! I can't win, Gran! Anything I do, I can't win! I might as well leave this flat! Maybe I should call social services. Ask them for a bed for the night.'

'You don't mean that, Lemar.'

'Yes I do! I can't stand it here! I get blamed for everything. They don't want me here! Can never do anything right and Mum and Elaine just switch all their shit on me!'

'Mind your language, Lemar! When I came into your room I wasn't bad-wording.'

'I *hate* it here, Gran. *Hate* it! They treat me like a kid!'

'There's a reason why your mother gets so upset about your father, Lemar, even after all these years since they split up.'

Gran tried to reassure me by squeezing my shoulder. 'You have to remember, Lemar. Your parents were childhood sweethearts. They've known each other since they were eleven.

When they were both fourteen your grandfather wouldn't let him in the yard! He wanted your mother to concentrate on her schoolwork rather than "de nasty boy dem"! When she turned sixteen all she ever talked about was your father *this* and your father *that* and how nice their wedding was going to be. Maybe we should have encouraged her to think of other tings. You know, life is not just about revolving around one person, even if that person is your life partner. But, yes, Lemar, they did love each other for true.'

'You're still not explaining why she takes out stuff on me, Gran.'

'I'm trying to explain why tings are so difficult for your mother now – why it's hard for her to move on. You see, your father was everyting to her. She never really had an ambition to be some big star or have some big career – she just wanted to marry your father and raise a family with him. That's all.'

Gran's eyes were watering, like she felt guilty about something. She took a couple of seconds to compose herself before she went on. 'So it was devastating when your father walked out. *Devastating* me ah tell you. Everyting she dreamed of, hoped for, gone. *Kaput!* And now with you going to Shirley's regular now, she feels she might lose you to her also—'

'But that's stupid, Gran! Mum's my mum.'

'Not stupid, Lemar, human.'

Gran squeezed my hand, stood up and left my room. I noticed that her movements were a bit slower than her normal self.

For the rest of the evening I didn't switch on my computer, turn my TV on or play any of my video games. I just lay on my bed, getting my stare on at the ceiling above me. I wished I was five, six or seven years old again, when Mum and Dad would spoil me on birthdays with a world of toys and all the chocolate mini rolls I could eat, and Elaine would lead me by the hand to show off 'liccle bro' to her bredrens. They would get their stupid faces on and say how cute I was. I felt important. Life was good back then.

I wasn't sure what time I fell asleep but sometime in the night I felt someone kissing my forehead. My eyes slowly opened and I realised I had slept in my clothes. I expected to see Gran's shape walking out of my bedroom but as the figure turned around I realised it was Mum's.

10

The Lion, the Tiger and the Bear

The big event at school the next day was Jonah showing off his new phone to everybody. Every time he got something new from his parents, he went all secretive on us and then suddenly revealed his new phone, game, trainers or shoes in the playground or in the dinner hall. Everyone would crowd around him, saying that they would get something similar to sex up their feet or whatever but they knew they couldn't afford to. Jonah would have his I-won-the-lottery smile on and drink in all the attention.

With his new phone, the interest Jonah got was ridiculous. Even Venetia King came over to where we were sitting for lunch and asked to see the damn thing. Her eyes lit up like she was holding the World Cup. Jonah couldn't have smiled wider if someone had banged an iron banana into his mouth. I wanted to snatch the damn phone, run over to the slop-out bin and drop it in there. We'd see how much Jonah got his grin on after that! Our IT teacher, Mr Lindsay, once said mobile phones should be banned in schools and I was with him.

'Oh, we've got a basketball game on Wednesday,' Venetia said to Jonah, totally ignoring us. 'Are you coming to watch? We could do with some support.'

Jonah got his nod on so much I thought his head was gonna drop off. His eyes had the same look of someone winning *The X Factor* or some other stupid singing show. Anybody would have thought she'd asked him to go to Hawaii with her. Meanwhile, Venetia reserved her gaze for Jonah's damn phone.

'What about you guys?' Venetia turned to McKay and me.

If it wasn't for Venetia loving Jonah's new phone, I would've jumped to the ceiling with a massive YES, but my jealousy was beating the shit out of my common sense. 'Er, I dunno, Venetia. Got things to do. I'm behind on so much homework you wouldn't believe it.'

Venetia narrowed her eyes, seeing right through my bullcrap. *God! She has never looked so fit and never been so far out of my reach. This is all Jonah's fault with his damn phone!*

Meanwhile, Jonah looked at me like he was trying to work out a cruel maths problem. I tried to think of a reason to boot him up on the way home.

'I've got things to do too,' said McKay. 'Like cook my dad's dinner before he gets back – and fix the boiler.'

McKay didn't even know how to turn his oven on and he could have written all he knew about boilers on Venetia King's baby fingertip.

'Shame,' Venetia said. 'As I said, we need all the support we can get. We're playing Joan Benson and you know what we feel about *them*.'

Joan Benson was the private girls' school where most of the parents who lived in Crongton Village sent their daughters. I didn't know why but every time they came down to our ends they seemed to love-up the attention they got from the Year 11 brothers. The girls from our school hated them though – something to do with the Joan Benson sisters getting their pose on with their name-brand garms the last time they visited for a match. There was also a rumour that Kiran Cassidy, one of the most popular boys in our year, kissed up one of the Joan Benson girls in the toilets.

We bounced home that afternoon with Jonah still in his most-popular-kid-in-our year zone. McKay and I tried to talk about anything apart from new mobile phones. We didn't want to encourage him.

'I haven't taken a pic of you bruvs today yet, have I?' said Jonah, taking his damn new phone out of his pocket.

'Cos I don't *want* my pic taken,' replied McKay. 'Aren't you happy with the pics you took of all the Year 11 girls?'

Jonah's smile was bigger than a tent-full of clowns.

'Yeah, I took a lot,' Jonah said. 'And I took four of Venetia King. Gonna upload 'em on my PC when I get home.'

'But did you get any digits?' asked McKay.

Jonah's expression switched. 'I could've if I'd wanted to. And why are you laughing, Bit? I don't see you with any digits.'

'My day will come,' I said.

'I'm heading back to my slab,' said McKay. 'Feeling kinda peckish. Gonna make myself a corn beef, chicken-slice, tomato and cucumber sandwich and slap some mayonnaise on it. Maybe I should wedge some pickle in the mother too – Dad bought some hard dough bread yesterday.'

Jonah and I watched McKay lope away. I was pretty sure both of us were imagining some kind of giant Monster Munch.

'Gonna stop by my yard and play some Call of Duty?' asked Jonah.

The invite was tempting, especially with all the shit happening in my place recently. Mum had made sure she was out of the flat by the time I'd got up. Elaine had hardly said a word this morning and Gran had kept on telling me, 'Nah worry, Lemar, everyting will be all right.' But that was better than Jonah telling me about all the freaking apps on his new phone and me feeling awkward if his sister, Heather, was around. Boy! She was fit … but not as pretty as Venetia.

'Nah, I've got things to do as well,' I replied.

'When's the last time you've been around to my place?' Jonah wondered.

'I'll come up Wednesday,' I said. 'Just let me get all this homework out of the way.'

'All right then.' Jonah nodded.

He took out his phone and played with the damn thing until we reached our slab. I promised myself that somehow I'd get myself a new phone and have a world of Year 10 and 11 girls giving *me* untold attention.

*

By Wednesday things had returned to normal at home. Elaine had even asked, 'How you doing, bruv?' at the breakfast table. She seemed to have forgiven me for bringing those baby clothes home from Manjaro. Mum had gone back to kissing me on the forehead when she came home from work or when I left for school and Gran got her nag on about my homework. The only interesting thing that happened in school in the morning was my art teacher, Ms Rees, telling me my work was being considered to appear at some local gallery near to Crongton Broadway. She said my art had 'an urban contemporary modern slant to it'. Wasn't sure what she meant but my self-esteem grew taller than the Statue of Liberty. Maybe Dad was wrong. Perhaps one day I *would* be able to make a living out of my art.

I felt proper proud and at lunch break I called Mum to tell her but her phone went to voicemail. I left a message. Meanwhile, the brothers were getting all excited about the basketball match between our school, led by Venetia King, and the Joan Benson girls.

I got a text in my afternoon geography class. I thought it was from Mum but it was from Manjaro.

What's gwarnin, bruv? Hope tings are on the level at home and at school. Say hi to Jerome for me. He must've grown large from the last time I saw him. Would love to see him. Will be in touch.

Something cold slide-tackled down my spine. *Does he want another favour? What will I say to him? Then again, if it's something minor like going to the shops or something, and he gives me a touch, then I could think about saving up for a phone like Jonah's. But he might want me to go on a mission up Crongton Lane again. Shit!*

The final buzzer sounded and Jonah shot up out of his chair and hot-toed out of the place like zombies wanted to eat him. McKay and me looked at each other and I wondered what to do. I got my fret on about Manjaro's text. I considered telling McKay but thought better of it.

We bounced through the school corridors towards the main exit. When we got there we saw the Joan Benson girls climbing out of their school minibus in the car park. They wore navy blue capes over their sky-blue uniforms. Quite a crowd had built up. Brothers were wolf-whistling and spitting bars as South Crong girls got their hate on. Their teachers looked at us like we were terrorists and they were spreading their arms and escorting the girls as if they were a president's security detail. We saw Jonah getting his jump on near the minibus, taking pics with his damn new phone.

'What we gonna do, Bit?' asked McKay. 'Are we gonna trod home or watch this mother?'

I thought of Venetia King in her school basketball kit. 'Might as well stay and watch. Got nothing better to do.'

By the time we arrived at the sports hall there was no space left on the spectators' benches. We had to sit on the floor. We spotted Jonah taking more pics with his blasted phone. Girls were sitting either side of him and he loved it up. Venetia and her teammates were warming up, getting their bounce on, and I had to admit that Venetia looked as if she'd give my dad a good game.

Fifteen minutes later, the Joan Benson girls emerged from their dressing room. A weird thing happened. Brothers from our school, including McKay, got their cheer on while the girls booed them. Maybe it was because the Joan Benson girls wore shorter skirts. Venetia King glared at McKay, and if McKay ever dreamed of getting it on with her, that fantasy chomped the mud.

The game started. It was more hard-core than I expected. Players were barged off the ball, squaring up to each other, hair-pulling, elbowing ribs and cussing worse than my mum on gas-bill day. Wasn't sure if the Joan Benson girls understood all the swear words but it was entertaining as hell. One Joan Benson girl had to go off with a bloody nose and one of our players was sin-binned for a wild kung fu kick – all good.

Joan Benson won by three points: 43–40. The supporters filed out of the sports hall, with the boys chatting about the fit girls on display and the girls talking about how Joan Benson girls were all bitches.

I heard someone bouncing a basketball. There was only one player on the court – Venetia King. I stood up and she noticed me. I could see that the pain of defeat was beating the shit out of her composure. She walked towards me, bouncing the basketball. If I was brave I would've stood up, hugged her and told her, 'Nah worry, sweet fitness, everyting will be all right.'

She stopped a metre away from me and asked, 'Fancy a one-on-one? I need a warm down.'

I unzipped my jacket and took to the floor. *Be cool,* I said to myself. *Whatever happens, don't fall over. And don't, don't, don't stare at her too much.*

'You go first,' she said, bouncing the ball to me.

OK, I said to myself. *This is no big deal. Look how many times I've had a one-on-one with Dad on Crongton Green. This is the same deal. It's not some mad black hole in the universe – spacecraft science. Just throw the freaking ball into the hoop. So what if my opponent is the fittest girl in my year.*

We played for about twenty minutes and she beat the bull-crap out of me. Some of my shots were even missing the backboard. McKay was cracking up on the floor with laughter. I couldn't remember playing so rubbish. She also cheated by pushing, barging and stepping on my big toe. When I glanced at her she had her 'I'm serious at this basketball shit even when I'm playing shorties' face on. I ended up on the floor twice.

Venetia beat me 20–4. I tried to make it look like my defeat and my big toe weren't hurting me.

'Thanks,' she said. 'Needed that. We lost today cos only one or two of my teammates wanna put in a hundred per cent. I got really pissed off when just before we left the changing rooms Sandra Robinson said, "If Kiran Cassidy's watching I hope I don't sweat too much." I mean, how we gonna beat Joan Benson with that attitude? They're gonna have to step up if they want to make something of themselves in sport and get out of these ends.'

I nodded. If she'd said that all the Joan Benson girls were lizards but had somehow taken on human form I would've nodded to that shit too. And what was with Kiran Cassidy? Apart from fifteen centimetres of height he had on me what else did he have?

'Bit, can you do me a favour?'

'A favour? What kinda favour?'

'You're good at drawing, right?'

'Yeah, I suppose so.'

'Yeah.' Venetia nodded.'I've seen some of your work in the art room. Ms Rees puts the best ones on the wall.'

My head started to get its swell on. It felt twice the size of the basketball. 'I work hard on it,' I said.

'Do you think you can do a portrait of me?' she asked.

For a very long moment my mouth was paralysed. *Did she actually say what I think she said?* I glanced at McKay. His eyes showed the same shock. I ran over her request again. *Do you think you can do a portrait of me?* It was like someone working at the fried chicken takeaway asking if McKay wanted some free wings. Didn't know why it took me so long to say yes but at that moment I felt a vibration in my pocket. It was my phone.'Er ... one sec, Venetia.'

I was embarrassed to pull the damn thing out as it was a million years older than Jonah's new one. McKay's nickname for it was 'liccle brick' – it rhymed with another moniker of mine – Liccle Dick. It was another text from Manjaro. I swallowed the saliva that had built in my mouth.

We'll catch up soon, Bit. Hope Jerome is all good. Might ask you to do a favour for me.

All of a sudden I got my panic on. *What?* With Venetia staring at me and Manjaro texting me, I felt the pressure.

'Liccle Bit?' Venetia asked. She offered me a look like a

nurse who's discovered a little kid has swallowed a toy car. 'The portrait? You up for it? What are you saying, Bit?'

'Er, what? Oh, yeah, course, man.'

Venetia's smile niced up my heart. My calf muscles felt all tingly. 'That's great! Where do you wanna draw me? In the art room? In the playground? Then again, nah, too many people might distract us. Shall I come around to your yard?'

Had I heard right? Venetia King wanted to come around to my yard. Would have to make sure Mum, Elaine and Gran weren't around. *Don't want them embarrassing my hide. Better get my scrub on in my bedroom. Better scrub the whole damn yard. What should I wear? Definitely need to get a trim. Wait a minute! I wonder what Manjaro wants me to do? Oh crap! Don't worry about that for now – Venetia King asked to come around to my flat. Let me soak in that heavenly glory.*

'So where's it gonna be?' Venetia asked.

I glanced at McKay again. His mouth was open wider than China. The muscles in my face wanted me to get my biggest smile on. I tried to fight the urge of grinning like a clown who's sunk a happy-clappy pill. I developed a serious twitch – Venetia must've thought I was coming off drugs or something, or maybe having a stroke.

'At my yard!' I finally said.

'Cool,' Venetia replied. 'I'll let you know when.'

'You might have to sit for two or three sessions,' I said in a rush. 'I wanna get it right.'

'Yeah, that's cool too. Thanks, Bit. Gonna get my shower now. See you tomorrow.'

I watched her step towards the changing rooms and

imagined her taking a shower. No other girl in human history had ever walked sexier than Venetia King ... maybe apart from Jonah's sister, Heather.

I tried to appear cool but my heart was doing this Olympic-gymnastic-jumping shit in my chest. McKay looked at me like I was an alien with bad breath or something. '*Why?*' he said. 'Why you? I mean ... you're so freaking short! Fit girls don't usually go for short brothers. It's just ... wrong. This doesn't make sense. Something's wrong with the world, bruv. Can't freaking believe it.'

I stepped out of that sports hall and, for the first time in my short life, I felt ... tall.

11

Breaking News

McKay was seriously mystified on the way home. 'It don't mean nothing,' he said. 'She just wants you to draw her, no big deal! Doesn't mean you're gonna get to first base or nothing.'

'But I'm on the field of play,' I said.

'You're just drawing her, right. She ain't gonna pose naked or anything and when you're done drawing her, that's *it*! She'll go back to ignoring your short ass.'

'You're just jealous! This is eating you up, bruv!'

'It ain't nothing, Bit. Look, I've gotta step home and clean up the castle before my dad gets back. See you tomorrow.'

I could understand why McKay wanted to step off. This must've been one of the worst weeks of his life. What with Jonah posing off his new phone and Venetia King stepping to my yard, McKay would probably crash out in his room, draw the curtains and ask his family not to trouble him. He might have been so upset he couldn't eat his dinner ... Then again, delete that, nothing would have stopped McKay from mauling a meal.

I remembered that I'd told Jonah I would check him at his place after school on Wednesday to get our gaming on. I wasn't gonna go but I had to tell him about my Venetia King news. If his sister was there then so be it. It would be worth the look on Jonah's face when he found out my shit. In fact, I hoped he'd take a pic of the moment on that damn new phone of his.

Arriving at Jonah's place ten minutes later, he led me to his front room where he had a fifty-inch TV on the wall. My TV seemed as tiny as a postage stamp in comparison. 'I'm gonna plug in the wires for the game,' he said. 'If you wanna drink or anything just step to the kitchen and help yourself.'

Jonah's phone made this musical sound. He paused the game and read his text. 'It's from McKay.'

'I bet it's about Venetia King stepping with her fit self to my yard.'

'No it ain't,' Jonah said. He put down the game console and reread his text message. 'Oh my days! Another brother's been deleted! Blazed by the old library. *Shit.* How many is that in the past—'

'Shot! Who?' I hoped it wasn't anybody I knew from Manjaro's crew. *Shit. What if it is?* 'You're one of us now,' the girl had said. 'Who got blazed? *Tell* me who?'

'He ... he didn't say who. He's on his way there now. Man! It's like a brother gets blazed every freaking week!'

Jonah hurriedly packed his game away. Damn! I had to leave my bourbons and my chocolate butterfly cake behind. We bombed down the stairs of our block and hot-toed a shortcut through the children's play area of our estate, around the skate park and eventually to the road where the old library building was located. Sirens were blaring in the distance and there was a helicopter hovering above. The feds were pushing back the crowds and trying to tape off the whole street. 'If you carry on obstructing us I'll have to arrest you,' said one grumpy fed to some eager brother. 'Now *back off* and let me do my job!'

We could hear a girl bawling at the front of the pack. Someone else was cussing.

'What is wrong with these young people? Shooting each other for *what*?'

'It's the North Crong–South Crong turf war again,' said another.

'I blame the parents,' an older woman said. 'Letting their kids run around the place with guns and knives. *No* discipline at home.'

'That's cos there's nothing for them to do around here,' a younger voice said. 'They've closed down everything.'

'That's *no* excuse for killing each other,' the first voice argued.

'Lock 'em up, I say, and fling the key into the sewers!'

I wished the ancients would just shut their beaks. They were getting on my nerves. They were always saying shit about us but my dad had told me there was nuff beef back in his day with brothers getting blazed and shanked. It wasn't like we were the first generation to have these worries and it wasn't like most brothers I knew wanted to go out and shoot somebody.

I know it's not the PC thing to say but being there at a murder scene was proper exciting. I got this surge of danger running through my veins like one of them mad bobsleigh riders bombing down an ice chute. People around me buzzed with their own ideas and explanations of what happened and who did it.

From what we could see, and cos I was a short-ass I had to jump up and down, the feds were talking to people from the computer repair shop next door to the old library. Other feds in yellow Day-Glo jackets were using chalk to draw around some bits that were on the ground. I was too far away to see but I imagined drippings of blood were wetting up the concrete. I nudged a guy in front of me. 'What ... What happened? Who got blazed? Was it someone from North Crong or South? Do you know—'

'Rest your lip, liccle brother, and I might give you an answer!'

'Sorry!'

'Drive-by shooting,' answered the brother. 'Some North Crong boy was stepping out of the computer repair shop when two guys on a motorbike rolled by and blazed him. Two shots laced him in the chest. Someone said they fired four shots and this other brother says three. One went through the shop window. An assistant got shot in the arm.'

'Drive-by!' repeated Jonah. 'Things are getting messed up.'

'Someone said it was one of Major Worries' close soldiers,' said the brother. 'If it was then this war ain't gonna stop soon.'

I had heard Major Worries' name being whispered a few times. He was Manjaro's number one enemy – the top G of the North Crong crew. I had never seen him before but McKay said he was broader than Chicago and taller than the Shard – all of him serious muscle. He walked around in a black vest and black tracksuit bottoms and had a king cobra tattoo nicing up his tree-trunk neck.

The feds asked us all to retreat further. I was still springing up and down trying to get a better view. I noticed that the steel shutters covering the doorways and windows of the old library were now daubed in North and South Crong graffiti. I hoped no one would ever spray my nickname anywhere. I don't wanna be a target.

'I'd never snitch to the feds,' said the brother in front of me, lowering his voice. 'But I reckon this is Manjaro getting revenge for Nightlife.'

Suddenly, I felt this cramping feeling in my stomach. I recalled my last favour for Manjaro when I collected a package from an address in Crongton Lane. I backed away a few paces. 'Jonah, Jonah, gotta step home.'

'Why?' Jonah replied. 'You're not gonna wait for the feds in the white jumpsuits getting their CSI on? And the TV news people will be stepping here soon.'

'No ... gotta step.'

I turned around and nearly bumped into McKay who had obviously been running. He was sweating and wheezing and offered me a messed-up look. 'Who got deleted?' he panted.

'Some North Crong brother in a drive-by. The feds are pushing people back. The war's erupted again, innit.'

He slowly shook his head, not taking his eyes off me. I could almost read what he was thinking. *You might've carried the murder weapon for this latest deletion!*

I stared at the ground to avoid his eyes. McKay reached out and grabbed my shoulder. 'Remember, Bit, some mother has to pull the freaking trigger – guns can't work on their lonesome. Believe that.'

I tried to force a smile but my face wasn't having it. I made my way out of the throng, deciding to head for the park instead of stepping home. When I got there the park was empty, apart from a dad playing football with his son. What else could've been in that parcel? It wasn't hot meals for the ancients. It had to be the gun. I sat on a swing and asked myself why had it been *that* package I'd picked up? But if it hadn't been me, Manjaro would've asked someone else. That didn't make me feel any better. I wondered who the guy was who got blazed. Who were his parents? Maybe he had an older sis who had a toxic temper too? He might've been good with his hands, making stuff, or liked watching old school kung fu movies like Jonah, McKay and me. If this shit didn't stop, that kid balling with his dad in the park might soon be in danger – and all his liccle bredrens too.

My phone rang. It was Gran.

'Lemar? Where are you? I expected you home an hour ago. Don't you know that someone else has been killed?'

'Yeah, I know. I'm in the park, Gran. I decided to step here after I went to Jonah's. On my way home now.'

'Be careful!'

I was more than careful. After every ten steps I glanced over my shoulder. I crossed roads when there wasn't any moving car in sight. The standard amount of kids weren't playing in the forecourts or hanging out by the grocer's compared to usual. I arrived home safely and let out a sigh as I closed the front door behind me.

Gran had cooked salmon fillets, pasta and niced up my plate with a sprinkling of cheese. We ate in silence. Mum was still at work and Elaine had been out all day visiting friends – she had called home to make sure everyone was OK after hearing about the murder. Both of them were going to take a cab home. I was seriously thirsty and I sank four glasses of water – Elaine had probably killed the rest of the blackcurrant squash.

'So are you going to give me the silent treatment all night or are you going to tell me what's on your mind?' Gran wanted to know. 'I guess this latest murder has everyone in a fret. Me don't understand where these foolish young people get their hands on armed weapons.'

Guilt kicked me in the chest. I had to stare into my empty plate. 'I … I don't understand either. But I'm … I'm all right, Gran.'

'You sure? You look like you've just seen me grandfather!'

'I'm just a liccle tired, Gran,' I lied.

Gran studied me hard.

'It's *me* you're talking to, Lemar! Not some foolish old

woman that don't know you. Now, tell me what is troubling you. You've hardly said a word since you reach home. Out with it!'

How could I tell her what was bothering me? That I might've carried something that placed other people in danger. That I might be one of *them.* And being one of *them* might lead to North Crong bruvs trying to blaze me. The cramping sensation in my stomach got worse. I could sense my forehead about to erupt with sweat beads. My heart did its best to free itself from my chest. I wanted to pour myself another glass of water but that might have looked proper suspicious. Gran seized me with her most lethal stare. 'I . . . I . . .'

'I what, Lemar?'

Guilt was stomping my conscience. I just couldn't tell all to her. She'd be so disappointed in me. 'I'm worried about the bad vibes in the flat. You know, between Elaine, Mum and me. Things are cool right now, but when's it going to kick off again?'

'Don't worry yourself about that.' Gran smiled. 'Every family has their ups and downs. Yes, we have our issues but in the end they'll be sorted out. No bad vibes last for ever.'

'There's . . . there's this girl coming around here soon. She wants me to draw her.'

'Is that what's prompted all this?' Gran laughed. 'You're a liccle nervous? Don't worry yourself, Lemar. We'll be on our best behaviour. I'll promise you that . . . Who is this girl? Is it the same one you've been sweet on for a while now?'

'Er, yes, Gran. Her name is Venetia.'

'Nice name! Now, when she comes around just be yourself. Don't try to show off and don't pretend to be someting that you're not.'

When Mum arrived home, Gran wasted no time in spilling my Venetia news to her. She came into my room while I was sketching something with a mad, proud grin on – like one a mum has when her child learns to ride a bike or something. She hugged me like I had a world of grade As in maths.

'Mum! I'm doing a new sketch!'

It was like being six years old again. 'You see, Lemar,' she said. 'If you concentrate on what you're good at, you'll be rewarded.'

'Yes, Mum.'

'What a day for you!' she continued. 'Your artwork might be on display at a gallery and you have a date with a nice girl. Blessings rain upon you today!'

'*Mum*, it's *not* a date!'

'Of course it's a date! Just remember to brush your teeth when you reach home that day. You don't want your mouth to smell frowsy-like! And also fix up your armpits.'

'*Mum!*'

'I'm glad something went right for you,' she added. 'So much terrible news these days! Your gran told me that you were worried about the gang war erupting again but try to concentrate on the nicer things, you hearing me? If we don't do that we would never step out of our flat and live our lives!'

'Yes, Mum.'

'*Don't* let these idiot boys who just want to kill each other spoil your good news.'

'All right, Mum.'

She kissed me on the forehead before she left my room. I got back to my sketch of the old library feeling another punch of guilt.

A couple of hours later, Elaine barged into my room, looked at me like I had grown a carrot from my ear and asked, 'Venetia King is coming here?'

'Yes.' I nodded.

Elaine shook her head, left my room and slammed my door.

I was falling asleep that night dreaming about kissing Venetia King on a sun-blessed beach in Hawaii when I heard my phone vibrate. There were three messages from McKay.

The North Crong brother who got deleted was Long Mouth Smolenko, Major Worries' right-hand man. He's a mixed-race yout. Think his dad is Polish or Russian or something.

As I read, the cramping sensation in my stomach returned. I thumbed down to the second text.

World War 3's gonna start, bruv. Better start digging your bunker. Major Worries is not gonna let this go. Brothers are saying he's looking to buy some AK-47s and rocket launchers and shit.

Had my collecting that package led to this? I opened the third text.

Breaking News

Dad's putting a curfew on my ass and pulling up the
drawbridge. Says that I can't step anywhere after school
and I must retreat to my castle.

I lay awake in my bed thinking of Nightlife and Long
Mouth Smolenko. How many more would get deleted? And
why did people call him *Long Mouth*?

12

Date Night

When Mum bounced into my room in the morning and slapped on the light, my eyes stung more than usual. She was filling my sock drawer, placing ironed shirts in my wardrobe and picking up pencils from my floor.

'Lemar! When you finish school this afternoon I want you to come straight home, do you hear me? No lingering or messing around, just bring your liccle backside back to this flat, you hear me?'

'I hear you, Mum.'

'I'm not having you getting caught up in this gang-war madness! It was on the local news last night. A drive-by shooting! Some poor boy got shot coming out of the computer repair shop up by the old library. He was only nineteen. God! I feel for his parents. You know I shop in the supermarket near there, don't you.'

She found a pair of boxers at the foot of my bed as she carried on tidying my room. She hardly looked at me but that was all good cos guilt was jabbing my head again.

'Yeah, Mum.'

'That could've been any of us!'

'I know, Mum.'

'I think I would turn fool if some madness ever happened to Elaine, Jerome or you.'

'I hear you, Mum.'

'Don't even *think* of wandering about after school near the town centre, Lemar. You hear me? In fact, you get your liccle self back to this flat.'

'All right, Mum. You already said.'

God! When is she gonna stop? The jabs of guilt had turned into uppercuts. She finally left my room and I could breathe easily. Tried to tell myself to stop thinking about that guy who got blazed away and concentrate on the good things in my life. Venetia King.

When I got ready for school I niced up my armpits with extra deodorant and got my aftershave splash on – a gift from my sister. It was the first time I had used it since I got it at Christmas.

Before I left I stared into the mirror in the bathroom to see how my moustache was getting on – not too good but at least there was a sort of shadow there. Man! Even Jonah was getting his bristle on. I needed some facial hair to sex up my face and I needed a trim to nice up my head.

The first thing I noticed on my way to school was the presence of fed cars cruising about the estate. I got my fret on about them stopping me, dragging me to the fed station and charging me with being an accessory to a murder. Jonah was jabbering away about his damn new phone and taking pics of the fed cars but I didn't hear or pay attention to him. I was wondering how hardback brothers would treat me if I ended up in a young offender institution.

English was the first lesson of the day. I could hardly string a sentence together. I sat next to McKay in history and he had a mad theory about the Smolenko deletion. 'It was a professional hit,' he whispered like he was a mega-snitch in a mafia movie. 'Smolenko's dad is a top G in Poland. He brings in all kinda guns, tanks and explosive shit from there. He's got men working at airports, seaports, train stations and shit. Manjaro wants a piece of that so Long Mouth Smolenko had to be blazed.'

McKay always had a world of crazy theories but this one had to be his worst. 'What you talking about, bruv?' I challenged. 'That's bull-crap. From what I heard today, Smolenko's dad is unemployed. The last job he had was stacking shelves at the supermarket.'

'That was his cover,' McKay insisted. 'I'm telling you, he's a top G. Man's got a fifteen-room mansion back in Poland with a swimming pool, Jacuzzi and cinema room. He's got a satellite dish the size of the one on top of the MI5 building.'

'You're being OTT.'

'No I'm not. Smolenko's dad had to get plastic surgery cos Interpol were after him.'

'Who are Interpol?'

'They're kinda like the FBI for Europe. A world of James Bonds but they don't get the cool gadgets and the sick cars.

They blaze first and ask questions later. They can delete a man with their telescopic rifles right between the eyebrows from three miles away. You can't mess with those brothers.'

'McKay, who tells you this shit? Don't you think that Nightlife getting deleted has anything to do with it?'

'It does a bit but it's not the whole story,' said McKay.'Who knows? Maybe Major Worries set up to blaze him cos he was about to snitch.'

That was the one theory I wanted to believe in cos it meant my package handling had nothing to do with it.

I was worrying about this Smolenko thing so much I was thinking of stepping home at lunchtime. I was sinking my school dinner of beef lasagne when I considered developing a chesty cough that I could go to the school nurse with. Couldn't go to her and say I'm stressed out – she wouldn't hear that or test that shit with a thermometer.

Meanwhile, Jonah and his damn new phone were still getting untold attention. This time Year 8 girls were swarming around him. Venetia King ambled through Jonah's audience in that sexy way of hers, but not to Jonah. 'What's happening, Bit? Everything all good?'

I straightened my back and put my best pose on. 'Yeah, yeah, yes,' I stuttered.

'How's tomorrow for you? Come around to your yard after school?'

'Yeah,' I replied. 'That's cool.'

'You don't mind doing this?'

'Course not!'

'Then I'll link you at the main entrance after school, yeah?'

'Yeah, see you then.'

My heart did a somersault and I grinned wider than the Mississippi. Jonah angled his eyebrows and McKay shook his head, saying, 'Why you?'

I couldn't remember the last time I had felt so bad but then switched to feeling such a good vibe. My ass was chained in a sewer bath and the shit was rising but at least Venetia was coming around to my yard. Because of her I could listen to the stupid pop songs that Year 8 girls sang in the playground rather than the feds turning up and dragging my ass to a fed cell. For the rest of the day I smiled at people I didn't even know. They probably thought either I was weird or had taken one of those pills that Manjaro's soldiers had been selling. Maybe I was overcompensating for the dread I felt in my stomach but it got me through the day.

Next morning I asked Mum if she was working late. 'Yes,' she replied. 'They got me on the twilight zone for three days in a row! Three days!'

'Sorry to hear that, Mum. It'll be good when we can share more time in the evenings.'

Mum offered me a wry look. 'Are you trying to sweet me up, Lemar? If you're building up to asking me for money the answer is *no*. I have nuff bills to pay.'

'I get it, Mum.'

Man! At least she wouldn't be around this evening.

Next on my list was Gran. She was doing some ironing in her room that she shared with Mum. 'Are you gonna be around later on, Gran?'

'Why you asking?' she interrogated.'You want the place free so you can get up to nastiness with your new girlfriend?'

'She's *not* my girlfriend! And no, Gran, it ain't like that.'

'Then tell me how it's like then.'

'I just ... just wanna sketch her in some peace and quiet.'

Gran grinned a knowing grin. God! A gran thinking about her grandson having sex is just ... wrong.'You just make sure you behave yourself and keep the snake in the cage!'

Last on my list was Elaine. She was feeding Jerome his bottle when I entered her room.'You gonna be around later on, sis?'

'What if I am?' she asked.

'Just asking! Man! Can't I even ask you a simple question these days?'

'I might be and I might not,' she finally answered.

I decided not to push her any further and left her room.

'Lemar, hold up,' Elaine called me back.

I returned and sat on her bed. She nudged the door closed with her backside while she continued to feed Jerome. He was making these cute gurgling sounds.

'You heard anything on road about Smolenko's deletion?' she asked.

'No, how would I know?'

'Cos you're on road more than me.'

'I go to school so how would I know anything? Who's gonna tell me shit?'

'Cool down your fever, bro! I only asked.'

'I haven't heard anything, sis.'

Jerome spat the bottle teat out of his mouth and Elaine

started to rub his back. 'I just hope that anyone I know is not involved.'

'As I said, sis, no bird has landed on my shoulder and chirped me anything.'

Elaine gave me a long look. 'Have a good day at school.'

The day at school was the longest ever. Maths went on for five hours, English went on for six and chemistry went on for eight years. I think I had slapped too much deodorant on as McKay and Jonah teased me all day about it. They pissed me off by calling me the 'armpit kid'. As the final buzzer sounded I hot-toed into the boys' toilets and almost drowned myself in the sink. I dabbed and shook the water off me but I still had a lingering smell of my deodorant polluting my personal space.

As I stepped through the school corridors towards the main exit my heart started to pound like an out-of-control wrecking ball. I stopped rolling, closed my eyes for a few seconds and tried to get my meditation on. Didn't wanna hot-step out of the school like a kid running down the stairs on Christmas morning. I resumed walking and attempted to strut as cool as I could. I pushed through the swing doors like a cowboy in those ancient western movies and immediately heard the messed-up laughing of Jonah and McKay. My heart sank to the bottom of my stomach. 'What are *you* doing here?' I asked. 'Step home!'

'Waiting to see you get humiliated,' answered McKay through his giggles. 'Venetia's not coming, bruv. She was playing with you.'

'No she wasn't,' I countered. *Shit. Maybe she* was *playing me? I mean, I'm a short-ass.*

'Do you see her?' asked Jonah. He was shielding his eyes from the sun like he was a sailor in the crow's nest looking for land. 'No sign of Miss Fitness, bruv!'

'I haven't seen her since dinner time,' added McKay. 'She must've come to her senses, bruv. She probably realised she was in a messed-up state of mind when she said she'd go back to your castle, started to scream, hot-toed to the school counsellor and sank untold pills.'

'Her mum probably picked her up and took her home,' laughed Jonah. 'She ...'

Just then Venetia King rolled out of the main school exit. She really did have the sexiest walk in the whole universe. She stopped for a moment to check something on her phone. For a second I closed my eyes and willed, *Please see me, please see me.* She finally waved at me. She looked proper gorgeous. I felt my heart pick itself up from the bottom of my stomach and rise like a beach ball in a swimming pool. My grin was broader than the USA. Jonah looked devastated. McKay stared at the ground and shook his head. 'Something's not right with the world,' he muttered. '*Why, why, why* you? You're ... Liccle Bit.'

McKay and Jonah walked away like they had just lost their entire families to cannibals on some faraway messed-up island. Venetia stepped towards me and my heart got its bounce on. I had such a boost of confidence that for a second I was thinking if I should get my Hollywood kiss on. I thought better of it. 'Sorry I'm late,' she apologised. 'I had to see my English teacher.'

'That's cool,' I replied. 'No problem.'

We stepped out of the school with some schoolmates getting their stare on. I didn't give a shit – Venetia King was trodding home with *me*!

'So how long you've been drawing?' Venetia asked.

'Oh, from primary school days,' I replied. 'For Christmas one year my dad bought me this sketch pad, colouring book and pencils and stuff. So it kinda started from there.'

'You're really good,' said Venetia. 'There's one that Ms Rees put up with some sad man sitting on the pavement with the old warehouses behind him. That's my favourite. What made you think of that?'

Kiss my granny's neck warts! She has a fave painting of mine! That means she must've seen 'em all.

'Er, I was just thinking of what happened to all the men who used to work there, you know. So I imagined one of them men just coming back to have a look at the place where he used to work.'

'Thanks for agreeing to do my portrait, Bit. I saw the one you did of your gran – *really good*!'

Oh my days, she thinks I'm really good. I should be recording this.

'Thanks. Do you want a profile or full-on?'

'Full-on,' answered Venetia.

'So where do you live?'

'On the other side of the estate – Somerleyton House. Fifth floor. Not too far from Wareika Way. It's near the Crongton stream and for some reason it stinks on a Thursday morning. My mum's always cussing about it.'

Date Night

'The smell could be due to the world of guys who, er, do their business in the stream after balling in the park.'

'Eeewwww! That's gross. Typical of what a lot of guys do around here – use the place like a toilet!'

'I wouldn't do anything like that,' I quickly added.

'I hope *not*.'

'Er ... have you got any brothers and sisters?' I asked.

'My sister, Princess, is twelve and I've got a living brat of a bro who's eight, Milton. They get away with all kinds of tings that I didn't when I was their age. So unfair.'

'I've got an older sister, Elaine. She's ...'

'Yeah, I heard of her. She used to link with Manjaro, right?'

I wished she hadn't brought that up. 'Er, yeah.'

'Ain't she got a baby for him?'

I'd hoped she wouldn't ask that. Was getting tired of people on the estate asking me if Elaine had Manjaro's baby. I hadn't expected it from Venetia. Better answer her though and move on. 'Er, yeah. Jerome.'

'Don't get me wrong,' Venetia said, holding my wrist. 'I'm not judging your sis or anything. Maybe she thought linking with a man like Manjaro was a way to get out of the ends.'

We swapped more small talk until we reached my slab. All the way I was checking if anybody I knew from my year was watching us together. Among other things, I learned that Venetia's mum works in a laundry shop, her dad fixes boilers and her sister, Princess, was always jacking her clothes.

As we climbed the steps to my flat I prayed that Mum would still be at work, Elaine was out visiting friends and

Gran was getting her nap on in her room. I turned the key in my front door and heard a world of cussing. Oh *double shit*!

'You don't run my life!' Elaine screamed at Mum. 'You can't tell me what to do!'

They were clashing in the hallway and Venetia and I just stopped in our tracks. I didn't know what to do or say. My heart sank like a torpedoed basketball.

'A part-time job would help me out, Elaine!' Mum argued. She had a chicken leg gripped in her left hand that she had just seasoned. Venetia's nose twitched from the curry powder and the pepper. 'It's just me in this yard paying gas bill, electric bill and every other kind of bill. Your gran helps me out with her pension but that's not much. Why can't you find a part-time job and contribute a bit?'

'Cos I want to *study*, Mum,' replied Elaine, waving Jerome's bottle in front of her. 'How many times do I have to tell you? I want to do business and accounting. That's what I wanted to do until Jerome came along.'

'So while you're taking yourself off to college, *I* have to pay for everything and feed everybody?' Mum spat back. 'Can't you fit in a part-time job with your studies?'

It was proper humiliating. The chicken leg versus Jerome's bottle. Lord knows what Venetia thought of it. I just hoped she wouldn't spill to anybody at school about it. I felt what chances I had with her were chomping the mud.

'Mum! It won't be for ever,' Elaine ranted. 'Gran has already told me she doesn't mind looking after Jerome. I thought you would support me on this but *oh no!* You just want me to end up in a dead-end job like *you*!'

'This dead-end job pays for the roof over your spoilt head! It paid for you to go through school, all the shoes you've worn out and all of your damn clothes!'

The chicken leg was flying dangerously close to Elaine's head.

'I know, Mum, and I love you for it, but I want to end up with something a bit more than just paying for a roof over my head and getting by.'

'So what I do isn't good enough for you? You have *no* respect for what I do, Elaine!'

Their noses were almost touching each other. They shared the same expression. Like mother like daughter. I prayed they wouldn't fight.

Venetia pulled my arm. 'Shall ... shall I come back another time, Bit?'

'Er, I don't know ...'

'I want to better myself and for Jerome, and *I* have no respect?' Elaine stated. She offered me and Venetia a quick glance. Then she glared at Mum. 'Sometimes I wonder if you're my freaking mother!'

Mum looked at us too then returned to eyeball Elaine. 'Change your out-of-order tone or see if this mother can still discipline her unruly daughter!'

At this point I proper hated my family. How could they do this to me? I wanted to take them to court and divorce their asses. I'd get my rage on in the witness box pointing at them madly like they did in serious court-case movies. I'd tell the judge and the jury how they deleted my chances with the girl who had the sexiest walk in the universe. I hoped the judge would be some evil, messed-up, medieval brother who sentenced them for seventy-nine years of mountain-breaking labour or something.

'Lemar!' Mum finally addressed me. 'And, er ...'

'This is Venetia, Mum,' I said.

'Hi.' Venetia introduced herself with a massive smile. God, she was gorgeous!

There was an awkward ten seconds.

By Mum's expression I could tell that she was relieved that I had bounced through the front door. Elaine crossed her arms and chewed the inside of her mouth – something she always did when frustrated. 'All right, Venetia,' she coldly greeted before hot-stepping to her room and slamming the door.

'Would you like something to drink or eat, Venetia?' Mum asked as if nothing had happened.

'Yes please.'

Mum disappeared into the kitchen. I sighed a giant sigh and led Venetia to the lounge. I slapped on the TV as Venetia made her fit self comfortable on the sofa. My God! Venetia King sitting on *my* couch. 'We've only got orange squash,' Mum called from the kitchen. 'Is that all right? I haven't cooked yet but I've got some bun and cheese that I picked up on the way home from work.'

'That's cool,' said Venetia politely. 'Thanks.'

I should've answered Mum too but I was too busy wondering why Mum was at home when she said she was gonna be working the twilight zone. Anyway, at least Elaine was raging so she'd probably be brewing in her room for the rest of the night.

'Nice place,' Venetia said, looking around the lounge. She was very polite. God! There was a pic of me on the wall when I was seven years old. I should've taken it down and burned it.

'Er ... where do you wanna sit? It's up to you.'

Venetia glanced around. 'I'll sit in your chair if you don't mind. There's a map of the Caribbean behind it and my family's from Trinidad.'

'That can work.' I smiled. 'When you finish sinking the cheese and bun I'll get my sketch pad and pencils.'

'Cool.'

I was proper relieved that Mum remained in the kitchen while I was sketching Venetia, and Elaine never left her room. Venetia hardly twitched a muscle and I could just stare at her. She had frizzy hair nicing up her diamond-shaped face and brown freckles sexed up her cheeks like brown sugar in a milo. Her eyebrows arched neatly and she had gold earrings the size of DVD discs in her ears. I struggled a bit with my curves and straight lines cos I was so nervous. There was something sad about her gaze though. I couldn't quite explain it. She'd posed for twenty minutes when I thought that was enough.

'That's it for today,' I said. 'With, er, everything that went on I couldn't, er, get in a vibe like I usually do.'

'Yeah, it was a bit ... tense,' she replied. 'But don't feel bad. You wanna hear the beef in my flat!'

I managed a smile. It was good that she was trying to make me feel better. Maybe my chances hadn't licked the mud.

'Next time will be better – trust me on that!'

'Can I see what you done so far?' she asked.

'No,' I said, quickly flipping over my sketch pad. 'You'll see it when I finish.'

'Come on, Bit. I'm sure it's all good.'

'*No,*' I insisted. I had my serious face on. She might've been the most kissable girl in my school but I didn't even allow Gran to take a peek of a portrait I was sketching before it was finished.

She stood up and stretched. I think she was brewing a bit. 'Thanks for starting this, Bit. When you're done I'll give you a liccle touch.'

'No, Venetia. I can't take your money. I'm doing this as a bredren.'

'You sure? I don't mind paying.'

I can't lie. Her insisting on paying proper vexed me. Anybody could pay me for a sketch. But somebody who I fancied? It just felt … wrong.

'Course I'm sure,' I said, trying to raise a smile. 'Nah, I can't take any money off you.'

If Jonah had heard this conversation he would've slapped each side of my head and then slapped me again. I could almost hear him cussing my hide. *What's wrong with you, Bit? The girl's offering you some money. Take it!* Like me, Jonah thought that Venetia King was hotter than a boiled egg in Jamaica but he wouldn't have any problem charging her top dollar for a portrait.

'You're generous,' Venetia said. 'Thanks again.'

My mind brought up an us-kissing-on-a-Hawaiian-beach fantasy and I had to give my head a shake to get rid of it.

'I'd better step now,' she said.

Date Night

'All right, I'll walk you out.'

Venetia stopped by the kitchen and said goodbye to Mum.

'Nice to have met you, Venetia,' Mum replied, between sips of her coffee. 'Lemar, you better walk Venetia home. *Don't* linger on your way back, you hear me?'

I was glad Mum mentioned the walking home thing cos I wasn't sure about asking.

'Thanks for stepping me home,' Venetia said as we moved out to the balcony. 'I've lived here all my life but I don't feel safe any more, you know, with all what's going on.'

'Yeah, I hear that. Some North Crong yout' called Long Mouth Smolenko got blazed the other day.'

'I heard about that,' Venetia said, folding her arms. 'Another family will wonder what is happening to them. People always forget what the families go through.'

'Must be horrible.'

'My cousin was shot by a stray bullet two years ago,' Venetia revealed when she stepped off the last stair of my slab. 'She was minding her own business at a bus stop when guns blazed from a car ...'

'I heard about that,' I recalled. 'Didn't realise she was your cousin. What was her name? Kay ...'

'Katrina King,' Venetia filled in. 'We were close, used to do everything together. Don't know how your sister could ever link up with a man like Manjaro.'

'I ... I don't know either. Er, shit happens.'

I made a mental note that Venetia must never find out about my package-carrying mission. *What was I thinking? Maybe Elaine's right. Sometimes I don't think before I act.*

'He's a good-looking guy but I could never link up with a man who's into G warfare and shit.'

What about me, Venetia? I wanted to scream. *Aren't I a good-looking guy?*

'Er, yeah, I hear you on that,' I said.

'You know what makes me sick?' said Venetia. 'There're people who know who fired the shot but they won't spill. It's some messed-up loyalty to their *crew*.'

'That is just wrong,' I agreed.

'One day though, Bit, that so-called bad man who fired the shot will be eating his food with plastic knives and forks for the rest of his days.'

'And I hear the food ain't too good in prison,' I quipped. 'The cornflakes are tough like ghetto gravel and the porridge is thick like hippo vomit.'

Venetia laughed out loud, almost tripping over herself. It felt good to know that I could make her crack up like that. When she composed herself, she said, 'Too many brothers from these ends finish up spitting through iron bars. *This* can't be the be all and end all. You got drawing, Bit, you can use that to get out of these ends.'

'And you've got your football and your dancing. With that you can get out of these ends too.'

'I've got more than that, Bit. You've gotta have a plan B. What happens if I mash up my leg?'

I thought about the conversation I had with my dad about plan Bs. *Maybe he's right cos Venetia's saying the same deal. But I'm crap at maths and English.*

We rolled on until we arrived at Somerleyton House – the

ugliest block of flats in the whole of Crongton. They'd painted it a dark blue that was just ... wrong. It was kinda messed up that the prettiest girl in Crongton had to live there.

'This is me.' Venetia smiled that gorgeous smile. 'I'll see you tomorrow. Thanks for walking me back to my slab.'

'No worries.'

I watched her perform the sexiest walk in history and go through the main entrance of the block. Man! Venetia King had been to my yard and I'd walked her fit self home. What a day. I wondered why she wanted me to draw her portrait. Maybe it was for her parents or something? But hey-ho! Who cared as long as she brought her fit self to my yard and I could roll myself into a position to get close to her.

13

An Inspector Calls

I bounced into my flat feeling a good vibe. I was sure Jonah and McKay were killing themselves with jealousy about me getting it on with Venetia King – that was why they couldn't bear to mention her name and why they were bigging up girls who they'd never bigged up before. Also, I hadn't heard anything from Manjaro for a number of days and the shadow of my moustache was definitely getting darker. The world was getting to be a better place.

I walked through the hallway and I heard unfamiliar voices in the kitchen. I stepped inside and I couldn't believe what I saw. The bounce in my step collapsed and my heartbeat decided to take a timeout. Two feds were sitting down at our small kitchen table, getting their sip on. Gran was serving them custard creams. Everyone looked at me.

'Hi, Lemar, how was school today?' Gran asked me. There

was no welcoming smile like usual and Gran's English always improved when there was someone official in the flat.

'Er . . . OK,' I answered.

I had to sit down before my legs gave way. My heart was right-hooking the front of my chest. The Atlantic Ocean was about to split open my forehead. I glanced at the officers and they smiled back at me. They lipped their teas again. I picked up a custard cream and sank it in two bites.

'These officers are just investigating the recent gang-war foolishness and are conducting door-to-door enquiries to find out if anybody has seen anything,' Gran explained.

I was barely listening. One of the officers was a woman and she gave me a look that said, *I know I'm smiling but we have evidence that YOU are involved with this shit, Lemar! And we're gonna make you spill!*

'It's just routine,' the male fed said. He sipped his tea once more. The female fed got her nibble on.

The Atlantic Ocean had burst and I had to swab it off my forehead. I heard a key crunching through the front door. Everyone looked towards the hallway. *Shit.* More feds? Didn't know why but I was thinking of that guy who crawled through a mile-long tunnel of shit to escape that mad prison in *The Shawshank Redemption* – another film that Jonah had downloaded illegally.

Elaine went by, pushing a screaming Jerome in his buggy. Then she came back and took a double-look at our guests in the kitchen. 'What's going on?' Elaine asked. 'Is Lemar in trouble?'

'No, no,' the female officer replied. 'We're just conducting door-to-door enquiries about the latest … incidents in Crongton. We think he may have seen something. Any little piece of information could be critical.'

'Gran,' Elaine called. Her voice now had its serious tone on. 'Can you look after Jerome? I think he needs changing. Might be best if I sit in for the interview – I know what they can't get away with.'

The feds glanced at each other.

'No problem, Elaine.'

Gran stepped out of the kitchen and she picked up Jerome from his buggy.

'You are over eighteen?' the fed woman asked Elaine.

'Yes, I am! Nineteen.'

The feds fake-grinned like they were taking pics with their least favourite aunt. The male fed had his notebook ready. Elaine glared at me – her eyes seemed to turn into gas rings. The Atlantic Ocean was still pouring out of my forehead and Niagara Falls was bursting through my armpits. Better keep my jacket on. The shit's about to slap the windmill.

'Is it Lemar Jackson?' the fed woman started. 'Can you confirm?'

'Yes it is,' answered Elaine.

'I'm sure Lemar can answer for himself,' said the officer.

'Yes, my name's Lemar Jackson,' I confirmed. I sat on my hands.

'We know that you were in school when Gregor Smolenko was shot dead outside the computer repair shop, Lemar,' she said. 'We've already spoken to your teachers. But I want to take you back a week or so before that.'

I could hear Jerome still getting his wail on in the lounge. It was beginning to scratch my nerves. Gran was singing one of her Bob Marley tunes, trying to comfort him. I closed my eyes and prayed that she could quieten him.

'He doesn't know anything,' put in Elaine. 'My brother was in school, you just said that. So how's he supposed to *help you with your enquiries*?'

'As I said,' the fed woman repeated. 'He may have seen something that may seem trivial but might well carry great importance.'

I glanced at the officers. Neither of them were loving my sister. I hoped she wouldn't make things worse. I wondered again why Smolenko was christened 'Long Mouth'.

'On the sixth of this month,' the fed woman continued, 'were you in the North Crongton estate area?'

'No he wasn't,' Elaine answered for me and crossed her arms. 'He was at our dad's. Tell 'em, Lemar. *Don't* let them intimidate you.'

The fed woman momentarily closed her eyes. I could see that she was getting her rage on. My heart was now uppercutting my ribcage. 'Perhaps Lemar can tell us better himself?' she said.

Everyone looked at me again. I felt the heat of their gaze. The shit was not only slapping the windmill, it was turning the green grass brown.

'Er ... I was just looking to play basketball with someone,' I said.

Elaine glared at me. I was sure that if the feds weren't there she would've deleted me like evil men killed poor kids in medieval days.

'Someone who matches your description was seen being chased by a gang of seven young adults,' the fed woman stated. 'Was this you, Lemar?'

Elaine's glare drilled holes in my forehead.

'Er . . . yes . . . I was chased.'

'Lemar!' Elaine yelled. 'What were you doing in the North Crongton estate?'

'Looking for a game of basketball,' I said.

Elaine was steaming. I looked away from her.

'Is it Ms Jackson?' the fed woman asked. Her lips were getting skinnier and skinnier.

'Ms *Elaine* Jackson,' my sister said with serious emphasis. A bit of spittle flew from her mouth.

The feds weren't the love of Elaine's life. I think it went back to the time when Elaine, fifteen then, jacked some perfume and shit from a store on the High Street. She was arrested and taken to Central Crongton fed station. They left her in a cell for six hours and apparently Elaine went through the whole dictionary of English and Caribbean swear words while she was in there. When Mum found out I think she cursed every bad-word from Hong Kong to Los Angeles. Gran picked up Elaine from the station. Elaine was all emotional when she got home. She and Mum had the mother of all ding-dongs when they clashed that evening. I kept out of the way. That night was the first time I had seen Gran put on earphones. For some strange reason Elaine grabbed a sleeping bag from the top of my wardrobe and slept on my bedroom floor that night – she never explained why but I heard her crying. I didn't know what to say to make her feel better. Something had happened to her. Maybe the feds traumatised her or maybe they forced her to watch *The X Factor*? But even back then, I knew better than to try to ask. If Elaine wanted to talk to me, she'd talk – but she never did.

'Can I resume interviewing your brother without too many interventions?' the officer asked.

Elaine nodded and chewed the inside of her mouth.

'Do you know why you were chased?' the fed woman continued.

'I dunno.' I shrugged.

I tried to look casual but the organs inside my chest were playing musical hot-chairs or something.

'Did you recognise any of the people who chased you?'

'No, I don't have any friends in North Crong.'

'Are you *sure* that you didn't recognise any of your pursuers?' the fed woman asked again.

'No ... I didn't.'

The feds whispered to each other. Elaine shot me another lethal stare. 'Why is it so important if Lemar recognised anyone who was chasing him?' she asked. 'That's what North Crong guys do. They see somebody who's not from their ends and they chase 'em. It makes them feel like men – brainless *pussies*! Why don't *you* investigate *that* instead of making my bro sweat?'

The feds continued muttering under their breath. Then the woman looked at me again. 'To answer your sister's question, one of the young adults chasing you *was* Gregor Smolenko. You already know that he was murdered outside the computer repair shop a few days ago.'

The crunching sensation in my stomach returned with a vengeance. I almost doubled up in pain.

'I'll ask you again, Lemar.' The fed woman leaned in closer to me. I noticed that her make-up was a bit OTT. 'Do you know why you were chased?'

I got my head-shake on. 'No ... like I said, I was looking for a game of basketball. They saw me and just started chasing. I didn't stop and ask why. I just hot-toed out of there. I had to leave my ball.'

Elaine shook her head and sent me an 'I'll chat to you later on' eye-pass.

The male fed scribbled something down and then they whispered to each other again. This was beginning to maul my nerves.

'OK, Lemar,' the fed woman said. 'Can you confirm that when you heard of an incident at Cowley Road, you decided to go up there to discover what happened?'

'How do you know that?' I asked.

'Just answer the question, Lemar,' the female fed pressed. 'Can you confirm that you were at the scene of the incident?'

'Yeah, I was,' I answered. 'But so was everybody else. We all hot-toed up there. Everyone wanted to know who got blazed. It was only later on that I heard it was ...'

'It's all right, Lemar,' the fed woman said. 'You're not under any kind of suspicion. We just need to know that when you made your way to Cowley Road, did you pass or see anybody acting suspiciously? Or just out of the ordinary?'

'Er, no,' I replied. 'Not that I can think of.'

'Are you sure? Nothing strange or odd?'

'He just said *no*,' Elaine put in. 'Are you deaf? How many times does he have to repeat himself? I thought he wasn't under suspicion.'

There was an awkward silence. I took the opportunity to wipe my forehead. *Elaine's not only flinging horse shit into the piss pot, she's throwing maggots in there too.* The male fed got his scribble on once again.

'Did you see any vehicles speeding away? A car or a motor-bike? Driving too fast maybe?'

'No,' I replied.

'Are you sure?'

Elaine, her arms crossed, was chomping the inside of her cheek.

'I'm sure.' I nodded.

The feds spoke quietly to each other once more. My fingers felt sticky. I let out a long breath. God! I was roasting inside my jacket.

'OK, Lemar,' the fed woman said. 'If you remember any-thing out of the ordinary on the day you were chased and the afternoon of the incident on Cowley Road, please let us know. Or, if you feel uncomfortable informing us, speak to one of your teachers or a responsible adult.'

She handed me a card with her name and phone number on it.

I nodded but looked to the floor. The feds stood up. I felt a touch of relief but I knew Elaine would get her interrogation on after they left.

'If anything comes to mind,' the female fed repeated. She

gave her card to Elaine. Elaine looked at it in disgust. 'Please let a responsible adult know ... we do offer provisions for your safety if you might feel threatened in any way.'

'I would if I knew something.' I nodded. 'But I don't know anything.'

Elaine kissed her teeth.

I saw the feds to the door. I wasn't sure if I should've felt well happy they left cos I wasn't under suspicion or shitting myself cos now I had to face my big sis. I crept back along the hallway and made for my bedroom. I needed a shower – my shirt was as wet as the *Titanic*.

'*Lemar!*' Elaine roared.

'I've got some homework to do,' I called back. 'But I'm gonna take a shower first.'

'Your BO's gonna have to wait! Get your liccle backside in here!'

'Elaine!' Gran called from my sister's bedroom. 'Quiet your mout'! I'm trying to get Jerome to sleep!'

About three months ago I'd asked Mum for a lock and key for my bedroom. She said she'd think about it and I forgot to ask her again. I kinda regretted that right now. No way was I gonna step in the kitchen and suffer Elaine spitting cusses at me. I sneaked into my room. Seconds later, Elaine barged in like she was one of them mad American wrestlers jumping into the ring for a death-match fight. She closed the door behind her. I sucked in a mighty breath. 'What's a matter with you, Lemar? What were you doing stepping to the North Crong estate?'

'I was bored ... just wanted to check the place out. Dad and

Shirley were with Steff and I just took a walk. It's a free country you know.'

I don't think Elaine liked my answer too much.

'*Don't* you know there's a gang feud going on? Didn't you hear about Nightlife? What is wrong with you, Lemar? They could've killed you! They should've killed you for your stupidness, you stupid dumb prick!'

Something in me switched. '*I'm* a stupid dumb prick? At least I didn't get myself pregnant by the top G in our ends. I don't make *them* kinda mistakes. That makes you more stupid than—'

I felt the punch as soon as the last word escaped my mouth. Elaine followed it up with a left hook to my jaw. I fell on to my bed. Elaine yanked me to my feet again. '*Don't* even go there! I'm telling you this for your own good and you're bringing up my personal shit? You must think you're grown now.'

She was raging but I could see the pain in her eyes. Something deep. *Shit!* I must've really stomped on a nerve.

I'd forgotten that when Elaine fought she fought like a man. When she had her rage on she could be some hardback, medieval, crazy-punching, Lemar-beating sister. She boxed me each side of my head and booted every cubic millimetre of my legs. I couldn't remember everything about my beat-down but I could recall the smell of Elaine's nail varnish. I dropped to the floor and Elaine jumped on top of me, getting her Tasmanian devil on. I heard the door open. Gran was holding Jerome. He was crying again. Elaine jumped off me and snatched Jerome from Gran. Thank God for my precious nephew! I staggered to my feet.

'Who you think you're talking to?' Elaine roared. 'Liberties! If you think you're a man, step to North Crong again and see what I do to your backside! Don't you *ever* say that Jerome is a mistake! You hearing me, Lemar? See I don't mess you up when you're home alone!'

'*Elaine!* Calm down! Madness ah take you.'

I covered my face with my hands as Gran ushered Elaine out of my room. The pains in my head felt like mini dodgems were crashing inside my skull. Elaine was cussing a world of swear words as she was escorted along the hallway. I started to wonder if even Manjaro could manage her in a fight.

I slowly stood up and every living cell of my body was aching. I squinted into my mirror on my dressing table. I had a throbbing jaw and I was cut just below the right eye – I looked a mess. Man! How would I explain my sister's beat-down to my bredrens? I could already hear McKay getting his mad giggle on.

I didn't go into the bathroom until Elaine stopped cussing. When I had crept there I ran a cold tap over my flannel and held it over my face to try to stop the swelling. I couldn't believe what had just happened. My sister had just beaten the bull-crap out of me. Why was it OK for her to call me a dumb prick but the minute I brought up *her* mistake she turned Ultimate Fighter on me? And I meant her mistake of linking up with Manjaro – not having Jerome. I was sick and tired of her taking liberties with me. If it wasn't her, it was Mum mauling my ears or blaming me for some shit. If it wasn't Mum then it was Elaine again. I couldn't win!

'You all right, Lemar?' Gran asked, poking her head around the bathroom door. She looked at me like how she might've looked on a dog that'd just crapped on her slippers. 'She says you called Jerome a mistake. How could you? What were you thinking? You know how she's sensitive about that.'

I didn't answer. Even Gran was on her side. Couldn't believe she was defending her after she beat me down.

'She's very sorry,' Gran continued. 'She's bawling her eyes out me ah tell you, holding Jerome tight to her. *Lord Almighty!* What a tribulation to strike this family.'

I still refused to say anything. What was there to say? I wasn't all right, I didn't tell Elaine to beat me down and inside I was raging.

'You want me to take a look at your eye?'

'No, Gran.'

'It's a nasty cut,' said Gran, leaning in to take a closer look.

'I'll be all right, Gran.'

'But it needs to be cleaned ...'

'Just *leave* it, Gran! Leave me alone!'

Gran shook her head and left the bathroom. As soon as she disappeared guilt boxed me in my head – I shouldn't have spoken to Gran like that. Moments later I heard Gran cussing Elaine. I went along the hallway and said to myself again that I had to get out of this madness. Gran had cooked chicken curry and rice but I refused it. Instead, I lay on my bed getting my stare on at the ceiling.

For the next hour or so, I remained flat on my back, studying the ceiling. Then I heard Mum entering the flat. Gran spilled to her in the kitchen and then Mum hot-stepped to my room. She sat down on my bed and looked at my face. The touch of her fingers made me feel better.

'Are you OK?'

'Yes,' I replied.

'You sure?'

'Well ... got a serious brain-ache.'

I could see her getting vexed. 'I'll be back in a bit,' she said.

She marched out of my room with serious intent. Seconds later, vocals erupted. Elaine started bawling. *Good!* After a short while I crept out of my room and into the hallway.

'I wanted to say sorry to him, Mum!'

'What do you think you're doing?' Mum roared. 'He's your *brother* for God's sake! You're gonna have to somehow find a place and get out of here, Elaine. I can't deal with your behaviour.'

'Mum, I didn't mean to—'

'Didn't mean to! You only stopped when your grandmother appeared with Jerome! What kinda example is that?'

'Something came over me ... I just saw red.'

'You can see the other side of the front door, Elaine!' Mum screamed. 'I want you out of here as soon as these stupid people find you a place. Do you hear me? *Out!* Go down to the Crongton Housing Department and tell them your own mother can't *take* you any more. Or talk to that social worker who came down here checking out the flat. What happened to her anyway? Why haven't they offered you a place yet? Don't they know this flat is *too* small? She saw that for herself didn't she? I can't take it any more! Let's hope they can find somewhere for you in weeks rather than months!'

Oh *shit!* I hadn't meant for this to happen. This had all got too serious. Didn't want Elaine to leave cos of me.

'Mum! It won't happen again.'

'You're too right it won't!'

'Didn't Gran tell you what Lemar said to me? He said Jerome was a *mistake*! I'm sorry for what I did to him but *he* kicked me off!'

I heard a door slam. I retreated back into my room, lay flat on my bed and pretended to get my nap on. Mum entered five minutes later. She slapped on my bedroom light. She had cotton wool, plasters and some kinda antiseptic bottle in her hands. 'Are you trying to fool me into thinking that you slept through all that carry-on? I'm your *mother*! Open your eyes and don't move your head, Lemar.'

Mum slapped a plaster on below my eye. The rest of my face stung like hell. 'Now you're gonna get up, go to the kitchen and get yourself some dinner. You hear me? I'm gonna go into the front room, watch a bit of telly and I *don't* wanna hear any more foolishness from you two! If I do then you'll soon find out who is the real crazy one in this yard. Do you understand me?'

I nodded. It seemed like Mum was on Elaine's side as well. I couldn't win. I couldn't remember Mum ever looking scarier. She had this Terminator gaze thing going on. I did what I was told and sank my dinner off a tray in my bedroom. I didn't care – I wanted to stay out of everyone's way. Gran and Mum were probably comforting Elaine and saying how out of order I was. But *I* was the one to get a beat-down! Mum would never kick her out.

14

Escape from South Crongton

It was after midnight and I was still brewing with all that had happened with my sister. Without thinking I started to put clothes in my sports bag. *How can I live in the same flat as her?* Five pairs of socks, four pairs of boxers, two jeans, five T-shirts and three tracksuit tops. I placed a towel on top and squeezed them all into the holdall. *I'm going on a mission. I'll crash at my dad's. He's more laid-back about stuff and Shirley won't maul my ears. And Steff proper looks up to me. It'll be me playing the big bro instead of the liccle bro. I can't wait until Mum finds out my ass is gone and she blames Elaine for the shit. Maybe Mum will bang her up the same way Elaine mauled me.*

I pulled on my trainers and sat on my bed. I stared at the carpet and my mind replayed my beat-down. I stood up, picked up my drawing case that contained my pencils and sketch pad and parked on the bed again. Mum would go nuts when she found me missing. But her beat-down couldn't be worse than Elaine's. Gran would be sad when I'd gone … I hoped she wouldn't hate my ass as much as the others. She must've seen it for herself though, the way Mum always defended Elaine no matter what.

I got to my feet then I walked two paces to the door. I pushed down on the door handle and pulled it towards me. I stopped when the door was ten centimetres ajar. I angled my head so I could peer through the gap. The light in the hallway was switched off – Mum always turns it off just before she goes to her bed. The kitchen door was closed but I could still smell Gran's chicken curry. All was quiet but my own breathing sounded like a dinosaur's asthma attack. To my right was the front door. To my left was a world of blame, cussing, favouritism and beat-downs. I took a deep breath. My heart started to have issues with my chest again. I stepped into the hallway, then paused. I closed my bedroom door carefully behind me. Walking in midget steps, I approached the front door. I turned the handle of the Yale lock. As I opened the door a fresh draught of cool air blasted my face. The smell of antiseptic came with me.

Stepping out on to the balcony, I gently pulled the door closed. I was out. *Should I call Dad before I arrive at his house? Nah, he will tell me to go back indoors. If I turn up on his doorstep he'll have to take me serious and take my ass in. And once he takes me in I ain't going back. Mum will have to accept it. I don't care if she hollers and screams like the woman did next door when the bailiffs called. Man! That was some drama.*

Peering over the balcony, I spotted some guys smoking

rockets inside a car in the forecourt. They were getting their giggle on as some rubbish guitar band was playing on their car stereo.

I took one last look at my front door and set off. I bounced down the steps of my slab with more care than I usually did. The night air was fresh. The unseen dogs seemed to bark louder at night than they did during the day. I read the graffiti on the walls. One joker wrote 'If you can survive living in South Crong, you haven't been here too long. If you think that nothing's wrong, your mind's long gone.' I kept to the estate paths rather than the roads – I didn't want one of Mum's friends who might be driving home from somewhere to see my ass. For a few seconds I did think about stepping to McKay's flat. His dad would be at work and we could get our gaming on throughout the night. But I decided against it. When serious shit slaps the blades McKay could be *too* sensible. He'd probably send my ass back to my mum.

I passed the empty factories at the north end of our estate – although council workmen were always boarding up the broken windows, tramps, runaways and rocket addicts always found a way in. Dad lived in Crongton Green, the east side of Crongton, so I avoided the town centre and the bus routes and made my way to his place via the quiet roads. Hardly anybody was about apart from a well-dressed couple getting out of a taxi and some zonked-out guy smoking something in his parked car. He gave me a messed-up look and I crossed to the other side of the road. My stepping went from brisk to rapid.

I arrived at my dad's some time later. There was an upstairs light on. Someone was still up. Strange. Usually Dad kills all the lights in the yard at about eleven. For a little while I simply gazed at his front door, wondering whether to knock or call him on my phone – I didn't want to wake up Steff. I decided to call and hoped I had enough credit.

Just as I groped for my phone in my pocket, someone slapped on a downstairs light. I retreated two steps. Suddenly the front door opened. Dad was carrying Steff to his van. She was covered in a blanket. Shirley was pulling a cabin case – the wheels scraping along the pavement made an ugly sound. I ran up to them. 'Dad! Dad! What's wrong with Steff?'

Shirley opened the passenger-side door of the van. 'Lemar!' she called out. 'What are you doing here at this time of night?'

I didn't answer. Dad looked at me. Stress was licking his forehead. Steff's eyes were half-open. She looked proper pale. I don't think she even realised that I was there. 'Lemar! Answer Shirley's question. What are you doing out on road at this time of night?'

'I . . . I . . . what's wrong with Steff?'

'She's sick, Lemar,' Dad replied. He laid her gently in the van, resting her head on Shirley's lap. 'We're taking her to the hospital.'

'Can I help?' I asked. 'Can I go with you? *Please.*'

'*No.* Go home! What are you doing out so late? Your mum will flip.'

'Er . . . I want to stay with you.'

'Have you lost your freaking mind? What's wrong with you? Can't you see I haven't got time for this? Steff needs to see a doctor.'

'Is … Is she gonna be all right?'

'We hope so …'

'I want to help,' I pressed again. 'She … she *is* my sister.'

Dad walked around the front of the van and opened the driver-side door. He climbed in and wound down his window. 'You can help me by *going home. Right now!*'

'But—'

'No buts, Lemar … what happened to your face?'

'I had a mad argument with Elaine and she beat me down today and Mum and Gran have taken her side and—'

'Well, you seem to be all right, so go home, Lemar!' Dad raged.

'I'm going! Tell Steff I love her to the max.'

'I will,' said Shirley.

'I'm … I'm sorry about what happened with Elaine,' Dad said. 'But you two have had scrapes before. You'll get over it.' Dad had lowered his voice. His eyes looked scared and his forehead was creased in worry.

'What's … what's wrong with her?'

'She's feeling very weak,' Dad said. His voice was calmer. He turned the ignition and the engine rumbled into life. 'They put her on this new medication but it's not working at all.'

'She'll be good, right?' I asked.

Dad took in a mighty breath and then switched on the headlights. 'Yes … she'll be good. Now *go home*. I'll call you in the morning.'

He shifted into gear, reversed and pulled away. I watched the van until it disappeared into a turning at the end of the road.

15

Rolling with the Crims

For the next ten minutes I parked my butt on the pavement. My right shoulder was tired from carrying my bag and my drawing case. *Now I have to step back to South Crong. Can't believe it! Don't wanna pass that stoned guy in the car again. What was he on?* I stood up, slung my holdall over my left shoulder and started trodding. *Man! What was I thinking? Maybe I should've planned this escape better. Maybe I shouldn't have hot-stepped out of my yard at all.*

I could hear sirens in the distance and the night whoosh of cars driving at speed. I didn't want to go home. Somehow, I wanted Elaine to pay for my beat-down. Why should she just get a cussing-down from Mum and Gran? I wanted her to feel some deep guilt slapping her head. Maybe I could hang out at the park until the morning and go straight to school from there. *Wait a minute! It's Saturday tomorrow. Then again, screw the park, some weird shit kicks off in Crongton Park at night-time. And it's not too far from where Nightlife got deleted. I'll just walk around the estate, find somewhere with decent light and sketch something. Yeah, I'll do that. It ain't too cold for my fingers. In the morning Mum will find out my ass is not in bed and she'll maul Elaine. They will all get their fret on. Yeah, I can work with that plan.*

I started off towards South Crongton, again taking the side roads. I had walked about a mile or so when I heard the rumbling of an engine. Headlights lit up the street. A car was driving slowly behind me. I looked over my shoulder. The ride was about fifty metres away. The headlights were bright. I stepped quicker. I could hear the car picking up speed. I looked to my left and to my right. There were no alleyways or cul-de-sacs to escape to – only people's front doors and front gardens. They weren't gonna let a brother in at this time of night. *Shit! It could be a North Crong crew. It could be Major Worries with his broader-than-Chicago shoulders and his airport-control-tower height.* He was probably still spitting blood over Long Mouth Smolenko.

I turned around and the glare blinded me. My heart raced. I pinned my head back and ran for my sweet life. The street was long – I couldn't even see the next turn-off or junction. Wished I was as quick as Jonah. The car easily caught up with me. I veered to my right, jumped over a low wall and burned into someone's small front garden. I made for the front door. I didn't care who they were or what time it was, they *had* to open the mother-freaking front door. The car shrieked to a halt and pulled up. Someone was climbing out of it. I was about to smack the letter box.

'Liccle Bit?' someone called.

It was a male voice. A voice that I knew. I strained my eyes.

'Liccle Bit?' the voice repeated. I heard a car door slam.

It was Manjaro. He was now sitting in the back seat looking out of the window – two of his crew were in the front. Manjaro's gold ear stud glinted under the orangey-yellow streetlights. A plain blue baseball cap covered his shaven head. It was a weird thing to feel, it being Manjaro, but I was as glad as a chicken seeing Kentucky Fried being bombed that it was him and not some North Crong brother.

'What you doing out on road at this time?'

'Er ...'

'Get your liccle butt into the car,' ordered Manjaro. 'Don't you know that peeps in these ends call out the feds even if they see someone smoking a cigarette?'

I thought about it. Someone slapped a light on in a room above.

'Get your liccle butt in the car!'

I did what I was told. He opened the back door for me. I climbed in. There was some sort of mint smell going on – it came from the air freshener hooked around the rear-view mirror. I placed my bag and my drawing case on my lap. A girl of about twenty years old was in the driver's seat. Her blonde hair was sexed up with red highlights. It was tied into a ponytail and she was wearing these glitzy diamond-shaped earrings. Next to her was the big brother I recognised from Remington House. He looked like he sank Rottweilers for breakfast. I didn't know there were that many veins in the human neck. The blue baseball cap he was wearing looked as small as a top hat on an elephant. He was getting his stare on through the windscreen. Manjaro moved over to make space for me. The driver indicated, pushed into gear and set off. 'Where to?' she asked.

'Business done for the night,' Manjaro answered. 'Roll to Liccle Bit's flat. You know, Elaine's yard. This is her liccle brother.'

'Oh, yeah,' she said. 'I remember.'

I wondered what kind of business. Didn't think it would be the best idea if I asked.

Manjaro turned to me. 'What's the score with you being out on road at this time, Bit?'

'I ... I was going to my dad's.'

'At this time?'

'Er ... yeah.'

'What happened to your face?'

'Had a fight.'

'Who with?'

I didn't want to answer.

'A North Crong yout'?'

'No.'

'Then who?'

I peered out of the window.

'*Who*, Liccle Bit?'

'My sister.'

I glanced at the driver's rear-view mirror. A flicker of a smile touched the guy in front of me. There was no emotion on the female driver's face.

'Elaine has a temper,' Manjaro said, letting out a breath.

'Believe me, I know.' I could hear the laughter in his voice and my cheeks burned.

We drove back to South Crongton estate. Jazz was playing on the car stereo. I noticed there was a briefcase beside Manjaro. He was working out something on a calculator while checking some numbers on a small notepad. I thought it was a liccle late to be doing some accountancy. Maybe he'd been driving around collecting money from all the people who worked for him? Again, I didn't want to ask.

The girl-driver and the big guy sitting in the front didn't say one word between them. We pulled up outside my slab.

'Your station, I believe,' Manjaro said.

I didn't move. Couldn't help but think of my beat-down and the possibility of another. My hands started shaking. I felt the sweat bubbling on my forehead. In my mind Elaine's fists turned into concrete-spiked wrecking balls. 'I ain't going,' I said.

I looked up to my floor and imagined the hell I might catch when I rolled into my flat. Manjaro seemed to spot my fear and shook his head. The girl-driver stared out the windscreen impatiently while kissing her teeth. The heavyweight in the front passenger seat drummed his thick fingers on the dashboard. There was a saxophone solo playing from the car sound system.

'Get out, Bit,' Manjaro ordered. 'It's best that you find your butt home.'

I kept my butt still. 'I ain't going ... not yet anyhow. I might go for a walk around the estate till morning then face them.'

'You really think I'm gonna take the rap for letting you step around the estate at these mad hours?' said Manjaro. 'If someting happened to you your sis would never forgive me. If you're not gonna roll home then stay in the ride!'

'But ...' I started to slowly reach for the door handle but didn't have the nerve to pull it.

Manjaro shook his head again. He tapped the female driver on her shoulder. 'I haven't got time for this,' he said. 'Don't wanna be seen in these ends at this time of night.' She indicated, expertly moved into gear and sped off again. No one said a word.

Shit! Maybe I should've got my bravery on and bounced out.

We were heading south, passing my school and beyond our estate to streets that weren't as rich as Crongton Village. The houses had decent-sized front rooms and I guessed three or four bedrooms. Crongton Heath. Dunno why they called these ends Crongton Heath when the heath itself was a further two miles south. There weren't so many four-wheel drives nicing up the roads but instead the kinda rides that my teachers drove. Manjaro was still working on his calculator. Suddenly, we pulled up outside this normal-looking semi-detached house. We all climbed out of the car. 'Lady P will drive your liccle ass to your slab in the morning,' announced Manjaro. 'You hear me, Liccle Bit? And she'll watch your ass enter your gates.'

I nodded as the heavyweight looked up and down the street as if he were looking out for assassins. I thought about a vengeful Major Worries and how much he wanted to delete Manjaro and anybody with him cos of the Smolenko blazing. Something chilled cold-toed down my spine.

'But until then,' Manjaro continued, 'your ass is staying with me. It's not safe to be stepping the streets at this time.'

Lady P opened the front door. She wiped her feet on a brown mat that said 'Welcome'. Carrying my bag and my drawing case, I followed Manjaro into the house. The heavy-weight closed the door behind us. Lady P walked up the carpeted stairs opposite the front door. The guy with the tree-trunk neck sat on the second stair. There was a framed black-and-white pic of some black guy in a white suit blowing a trumpet hanging from the staircase wall. Manjaro walked along a hallway that led to a kitchen. I followed him. He switched on a kettle and I sat down at a small kitchen table. Three of the day's broadsheet newspapers were resting beside a toast rack. I put my bag and drawing case on an empty chair.

'Cup of tea?' he offered.

I took a rapid sweep of my surroundings. Didn't know why but I was expecting to see rice-bag sizes of cocaine, and cookie jars full of weird-shaped pills and tablets. There was none of that – just the everyday shit you find in any kitchen. He even had cartoon magnets on the fridge and some super-market calendar hanging on a wall. Gran would've approved.

'Cup of tea?' he asked again.

'Oh, yeah. Yes please.'

'How many sugars?'

'Er ... two please.'

This was weird. Manjaro was behaving like normal. It was freaking me out. And this was all nuts! I could barely step up the stairs of my slab if I knew Manjaro was on the staircase but here I was sitting down in *his* yard! In his freaking kitchen! McKay, Jonah and Elaine wouldn't believe it. The shit was rising above my nose. Had to think of an excuse to get out of here. McKay said Manjaro had deleted people but here he was making me a mother-freaking cup of tea.

'Do you want any biscuits?' he asked.

'Er ... yeah,' I replied. I was getting tired but knew I had to be wide awake.

'Behind you there's a cupboard. Open it and you'll find a biscuit tin.'

I did as I was told. I took out three chocolate digestives and got my nibble on. By the time I started to sink my second biscuit, Manjaro was stirring my cup of tea. He made himself a mint tea and joined me at the table. I took a rapid sweep of the kitchen. He had juice makers, some sort of coffee machine and cookery books on a shelf. 'This is my yard,' he said. 'Worked hard for this shit. And the brothers and sisters who run with me, I'm gonna help them buy their yards, you receiving me? That's the plan. If they try and follow the system they'd never have a chance of buying shit, you receiving? I wanna help brothers and sisters step up.'

I nodded. I couldn't help but admire him for owning his own yard at his age but he still made me as nervous as a fat sheep stuck up a skinny tree with nuff lions on the ground.

'Take Pinchers,' resumed Manjaro. 'He doesn't chat as much as the others but I trust him the most. He's the brother sitting on the stairs – some of my bredrens call him Big Yout', but I like to call him Pinchers. You know why?'

'No,' I answered. I tried to fight my weariness but my eyes were screaming to close.

I imagined that he was called Pinchers cos he could seize a man's head with his mountain-breaking arms and get his crush on. If I were a gladiator I'd rather face the lions than him.

'Because when he's taught something,' Manjaro explained, 'he doesn't forget. It takes him a while but once he gets it, it stays in his hard drive, you receiving?'

'Er, yeah.'

'Pinchers had trouble at school, teachers couldn't handle him, but since he's been with us he's got his education on. You see, Bit, *they* don't understand that everybody learns at a different pace. All because some are slower it doesn't mean they're as dumb as shit, you receiving? Pinchers is with me most of the day and I teach him maths and business when I have time. When Lady P has time she teaches him English. You can't study a damn ting if you haven't got good English. In about a year or so he'll be ready to step to college.'

'That's . . . good,' I managed. I glanced into the hallway and wondered if Pinchers could hear our conversation.

'What I do *is* a business, Bit, and any brother or sister who's gonna work for me *has* to know something, you receiving?'

'Er, kind of.'

'I'm *not* like the Major,' Manjaro stressed. He sipped his mint tea. For a micro-second his eyes blazed with hate. He then moved his head in a circle as if he was relieving some pain in his neck. 'He's all about brute strength – he doesn't teach his brothers any shit. But sometimes we *have* to match that brute strength, you receiving? He *has* to know that he can't take liberties with us.'

I nodded again, hoping that he'd stop chatting about Major Worries. He sipped his tea again and let out a sigh.

'So you're a good artist?' he asked, looking at my drawing case. 'Elaine used to say that you were always getting your sketch on.'

'Yeah,' I replied. 'I … I like sketching landscapes and portraits.'

'That's good.' Manjaro nodded. 'Very good. Maybe one day you can do a portrait of me and I'll give you a nice liccle touch. When you finish school you'd better find your short ass in art college or something, you receiving?'

'Er, yeah.'

'You've been blessed more than most,' he said. 'Most youts in Crongton don't know what they're good at.'

Manjaro stood, picked up his tea and left the kitchen. I stared at the lip stains on my mug and wondered if I should hot-step it out of there or stay to hear more from Manjaro. He was scary as a shark to a legless frog but kinda intelligent. Mum would probably beat the bull-crap out of me whatever I did so I decided to stay.

Ten minutes later Manjaro returned. 'Finished your tea?' he asked.

I nodded.

'Come,' he ordered.

He led me back along the hallway and opened a door on the left. He ushered me into what looked like a half-lounge, half-office. There was a two-seater black leather sofa and I parked on that. In a corner was a desk with two computer screens on it. The shelves above the desk were full of textbooks, files and folders. Hard drives were blinking below the desk. There was a flat TV screen fixed to the wall on the other side of the desk but it was only as big as a Monopoly board. I couldn't understand why a top G like Manjaro only had a small TV – maybe he had a bigger screen upstairs.

In the other corner was a chequered-topped wooden table. It looked heavy and expensive but what I saw propped on top of it proper shocked me. There were framed pics of Elaine and Jerome. Jerome must've been a few days old and Elaine looked as if she had gone ten rounds with a Tasmanian devil. There was a name tag on her wrist so the pic must've been taken at the hospital. I just couldn't remember seeing Manjaro at the hospital after Jerome was born. In one shot he was holding Jerome while grinning wider than the White House.

'When we were … together,' Manjaro started, 'I was always encouraging your sis to continue her education. She's well brainy, Elaine. She got pregnant with Jerome but that shouldn't stop her, I told her.'

For a moment I was gonna say that Elaine had a raging argument with Mum about her going back to college but I thought better of it.

'They're trying to make it hard for us,' Manjaro resumed. His expression told me that whoever *they* were, he hated them with a passion and a half. 'By jacking up uni fees and deleting college grants *they've* made it impossible. So what I do is important. You see Lady P upstairs? She's taking a year out but when she goes to uni she won't have to fret herself about uni fees cos she's been working with me, you receiving?

She'll be able to afford it and won't have to stress out. She'll do good whatever she decides to do for a career cos she's sharper than a grade-one hair-trim.'

Wasn't sure what he was talking about but I nodded anyway.

'The remote for the TV is on the small table to your right,' he said. '*Keep* your ass here until the sun blesses the morning, you receiving? Can't have my *brother-in-law* roaming the streets at mad o'clock.'

He was gone before I could reply, pulling the door closed behind him. He returned ten seconds later. 'I know what people say about me so don't judge me, Bit. *They* allow people to buy alcohol, cigarettes and let them have addictive prescriptions and shit. That messes up people's bodies but *they* don't mind that. I'm not doing anything different from what the big alcohol, tobacco and chemical companies are doing. Even your sis agreed with that.'

Then he was gone again. I fiddled with the TV remote and flicked through the channels. But I wasn't really looking at the TV; I couldn't take my eyes away from the pics of Elaine and Jerome.

Five minutes later Lady P appeared with a duvet and a pillow. She handed them to me. 'I'll be leaving about eight in the morning,' she said. 'So if you wanna ride back to your slab be ready by then.'

'Yes, thanks.'

I found a music channel I liked and settled on to the sofa with the duvet covering my body up to my neck. I didn't know whether to feel scared or comfortable. *He* called me his brother-in-law! He wouldn't beat-down his brother-in-law would he? I wondered how my sis and Manjaro got together. She must've spent time in this room watching TV and playing or working on those computers in the corner. Did she really agree with all the reasons behind the shit that Manjaro had been up to? The top Gs of big alcohol, chemical and tobacco companies didn't do drive-by shootings. Elaine must've suspected that Manjaro was involved in the Smolenko deletion.

16

A Full Crongton Breakfast

I think I dropped off for the next couple of hours or so. When I woke again I realised someone had switched off the hallway light. I wondered if Pinchers was still parked on the stairs. Maybe he was Manjaro's bodyguard. I considered whether Mum had discovered that my ass was missing and if she had mauled Elaine. I thought about Gran. Maybe she'd be the one to find me missing. *Shit!* I hoped it wouldn't stress her out. She'd be proper worried. *Maybe I should step back to my slab before everyone gets up. What am I thinking? Forget that mission. Don't wanna vex Manjaro. Who knows what could happen to me.*

A little while later someone pressed the doorbell. It was answered immediately so I guessed Pinchers must've been on that hardback stair all this time.

I turned the TV down and I heard many different voices. I didn't dare open the lounge door. Someone was laughing but someone was scared. '*No! No!*' I heard a brother wail. Something dropped to the floor. I guessed it was a pair of knees.

Suddenly, Manjaro entered the front room and closed the door behind him. He switched off the light. 'Turn the TV volume *up*,' he ordered. 'And stay in here, you receiving?'

I nodded.

Manjaro shut the door behind him. I did what I was told but didn't raise the volume too much. Something icy shot through my veins again. My heart started to pound in my chest. I just had to hear what was going on.

I edged along the sofa to be closer to the door and tried to listen in to the conversation taking place.

Manjaro was speaking. 'You think I wouldn't notice?'

'No,' came back a reply.

'Do you think I'm too dumb to work out that you've been jacking my shit off the top?'

'No, Manjaro.'

'Do you think it's only me you're robbing from?'

'No, Manjaro.'

'*What* did I say to you when you first came to me? You remember? When I told you and the others to listen *very* carefully cos I had important shit to say? *What* did I say?'

Jesus! I wondered who this guy was. He sounded about sixteen, maybe seventeen. His voice seemed proper desperate, terrified. I wondered if his family knew where he was. *Damn!* Maybe I should've stepped home but how would've I got past walking-castle Pinchers?

'Er ... every loss is our loss and every profit is our profit,' answered the boy.

There was a pause. My heart punched my ribcage again. I heard footsteps climbing the stairs and stepping to the kitchen. Then they returned.

'So you remember,' said Manjaro. 'So you *know* you're robbing off everybody, not just me. *Why?*'

There was no response. Everything went quiet. I'd rather suffer a beat-down from Elaine than explain shit to Manjaro, Pinchers and whoever else was there standing in the hallway.

'WHY DID YOU ROB FROM US?' Manjaro suddenly exploded. His voice made me shudder and that icy thing was now cold-toeing down my spine. 'WHY? HAVEN'T WE TREATED YOU GOOD? WHO PAID FOR YOUR NEW LAPTOP THAT YOU STUDY ON? ALL OF US!'

'My … my … mum has been having trouble paying the rent and bills,' the boy finally replied. 'So I … I meant to pay it back.'

'Then why didn't you come to me?' Manjaro asked. His tone was calm again, like a worried uncle. Manjaro had some kinda Jekyll and Hyde deal going on. 'What did I say to you about this kinda shit?'

'That … that if we have any worries to come to you.'

'Then why didn't you?'

'I … I … dunno. I didn't think …'

'Aren't I approachable?' Manjaro asked. 'Don't I look after my people?'

'At all times,' said a girl's voice.

'Twenty-four-seven!' added a male voice.

'You know it!' added the girl.

'But … but you haven't got a mobile,' said the boy.

'But you *know* the mobile numbers of Pinchers and Lady P, don't you?'

'But ... but they keep changing.'

The boy's voice was getting lower and lower. I could hardly hear a damn word of what he said.

'Aren't you told when the numbers change?' Manjaro raised his voice. 'TELL ME! AREN'T YOU TOLD WHEN THE NUMBERS CHANGE?'

I didn't hear any reply. God! I felt the boy's fear – it seemed to seep through the centimetre gap beneath the door. I grabbed the pillow and dug my fingers into it. I glanced to the window and wondered if it could be a possible escape route. So *this* was how he paid for his house? How Lady P could take a year out? *Bull-crap!*

'Pinchers!' Manjaro called.

I heard footsteps and someone being dragged to the kitchen. The boy was groaning, sobbing. Then the beat-down began. The boy squealed from the first three blows. Then he was silent but I could hear the thudding and walloping. I had this mad urge to take a look but my ass could've been next. I closed my eyes. Footsteps returned to the hallway. My hands were shaking and I had this sickly feeling in my stomach.

'I didn't want to do this,' said Manjaro. His voice was now slow, as if he were typing every single letter into the boy's brain. 'Don't ... ever ... jack from me ... again.'

I didn't know about the boy but Manjaro's lyrics scared the bull-crap out of me.

'Make sure you keep up your IT studies,' added Manjaro. 'It's important ... Take his ass back to his slab. Give him something for his nose. Someone clean up the shit on the floor – I don't want it stained.'

Somebody opened the front gate. A cold draught blew under the lounge door, chilling my ankles. Seconds later, I heard a car pull away.

The lounge door opened. I groped for the TV remote to turn up the volume. Manjaro stood under the door frame for a few seconds. He was wearing a black glove on his right hand and nothing on the other. He glanced at the TV and then turned to me. 'If a business is going to work you need discipline,' he said. 'And a loyal workforce. When you finish watching the TV, switch it off at the socket – I don't like to waste electricity. Oh, and when you're ready to sleep *don't* put your trainers on the sofa.'

'All right.' I nodded.

He pulled off his black glove and caressed his knuckles. I took in a sharp intake of breath. *Try not to look too scared, Lemar,* I willed myself.

'I hope you can work out things with Elaine when you get back to your slab.'

I nodded again but my hands underneath the duvet were still shaking.

Manjaro closed the door behind him and I got up and turned the TV off at the socket – I didn't want to forget. I sat back down on the sofa and looked again at the framed photographs of Elaine and Jerome.

How had it got so bad between us? Once, she'd been the perfect big sis, taking me out to the movies, to funfairs, paintballing and other stuff. She was the one who picked me up from school in my early days and I would spend most of my time in her room. I could never beat her at that Connect Four game. I would lie on her bed watching cartoons on her small TV while she was doing her homework. Maybe I could've been more supportive when she got pregnant though. Mum and Gran gave her a hell of a time. Some days I sensed she was crying in her room but I didn't go to her. I remained in my room playing my games, trying to forget the mad tension in the yard ... Now she was beating the bull-crap out of me.

I lay down on the sofa but I was too scared to sleep. I heard every toilet flush, every door creak and every footstep. I looked to the window but the dawn was dragging its ass. I must've turned over about fifty times.

Finally, the morning rolled in. I sat up and slapped on the TV. I decided to watch the news channel. I heard someone bounce down the stairs and enter the kitchen. Minutes later, bacon was saying hello to my nostrils. The lounge door opened. Manjaro appeared in old trainers, baggy tracksuit bottoms and a tatty T-shirt. He didn't look much like a gang leader – but that didn't stop me being scared of him. 'Bacon, eggs and toast?' he offered.

'Er ... yeah ... thanks.'

'You sleep good?'

'Yeah,' I lied.

'Step to the kitchen and sink your breakfast.' It was as though no beat-down had ever happened last night.

I sat up, yawned and followed Manjaro to the kitchen. I parked myself at the kitchen table where a plate of two fried eggs, toast and two strips of bacon were waiting for me.

Despite how nervous I'd felt all night, hunger still rolled over in my stomach.

'What kinda juice you want?' asked Manjaro.

'Er ... what you got?'

'Orange, apple, cranberry or mango.'

'I'll have mango, please.'

Manjaro poured me a glass of mango juice. I sank my breakfast in silence. His eyes barely left me, as if he was thinking of some other favour that I could do for him. Why had I allowed him to bring me to his yard? Now I owed him big-time – again. I'd been a damn fool to ever leave Mum's flat. When I finished, Manjaro collected my plate and started to wash it up. 'Just wanna say thanks for collecting that package for me the other day,' he said with his back to me.

'Er, yeah, that's all right.' *No!* my head screamed. *Not this again!*

'It was ... important, Bit,' he said, looking into the sink. 'Very important.'

My insides churned like I had sunk five-day-old school custard. Part of me wanted to ask if there was a gun inside the parcel but I knew I couldn't. I didn't really need to ask. I knew the answer. *Shit. I'm in this up to my eyebrows.*

'Lady P will drop you home,' Manjaro said. 'If you want you can use the bathroom upstairs to nice up your armpits.'

'That's ... that's all right. I'll get my wash at home.'

'Your choice.' Manjaro shrugged. 'But I laid out a clean flannel and towel in the bathroom if you wanna use it.'

'Thanks but I don't wanna hold up Lady P. She said to be ready by eight.'

He was drying the dishes and placing them back in the cupboards. It didn't seem real. If he went a step further and pegged the washing to a clothes line in the garden I would've freaked out.

I was still sipping my mango juice when he turned to me. 'Remember, Bit, you *owe* me one, you receiving?'

As if I needed reminding. 'Er, yeah. Course. Thanks ... thanks for putting me up last night.'

'I'm glad we understand each other.'

'Yeah, we do.' *We understand each other all too good*, I thought. I'd been a stupid dumb prick, putting myself in this situation. Elaine wasn't wrong when she said that about me.

'That's all good. When you get back make sure you settle things with Elaine. She can lose her temper but she doesn't mean what she says when she's vexed.'

'I ... I know.'

'Don't *do* or *say* anything stupid, you receiving?'

'Yeah.'

'Good! I'm going for my run.'

He poured himself a glass of cranberry juice, sank it in one gulp, placed the glass in the sink and was gone out of the front door. It seemed weird that the top G of my ends went out to get his jog on in the morning.

I closed my eyes and breathed out a long sigh. Before I finished my mango juice, Lady P came down the stairs, entered the kitchen and asked if I was ready. She was wearing jeans, a blue pullover and she had her blonde hair tucked into a sky-blue beret. Silver teardrop-shaped earrings niced up her face. I didn't have to be asked twice. She led the way outside.

She opened the front passenger door of her car and I climbed inside. She started the engine, inserted an R & B CD and pulled away. 'He looks after us, you know,' she said, without looking round at me. Why did her voice sound so defensive? Maybe she had issues about the beat-down too.

I didn't respond. Instead I just stared out of the wind-screen – the thudding and the walloping crashed back into my mind. I wondered who that poor boy was who'd been beaten up.

'And he had a big thing for your sis,' she added. 'He'd do anything for her and Jerome.'

She didn't say another word. She didn't need to.

17

Facing the Music

I climbed out of the ride slowly. Lady P offered me a half-smile. As I reached the first floor of my slab I could see her get out of the car and get her surveillance on. Elaine's fists had grown large in my mind and they were now as big as two rocky moons. My heart woke up and started drumming. I arrived at my floor and I midget-stepped along the balcony. I paused and saw Lady P still watching my ass. Manjaro had promised me she wouldn't leave until she'd seen me go inside – and he wasn't wrong.

I stood outside my front door and took in a deep breath. I pulled my front-door key out of my pocket and opened the door about fifteen centimetres. I looked along the hallway. Mum was there. She was talking on her phone but once she spotted me she broke off her conversation. She stared at me in shock for two seconds, her mouth open. I gently closed the door behind me and readied myself for a cuss attack. Her eyes looked tired and her skin dry. I braced myself for the mother of all beat-downs.

'Oh my Lord!' she exclaimed. 'Come here! My beautiful boy!'

Mum rushed and bear-hugged the sweet air out of me. I think she crushed three of my ribs before she let go but I was so relieved she didn't get her rage on. 'Where've you been?' she asked frantically. 'I rang your father at six-thirty this morning and he told me you'd been around his in the early hours. Elaine's out looking for you. She's been gone since half-six. Your gran nearly had a heart attack this morning when she found you weren't in your bed. *How could you do that to her?* We tried calling you but your phone was switched off. I phoned the police and they said to check with all your school friends. I went downstairs to Jonah, woke his family up, but they hadn't seen you. I called McKay – you weren't around there either. I was trying to find that girl's number. What's her name? Venetia something. That nice-looking girl who you sketched the other day. Couldn't find it! Christ! Lemar! I've been in a state. I'd better get hold of Elaine. Have you had something to eat? Are you OK? Where've you been all this time? Has anybody done something to you? *Don't* you do anything like that again, you hear me! You scared the freaking devil out of us!'

Mum finally paused for breath.

'I . . . I went for a walk,' I said. 'Needed some air. I decided to go to Dad's.'

'I know you were scared, Lemar, but Elaine won't do it again. I've had a long talk with her – if she does something like that once more she'll be gone for good. She's on her last warning. You're safe now, back home. Thank Christ. God! And I'm sorry if you thought I was a bit rough with you or was blaming you for everything. Really sorry. I've got to let the police know you've come home safely. No, let me get hold of Elaine first – she's looking for you.'

'But when I got to Dad's he and Shirley were taking Steff to the hospital,' I said. 'Hope she's all right.'

Gran emerged from the front room and she slowly walked towards me. She looked like she had seen a bad weepy movie or something. I couldn't remember the last time she had so much disappointment in her eyes – maybe when Granddad passed away.

'Mor-morning, Gran,' I greeted as she approached me. Man! I felt proper guilty. I could hardly meet her gaze.

Without warning she slapped my face hard and seized me with a mad glare. 'Do you know what you put me through, Lemar? I thought me very heart was about to jump out ah me chest! I did think I turn fool so me check your bed again to see if you was there. Lord Almighty, me get one shock this morning! *Don't* you *ever* do that to me again!'

'I won't, Gran . . . sorry.'

I followed Mum and Gran into the kitchen. 'You want sausages and beans with your eggs?'

'Yes please.' *Damn! How am I gonna sink Mum's breakfast on top of Manjaro's fry-up?*

I glanced at Gran but she was still looking away from me.

I was puncturing my second fried egg with my fork when Elaine returned. She glanced at me but didn't say anything.

'Jerome's still sleeping,' said Gran.

'Thanks,' Elaine replied before taking a chair next to me.

'You want some breakfast?' Mum asked.

'Yes please,' Elaine answered. She then turned her attention to me. 'Been out looking for you for the last couple of hours.'

'Sor-sorry.'

'I looked everywhere! Where were you?'

'Just be happy he's home, Elaine,' Mum said while pouring a glass of orange juice. 'It could've been worse.'

'I just needed to get out,' I said, staring into my plate. 'I ended up at Dad's but he was taking Steff to the—'

'Yes I know,' Elaine said. 'I'm fretting about that and Gran was sick with worry about you. We all were. You made tings *worse*! I was thinking all sorts and bad endings!'

'Please stop it!' said Mum. Her voice was weak, as if all the energy she had was suddenly sucked out of her.

There was a crashing sound. Mum had smashed the glass she was holding against the kitchen table on purpose. She had an 'I can't take any more of this crap' look going on. Orange juice and blood rippled near to my plate. Mum gripped the table and closed her eyes. Her body stiffened. Her forehead creased. I don't think she noticed the blood that was oozing from her hand. Elaine was the first to react, leaping out of her chair and ripping off three kitchen towels.

'Get her to sit down,' said Gran.

Elaine snatched a chair, placed it behind Mum and eased her into it. Mum's eyes were still closed.

'Take her hand and press down hard with the towels,' Gran instructed.

As Elaine saw to Mum's hand, I got up and wiped the table. Shards of glass were all over the floor so I used a dustpan and brush to sweep them up. I emptied the debris into the bin and looked at Mum. She still had her eyes closed and one hand clutching the table. She was hurting but I didn't think the pain was coming from her hand. Elaine was stemming the blood and trying to see how bad the cut was. 'You're gonna have to step to the walk-in surgery and get a couple of stitches,' she said. 'Lemar, go and get Mum's jacket.'

'Shouldn't we call a cab and take her to Crongton General?' suggested Gran.

'No, Gran,' Elaine replied. 'If she goes Crongton General she'll be waiting for ever and a week.'

I gazed at the reddened tissue that Elaine was pressing on Mum's hand. The stress of her worrying about my ass must've led to this. Felt really bad.

'*Move* your liccle ass, Lemar! Let's take her to the walk-in surgery!'

Mum seemed to be out of it. She was just staring into space and asking in a whisper, 'Is Lemar all right?'

'I'm OK, Mum,' I kept on repeating. 'I'm all good. Don't worry about me.'

God! Guilt was giving me a worse beat-down than that brother who'd suffered at Manjaro's last night. My stomach was feeling woozy, as if tiny gremlins were playing rugby or something in there.

We made it to the surgery twenty minutes later. Elaine explained to the receptionist what had happened and we sat down in the reception area with Mum between us. She still had this strange expression that scared the shit out of me. I glanced at Elaine and judging by her eyes she was petrified too. A nurse called for Mum within half an hour and Elaine helped her to the nurse's room before returning to her seat.

'She'll be all right,' my sister said. 'Just a couple of stitches she needs. Don't fret, Lemar, she'll be back cussing our asses in no time.' She glanced round at me and we shared a smile for the first time in ages.

'Why do you think that happened?' I asked. Mum wasn't the fainting kind.

Elaine gave a deep sigh and stared at her feet. 'Could be any number of reasons. Working too hard, being on her own ... us.'

I winced then looked at Elaine. She was staring blankly ahead and tears were falling down her cheeks.

'What's a matter, sis?' I asked.

Elaine didn't respond. She didn't even turn around to face me. The tears kept coming.

'Elaine! What is it?'

I looked around to see if any other patients had seen my sister crying. There were two old ladies chatting to each other and a young mother with a toddler. Two girls were parked in a corner glancing at us and talking into each other's ears. The receptionist was busy writing something down in a book.

'I've made a mess of things, haven't I,' she said quietly.

'So have I,' I said. I so wanted to spill that I'd been at Manjaro's place but thought better of it.

'Sorry for yesterday,' she apologised. 'Look what I've done

to your face! Don't know what came over me. You must be thinking your sister's gone way off-key but trust me, I didn't mean it.'

This was a biggie! Elaine *never* apologised, or not that I could remember. Maybe it was time for me to get my diplomacy on. *Man! Where do I start?*

'Sorry for saying ... you know, the mistake thing. I love Jerome to the max, you know that, right? He could never be a mistake.'

The tears kept falling.

'There I was,' Elaine continued in a near whisper, 'not doing too badly at school. Let me rewind that – I did proper good at school. Teachers always expected some good shit from me. Had some good friends. I loved going to the movies with them on discount Wednesday nights. We used to get nuff jokes trying to get one of us in for free. They were good days. We would draw up our lists of who were the waste-men and who were rocking. It was all good. I wanted to go college and get my study on, maybe do a bit of drama ... then I met Manjaro. I didn't listen to any of my friends who said he was a world of trouble. I felt ... it was like ...' She glanced at me, shame flooding her face. 'There was that time in the fed station. They made me feel ... feel so ...'

Something messed up filled her eyes. She shook her head and composed herself before resuming. 'Remember, when I cried afterwards in your room?' She shrugged. 'This might sound mad, but Manjaro made me feel safe. At the time he had a world of choice and I thought he wanted *me*. I thought nothing like what happened in *that* fed cell could ever happen to me again. Then, I started seeing what he was doing.' She wobbled her head again. 'It was all jumping out of a plane without any parachute.'

'It's not the end . . .'

I tried desperately to think of something to say to make her feel better. But it wasn't happening. McKay was good at this but I wasn't.

'And now my life has crashed,' resumed Elaine. 'I don't know if I'll ever be a good mum, they'll probably send me to live in some shitty flat, Jerome's dad likes to sample all the cakes in the box and Mum can hardly bear to look at me – she wants my ass out of the flat. The true friends I have now I can count on *one* hand. And what's more, I can't remember the last time I went to the freaking movies.'

'What about going back to college?' I managed.

Elaine chuckled and wiped away her tears. 'You'd never believe who'd encouraged me to go for that.'

'Manjaro?'

Elaine nodded. Surprise marked her forehead. 'How'd you guess that?' she asked.

'If it was Gran or Dad it would be standard so it had to be someone unbelievable.'

'Nothing wrong with your brain.' She smiled again.

'You should go for it, sis,' I encouraged. 'You've always been brainier than me.'

'And you've always been more artistic than me,' she said. 'I can't even put my make-up on right let alone draw good.'

'But you were tops at school though.'

'Wasn't tops when it came to *men*,' she said. 'The bitches

round here don't think I notice their snidey looks. I know what they're saying, Lemar. I *know*! "There's that slack bitch that gave up her crutches for Manjaro and bred for him. Doesn't the stupid bitch know that he's got girls all over the place? She just wanted his money but she got a pickney instead! Damn fool! Serve her right."'

I glanced at the two girls in the corner – they were still chirping into each other's ears.

'They don't say—'

'*Yes they do*, Lemar! I'm not an idiot! I hear them whispering in the shops and on road when Jerome's with me. They don't say shit to my face though cos they know I'll get hard-core on them.'

'How ... how did it end with Manjaro?' I asked.

Elaine glanced at me and then gazed at the floor. 'I couldn't ignore what was all around him, the things I seen him and his bredrens do. It scared the shit out of me! He can be proper gentle when he wants to, when it was just me and him. But he's got ... he's got a violent side. I think he needs help.'

'So everyone says,' I said, trying not to think of that poor boy's beat-down a few hours earlier.

'But he had a hardback life,' Elaine resumed. She wiped her face with a kitchen towel. She took a sip from my bottle. 'He had to drop out of uni cos of money worries and issues at home. He never talks about it with anyone else but his dad was a woman-beater. His dad messed up his mum, burst her eardrum. She's on incapacity benefit or something but the government are trying to force her to work. His dad used to drink too. When his dad died Manjaro used to say that his tombstone stank of alcohol and echoed of past beatings. Life in his yard was never blowing your candles out on birthdays and no rolling snowballs with Dad.'

'We used to do that,' I recalled.

'Yeah.' Elaine nodded. 'Not any more though. Dad left, I've got a kid and Mum never buys birthday cakes now ... She has issues. Mostly with Dad.'

'You think she'll be all right?' I asked.

'Not sure,' Elaine replied. 'She has to face the fact that Dad's never gonna come back.'

'Are *you* gonna be all right?'

There was a long pause. Elaine's lips moved but she didn't say anything. Her cheeks were glistening with tears again. 'I ... I was pregnant with his baby. And ... I rolled up to his yard unexpectedly and his bitch was hiding in the bathroom. I wanted him to come to a doctor's appointment I had.'

Elaine wiped her forehead and looked at me hard. 'I swear if my belly wasn't fat I think I would've deleted him. The bitch even knew I was carrying his baby ... they didn't care. He didn't want to give her up. He kept on saying he'd "look after me and the baby once it's born". After the second time he said that I punched him in the face. I raged at the bitch but she kept the bathroom door on lock. After that I bounced out of the yard and left 'em to it.'

'You *beat down* Manjaro!' I started to hum the theme tune of *Rocky* but Elaine wasn't loving it.

She stopped talking, dropped her head and covered her eyes with her palms. Suddenly, she hot-stepped out of the surgery. At that moment I proper hated myself for liking

Manjaro before the beat-down of that poor boy. I went outside to look for Elaine. She was sitting on a concrete bollard near the back of the surgery. She was wiping her face with another kitchen towel. I sat down beside her. For the next few minutes it was just too painful to look at each other. She finally glanced at me.

'I don't think it would've worked, sis.'

Her expression was full of trauma. I could feel my own tears forming so I made an effort to calm myself.

'How did I get pregnant for a G? What do I call you, Lemar, when I get vex with you?'

'A stupid dumb prick,' I answered.

Elaine chuckled again. 'Truth is, *that* is what I call myself.'

'You're *not* to blame, sis. Shit happens. Gran always says we have to learn from it.'

Elaine stood up abruptly. 'We didn't have this conversation,' she said. 'Let's see if Mum's ready.'

I followed her back into the surgery. We sat back down and Elaine dabbed away any evidence of tears. She closed her eyes for about five minutes as if she was trying to delete what happened with Manjaro from her mind.

'You know Mum's strung out to the max, right?' she said as she opened her eyes again.

I nodded.

'So we can't stress her out any more. I need to control my temper and you need to get your head down to your studies and stop running off. You hearing me, Lemar?'

'Yeah, I'm hearing you.'

Mum came out ten minutes later. Her hand was bandaged

but in the other she was carrying a brown envelope. Before she reached us she put the envelope into her handbag. She managed a half-smile. 'I don't know how I'm going to work with this,' she said, holding up her injured hand. 'Someone will have to help me with the deliveries.'

'Me and Lemar will do more in the yard,' said Elaine.

'You should do more anyway,' Mum replied. 'And why does it take the two of you to walk me to the surgery?'

'We were worried,' said Elaine.

'Worried? It's just a liccle scratch me get, not that serious. The nurse only gave me three stitches.'

'Be careful with it, Mum,' Elaine replied.

'Be careful? It's Saturday! Shopping has to be done, our flat has to be cleaned and I have to iron my uniform for work tomorrow.'

'Lemar and me will do the shopping, Mum,' Elaine offered. 'And when I get back I'll iron your work uniform.'

'I have to almost slice off my hand to get you to do the shopping?' Mum gave a brave laugh. 'Maybe I should chop off the other one!'

When I arrived home Gran told me that Dad had called. He dinged me again when I reached home from shopping and all I managed to say was 'Hi, Dad,' before he busted lyrics on me.

'Don't you ever do someting like dat again,' he roared down my mobile. 'You hear me, Lemar? I can't believe you're so damn stupid!'

'I'm sorry, Dad ...'

'If someting did happen to you,' Dad went on, 'how could

I ever tell Steff? Tell me how?'

'How ... how is she doing, Dad?'

There was a pause. I could hear him breathing. When he spoke again his voice was softer and full of emotion. 'She's doing OK, Lemar. Your liccle sister has some fight in her. We're so proud ...'

He went silent again.

'Tell her I love her, Dad.'

'I will.'

18

The Horrible Laugh
of Godfrey McKenzie

As I knew he would, Jonah called for me the next Monday morning before school. He took one look at my face, took out his damn phone and took a pic of me. 'Are you alive?' he joked. 'Or are you now one of the walking dead?'

'Step off, Jonah.'

'After I post your pic I'll let people on Facebook decide. I can't quite work out if your face looks like the Himalayas or that mountain range in *The Lord of the Rings*.'

'I swear,' I threatened, 'if you post that on Facebook I'm gonna fling you over this balcony with a toilet chained to your feet!'

'It looks like somebody flung you over the balcony already and the concrete kissed your face,' replied Jonah. 'Man! You look proper ugly. What happened to you? Your mum was banging on our gates at mad o'clock like paedos had kid-napped you. My mum was well vex.'

'I went to my dad's,' I admitted.

'Did he beat you up?' asked Jonah. 'If he did you should sue his ass! Trust me, Bit, if you sue him he'll have to sell that house in Crongton Green and give you nuff money. I always thought your dad was weird.'

'No, no! It wasn't Dad. What do you mean my dad is weird?'

'Then who messed up your face, Bit? When you play base-ball you're meant to bat the ball – not your face. Damn, you look *ugly*, bruv! Not sure if I should walk on road with you – you might scare away the chicks.'

My days would be over when he found out my sister gave me the beat-down. And I couldn't lie to him cos he was bound to bounce into Elaine, Mum or Gran sooner or later – they wouldn't lie to hide my shame.

'Chicks *don't* step up to you, Jonah,' I joked, trying to change the subject from my bruised-up face.

'They definitely won't if I'm seen with you.'

'Venetia King steps with me.'

'Only because she wants a free drawing. If that was me I wouldn't care how super-fit she was, I'm giving her a mother-freaking invoice.'

McKay was waiting for us at the bottom of our slab. He had this low-down, mischievous grin on his face. *Man!* I didn't need this.

'What's been going on in your castle, Bit?' asked McKay. 'Your gran been breeding vampire vultures and they escaped from their cage? Or did you try and shave yourself with a lawnmower? Damn! I dunno if I should roll to school or take you up to Crongton Village and start begging like the lepers did in Bible days! Trust me, your face will help.'

'Funny!' I replied.

'So who mauled your face?' Jonah asked again. 'Your mum? What did you do? Shit in her hair-grease tub or something? Flush her hair extensions down the toilet? Sink her secret bottle of rum?'

'No! It wasn't Mum and she *doesn't* use hair extensions.'

'Elaine!' yelled McKay, play-slapping Jonah's head in celebration.

'Get your fat hands off me!' protested Jonah.

'Am I right or am I right?' said McKay gleefully. 'You know I'm right. She's savaged your face, bruv! Ain't too late to step back home and get one of them environmental shopping bags. Me and Jonah will help you cut out two holes for the eyes.'

'Elaine?' Jonah repeated, eyes wide. 'She mashed up your face?'

For a moment I thought about telling my bredrens that it was Manjaro who mashed up my face. At least I would get street props if that were true. There was some brother limping around following a Manjaro beat-down and it was the real deal. I finally shrugged, which was as good as admitting they weren't wrong. 'She attacks like a cage fighter,' I said. 'Trust me, if she went for boxing in the Olympics she's winning gold.'

'You let Elaine maul you?' said Jonah, shaking his head. 'Didn't you fight back?'

'Rest your lips, bruv! You think you could handle her?' I challenged Jonah.

Jonah thought about it.

'Sorry, Jonah, but my money's on Elaine, bruv,' said McKay. 'In fact I would put all my games, my kung-fu DVDs and a fried chicken takeaway bucket on it.'

'You think I can't beat-down Bit's sister?' Jonah protested.

'*No!*' McKay shouted. 'Didn't you see Elaine beat-down that thick-eyebrow girl in the park about three years back? You remember that girl? If you could get away from her eyebrows she was kinda cute but she had moustache issues.'

'Oh yeah,' Jonah remembered. 'You weren't there, Bit. Man! Someone should've stopped that shit. Very entertaining though.'

'Can you keep this on the low profile tip?' I asked, glancing over my shoulder. 'I don't want the whole school to know that my sis mauled me.'

'That's good with me, Bit.' McKay nodded. 'Ain't nothing gonna spill from my lips.'

'And nothing's gonna leak from my tongue,' said Jonah. 'My lips are zipped.'

By the time I sat down for my art class in the period before lunchtime, the whole world and astronauts exploring planet Zod knew about Elaine savaging my ass.

Godfrey McKenzie, this boy in our year who giggled at anything, just got his chuckle on every time he looked at me as I tried to concentrate on my clay work in art – my hands weren't as steady as usual. His laugh was a horrible mocking sound, like a cross between a donkey's braying and a pig's oinking.

'Mr McKenzie!' Ms Rees rebuked. 'You've had your last warning! Get out of my classroom and stand in the corridor! I'll see to you after the lesson's finished.'

Godfrey made one more animal sound before he left. Ms Rees huffed and puffed and shook her head as snorts of laughter rippled around the room. Man! Life couldn't get any worse when Godfrey McKenzie was pointing and laughing at your ass.

By the time the buzzer sounded for lunchtime I was proper depressed. For a second I was thinking about paying the school counsellor a visit but thought better of it. If anyone spotted you rolling into her office your life was made a misery. I was about to step home when Ms Rees called my name.

'Mr Jackson! Oh, Mr Jackson!'

Ms Rees always called everybody Mr that or Ms this, even kids in Year 7. She was wearing this flowing orange and green headscarf which didn't match her sky-blue cardigan and brown skirt. Bits of clay and paint were messing up her hair but I guessed she liked it that way.

I approached her, thinking that she was gonna complain about my work in class today. I was trying to make a face profile out of clay but it was all going wrong – it was hard to concentrate with Godfrey McKenzie getting his giggle on behind me. But Ms Rees had this big grin on. 'Congratulations!' she said. 'The art department have selected your work to represent the school at the new gallery in Crongton Broadway in a few weeks' time – the twenty-seventh of this month.'

'Me?'

'Yes! You! Aren't you happy? It's quite an achievement. You should be proud of yourself, Mr Jackson.'

It didn't quite sink in. I couldn't quite concentrate cos some Year 9 girls were having an argument in the corridor. 'What about all the other Year 10 students and the Year 11s? Didn't you want to go for one of them?'

'We thought you displayed the most promise and also your work had the added flavour of a local slant to it. There'll be students there from other local schools, a couple of tutors from Ashburton Arts College, the gallery owners and their friends and the mayor!'

'The mayor!' I repeated. I could hear the Year 9 girls swearing and stomping along the hallway but Ms Rees seemed not to notice. Her eyes never left me.

'Yes, the mayor, Mr Jackson. Isn't that great? So make sure you invite your family down. There'll be a buffet and wine – you can't drink the wine but there'll be soft drinks for the students. They're trying to get someone along from the local newspaper.'

It started to sink in. Me getting my pose on in the local newspaper! Even McKay couldn't take the piss out of that. I had this tingly sensation in my chest. This would make my family feel better after everything that had happened. I only hoped the wounds on my face would clear up by then.

'You're allowed four works of art each,' said Ms Rees. 'Can I suggest two of your portraits and perhaps two landscapes? That one from the perspective of your balcony should be included. I like to call it "Concrete Jungle".'

'I really don't mind, Ms Rees, any of 'em will do. You decide. I have to phone my mum and tell her.'

'OK, you can call her as it's lunchtime but *don't* use your mobile in anybody else's class. You know the rules.'

'Thanks, Ms Rees. I've had a crap day but your news has just niced it up.'

'And I will try and get the head of year to come along – maybe even our headmistress too – the wine will help in her case. Whatever happened to your face?'

At least there was one person in the school who had yet to hear about Elaine mauling my ass.

I made my way towards the door, dodging the question – I just had to call Mum.

'Can you ask Mr McKenzie to come in,' asked Ms Rees.

I looked into the corridor. 'He's … gone. The girls who were making all that noise have gone missing too.'

Ms Rees slapped a hand against her forehead and wobbled her head. I think she mumbled a swear word. I called Mum.

'Mum, Mum!'

'Are you OK, Lemar? Are you in trouble?'

'No, Mum.'

'Then why are you calling? You know I'm at work and I can only talk on my phone if it's an emergency. It's not my dinner break yet.'

'My artwork's gonna be displayed at that new gallery on Crongton Broadway! My art teacher, Ms Rees, just said so. I'm gonna represent our school. She said I could invite the whole family. There's gonna be a buffet and wine. The mayor's gonna be there.'

'That's brilliant, Lemar!' I could hear her getting her joy on, but then things went silent. 'I can't talk. Got to go. Tell me all about it this evening.'

Mum killed the call. I stared at my phone, wondering why she couldn't have found just a few more words for me. I noticed Ms Rees looking at me from her desk. She offered me a half-smile before I stuffed my phone back in my pocket and made my way to the dinner hall.

McKay and Jonah were sitting together at a table. They had saved a seat for me next to them but opposite my place was Venetia King. She was chatting to a friend of hers and she was looking as gorgeous as ever. Suddenly, I remembered the mountain ranges, the bloodshot left eye and the split nose that uglied-up my face.

I stopped in my tracks and suddenly I wasn't feeling peckish.

'Scream,' shouted McKay, beckoning me over. 'We saved a place for you.' I walked over and Venetia King's eyes widened. 'It's true,' she said, staring at my face. 'I was ... I was gonna ask if I can come around after school on Wednesday for you to finish my drawing,' said Venetia. 'But it can wait.'

'*No!* Wednesday will be cool,' I said. 'My face aches a bit but there's nothing wrong with my hands.'

'You sure?' Venetia asked.

'Course I'm sure.'

'That's all good. I'll link you outside the main exit after school.'

I noticed Jonah and McKay had stopped sinking their food

and were glancing at Venetia and me. *Listen and weep!* I wanted to roar.

'I'll be there.' I nodded.

'You ... you OK?' she asked.

'Yeah, course. Believe me, it looks a lot worse than it feels.'

'Ignore Godfrey and the rest of 'em.' Venetia lowered her voice. 'Me and my cousin did fight all the time when we were young and, trust me, sometimes I came off worse than what you look like today.'

It was nice for Venetia to try to make me feel better. I felt a warm glow inside and I had to stop myself from grinning. I might've been mauled by my sister, Manjaro might be chilling in a corner of my brain but at least Venetia King's gonna be getting her pose on in my yard on Wednesday afternoon.

On the way home from school that day, I wanted to boast about Venetia coming to my gates again but McKay was talking about some documentary film he had seen in his history class. *She was so chilled with me at lunchtime and tried to make me feel good. Man! Maybe I do have a chance with her. Why does she keep sitting opposite me? If it was just a painting thing she could check me in the playground about that. Perhaps this sketching is for her to see if I'm on point before things get to second or third base. Lemar Jackson! Don't mess up the programme.*

By the time we reached our slab, McKay and Jonah were still arguing whether man ever stepped on the moon. I entered my flat and made for the kitchen. Gran was in there sticking a few candles in a chocolate cake. She was singing away. 'Rise up this morning, smile with the rising sun ...'

I cautiously sat down, out of her slapping range. 'Hi, Gran,' I greeted. 'Whose birthday?'

'Nobody's.'

'Then what's the cake for?' I asked.

'For you.'

'For me?'

'Isn't that what me say? Your mother called me earlier during her lunch break and told me the news about your art being included in this big gallery event. So me decide to buy you a chocolate cake so you can celebrate.'

'Thanks, Gran. Really nice of you. Did Mum tell you the mayor's gonna be there?'

'Yes, she told me.'

'And wine and a buffet's gonna be served.'

'She told me that too ... she's very proud.'

'What time is Mum coming home from work today?'

'She's working late, till eight.'

'Is Elaine around?'

'She went to Crongton College today to pick up a ... what you call it? A prospectus. Then she went to see Stefanie. But I called her and she sends her congratulations.'

Gran lit the three candles on the cake and invited me to blow them out. 'For more opportunities to come your way,' she said. 'Keep up the good work.'

She gave me a hug, then sliced the cake and we got our nibble on.

'Can I save a slice for Venetia?' I asked.

'Oh?'

'She's coming around Wednesday. Gonna finish my drawing of her.'

Gran raised her eyebrows. 'Of course,' she said. 'I'll cut a piece and wrap it in foil. A good way to a girl's heart, right?'

I sunk half of my cake, glad that Gran's eyes had lost their Terminator-like intent to delete me. 'How ... how was Mum this morning?' I asked. 'I didn't see her before I left for school.'

'She's ... better,' Gran replied. 'It's just a case of her accepting that she has a problem about stressing herself too much over stuff and being sensible enough to ask for help. There isn't any shame in that.'

'I think I know what you mean,' I said. 'I'll offer to do more chores in the yard. It was kinda scary her losing it like that.'

'Yes it was but she's getting there,' Gran added, placing her hand on mine. 'But me also worried about your sister. You don't know what's eating at her, Lemar?'

'No, Gran,' I lied. 'Elaine doesn't tell me anything.'

'You two were so close one time.'

'Yes, we were,' I agreed.

'At times like this we have to stick together,' Gran said. 'Sometimes we're like separate trees, standing in our own fields. But when you're isolated you're exposed to the rain, snow, wind and everyting.'

'I hear you, Gran.'

'But if we grow together,' Gran continued, 'we can help to shelter each other from the storm. You understand me, Lemar?'

'I understand, Gran.'

'*Good!* Remember that.'

She hugged me again like I was Jesus and this time I tried

not to wriggle free. I knew how much my gran loved giving me hugs and I let her words sink into my heart. *We have to help each other ...* Gran wasn't wrong. Elaine, me, Jerome, Mum, Gran – we were family, right?

19

First Cut is the Deepest

Wednesday afternoon could not come quickly enough. I thanked all the gods when the final school buzzer sounded. Thankfully, McKay and Jonah were not around at the main exit. Venetia was waiting for me. She looked as hot as a hot chilli served under a mad sun in Mexico. My Hawaiian beach fantasy blasted away everything else that was in my mind. *Should I kiss her on the cheek when I finish sketching her? Should I show her my room? Better hide all my computer games. Don't want her to think I'm a geek. In fact, I'd better stop the kissing mission cos I don't wanna mash up my chances of getting to base camp two and three. Maybe in a couple of weeks we can take in a movie or something. Yep, I'll blitz her lips then. After that, she might ask me to roll to her yard. I'll get to know her fam. I definitely need to get a head-trim before that.*

'Thanks, Bit,' Venetia said. 'Will really appreciate it if you can finish the drawing today. The rest of the week I've got dance and basketball practice.'

'No worries,' I said.

'So, what really happened to your face, Bit? Did Elaine maul you up for real?'

I looked into Venetia's eyes and I couldn't lie to her. 'Yeah, she did. Her temper is toxic. She can box down a four-storey slab when she's in a fever.'

'So you and her are good now?' she said. 'Don't wanna step into your yard and you two are still Game of Throning.'

'No, we're good now,' I replied. 'We had ... we had a long talk.'

'So much madness and violence around here,' Venetia said. 'Sick and tired of it. My dad knew Nightlife's family so we all went to the funeral. It reminded me of going to my cousin's. There was people crying and making up their noise as they lowered the coffin into the ground. Nightlife's mum almost dropped to the ground – the poor woman could barely walk. You know what, Bit? When I check it I've been to more mother-freaking funerals than weddings! It's messed up, Bit, for someone as young as Nightlife to go like that. I swear, when I get a chance I'm moving from these ends. Trust me on that. If I settle down with someone I don't wanna raise kids here.'

'I hear you on that.' I nodded, hoping that someone could be me.

When we arrived home Gran was wearing a smile the size of the Caribbean and an apron with a mango and a green banana on it. 'Lovely to see you again, Venetia! My, my! Me grandson has very good taste – just like his grandfather! Me just cook the chicken curry as me know you was coming. So come sit down and tell me what you think.'

I wondered if Gran had sampled any rum before I reached home but Venetia could do nothing but laugh as we sat down at the little round table in the kitchen. Gran served us our curry and rice. 'Lemar thinks I'm cranky and old, Venetia,' Gran revealed. Man! This could get embarrassing. 'He can't even imagine that *I* was young once. Oh yes! When I was a liccle older than you are now I would *borrow* my mother's gin, sneak out of my yard and go to pyjama parties. Oh yes! Those were the nights, whining and crubbing away like you wanted to start a fire with your dance partner! Me had to sneak back before it get light and my father would catch the blame for the missing gin. And why would they blame me? I was a nice, liccle Christian girl.'

Venetia and I almost choked on our curry laughing.

Venetia chased her dinner down with the slice of chocolate cake that I had kept for her in the fridge. She sank it in no time. 'You know, Bit,' she said, licking the crumbs from her lips. 'You being selected for this gallery thing? It means that you're the best artist in the school. Trust me on that and *don't* let anybody tell you different. You're riding places! You'll be out of these ends one day. And I'm on the same programme. Maybe your portrait of me will be worth something in the future!'

'You're not bad yourself,' I said. 'You're the best girl basketball player and footballer.'

She smiled that gorgeous smile. 'I'm good at English, IT and sociology too!'

First Cut is the Deepest

It was all good cos by the time Venetia got her pose on, she was looking very relaxed and oh-my-God-beautiful. I took my time sketching in her eyes and her cheekbones – I wanted to get them just right. Her neck was longer than most chicks of her age. She was a good model too cos she sat down without twitching for nearly an hour – Gran could barely manage five minutes. To finish off I had to mix my colours to get her smooth caramel complexion on point.

'*Done!*' I said when I'd finished.

'Let me have a look,' she said, jumping out of her chair. 'Oh my God! That's brilliant, Bit. Thank you so much. That's ... me!'

She gave me a warm hug and my Hawaiian beach fantasy played again.

I went to fetch her a drink. In the kitchen I was trying to get my cool on. 'This is *it*,' I whispered to myself. 'Millions of bruvs around the world do this shit every day. It's not as hard as Year 1 maths. It's just a few words. *What do you say about taking in a movie next week?* Why would she say no to that? She obviously likes me.'

When I returned she was busy texting on her phone. 'One second,' I said.

I carefully rolled up the sketch, went to my bedroom and pushed it into one of my drawing tubes. I returned to the lounge and presented it to Venetia. She accepted it, smiled and gave me a quick hug. 'Thanks so much, Bit!'

Man! I felt all tingly inside. I think my heart doubled in size. *I'm* definitely *gonna ask her to link me for the cinema. Maybe I'll get to base camp one this evening if I play my dominoes right.* 'Do you want me to walk you back to your slab?' I offered.

'No, it's all right, someone's coming to pick me up.'

'Oh. Who?' My mission had hot-toed down a sinkhole.

'A friend.'

'OK, I'll walk you down the stairs then.'

'Thanks, Bit. I've got a touch for you.'

'What did I say about paying me? I'm not taking your money, Venetia.'

I opened the front door and she followed me outside on to the balcony.

'Please take it, Bit, I've got ten pound for you. An artist should get paid for his work just like my dad gets paid for fixing boilers – it's your trade. Your pencils and stuff are your tools. They're your ride out of here.' Venetia seemed so set on getting out of this estate. Yeah, it was far from the big gated yards at the top ends of Crongton Heath, but it was still home.

I closed the door behind me. Venetia took the ten-pound note out of her purse and waved it in the air. I shook my head – if Jonah had seen this he would've booted me in the nuts, scratched out my eyes and slapped my forehead with a plank. She then tried to push it into my trouser pocket. I dodged her. '*Stand still!*' she insisted, raising her voice. She looked a bit vexed.

'I *can't* take it, Venetia,' I said. I took a deep breath and rolled on. 'I did your sketch cos ... I like you.'

She took a step back from me. Suddenly, she found the graffiti on the walls very interesting. She was a bit quiet when we bounced down the stairs of my slab. We passed my next-door neighbour, Ms Harrington, who was pulling up a trolley of shopping. 'Afternoon, Lemar,' she said. 'I heard about what Elaine done to you.' She paused to take a look at Venetia and then she turned to me again. 'Girlfriend of yours? That's nice.'

Venetia glanced at me like she wanted to say sorry and then jumped down the steps two at a time. I had to leave Ms Harrington standing and get a rush on to catch up with Venetia. I was thinking maybe I had upset her by not taking her money but how could I take her touch when I wanted her to be my girlfriend? The Hollywood kiss I'd had on my mind chomped the dirt.

Someone was revving a motorbike in the forecourt. When we reached ground level I spotted who it was – some Mediterranean-looking boy. He looked about seventeen. He was wearing these black leather boots that almost reached up to his knees, black jeans and a white shirt with black buttons. Some sort of silky black scarf was wrapped around his neck. I don't think he was from the ends. Venetia ran over to him, pulled out my sketch from the tube and showed him the por-trait. 'Bit, Bit! Come and say hello.'

He unfurled the sketch, got his gaze on and grinned wider than Rome. He then placed a hand on Venetia's cheek and kissed her on the mouth.

I had that five-day-old school custard feeling going on in my stomach again. I could barely force myself to look at the guy but there he was in his fancy black boots, stupid skinny scarf and black jeans. He had toothpaste-advert teeth and don't-mess-with-me arms. He offered Venetia a helmet to put on and kissed her again. This time longer. Much longer. She threw one arm around his neck and closed her eyes. I didn't know whether to cry or to find a suitable spot in the estate to delete myself. Finally they came up for air. I wanted to shoot an acid-tipped arrow through his tongue. She rolled up the sketch again and placed it back in its tube. 'Bit!' she called. 'I want you to meet Sergio.'

In all my days I had never hated anyone who hadn't done me any wrong as much as Sergio. I despised everything and anything about him, even his first pair of baby shoes, his gran, his distant third cousins and his toddler bredrens at nursery. I wanted the moon to drop from the sky and land on his head. When he was concussed I wanted some mad Brazilian swamp cannibal leeches to suck out his lips and eat his eyes. We'd see how he got his kiss on after that.

I didn't want to look as if I was dying inside so I walked over slowly. God! It was like meeting the zillionaire lottery winner who was one place in front of you buying his winning ticket.

'It's Sergio's birthday on Saturday and I wanted to get him something different,' revealed Venetia, holding up the tube. 'Thanks so much for this. You're an incredible artist.'

'I'm gonna frame it,' said Sergio in some sort of accent. 'And I'm gonna hang it up in my room over my bed.'

I now wanted the moon to land on my ass and delete me. I managed a quarter-smile but in my head I was screaming, *I didn't sketch Venetia to nice up a wall in Sergio's bedroom!*

'Are you sure you don't want a touch?' asked Venetia again. 'Take the ten pounds. *Please.*'

I glanced up at her and it was damn hard to stop the tears.

She held my gaze for a long second. I think she could see the grief in my eyes – it was like trying to hide a gorilla behind a skinny spiderweb.

I thought about the money. I was crushed, but I supposed that having ten pounds with a stomping feeling on my heart was better than just having that stomping feeling.

I took Venetia's note. She pulled on her helmet, sat on Sergio's bike and wrapped her arms with the sketch tube around his waist. She rested her head on his back. God! I hated Sergio's back and I hated his motorbike. 'Thanks again, Bit,' she said.

Sergio revved the engine loudly before pulling away. Before they left the forecourt of my slab, Venetia turned her head and offered me a wave. I stood still for the next minute or two, wondering what the hell had just happened to me.

I eventually climbed the stairs of my slab like I had motorbikes chained to my feet. Once inside I made straight for my bedroom. I lay flat on my back and stared at the ceiling. *Why didn't I think that Venetia might have a boyfriend?* A super-fit girl like Venetia was bound to have a guy. *What was I thinking? Oh shit! What am I gonna tell McKay and Jonah? If they find out about this they'll be getting their giggle on till I need a walking stick to climb my slab.*

I didn't feel like watching TV or playing games. I usually got my sketch on when I was on the down-low but I didn't even wanna do that. I just spent the rest of the evening feeling sorry for myself. Gran asked if I was OK but I just said I was tired.

Just after ten o'clock, Jonah texted me.

How did it go with Venetia? Did you get to first base? Did
you get to kiss her up? Do you even know how to kiss a
chick? Forget I asked. Of course you never kissed her up.

It took me an hour to reply.

I just finished her portrait. She's well happy with it. And
she gave me a ten pound touch.

Half an hour later, I heard my mobile vibrate again. I
guessed it was Jonah looking for more information or McKay
expecting some kinda hug-by-kiss account. For a second I
thought about lying and sexing up my reputation but no –
Venetia would probably come around here and maul me up
like Elaine did. I ignored the text for the next hour or so but
then I thought they'd keep on about it at school. I picked up
my phone and was about to reply.

But the last text I received wasn't from McKay or Jonah. I
didn't recognise the number.

I opened it.

The man wants a favour from you. He'll give you a nice
touch. You receiving? P

P? That must be Lady P. My heart started to box my ribcage.
Suddenly, my head felt all hot. I reread the text, hoping that
it would just disappear. But it didn't. God! What am I gonna
do? I can't get myself hooked up with Manjaro again. But I
don't want a beat-down like what that poor brother had to

suffer. But if I deal with Manjaro then what kinda brother am I? Maybe if I'm proper polite they might just leave my ass alone. Gotta try it.

Five minutes later, I replied to Lady P's text.

No disrespect but I really don't wanna get involved in what you do. I'm not no snitch so have no frets about that. Not even my shadow knows shit. My tongue's stapled.

I sent the text and placed my phone on my dressing table. I stared at it for a while, thinking that Manjaro's fist might come exploding out of it. Twenty minutes later I climbed into bed. I switched off my light and thought that surely Manjaro would ask someone else to do his favour.

I tossed and turned and I lost count of the amount of times I flipped over my pillow. It was useless. I couldn't sleep. I slapped on my computer and played Dungeons & Dragons. I had got through to the third level when I heard my phone tremble. I picked it up. It was a text from Lady P. The time was just after two-thirty in the morning. I paused for a moment and then I opened the text.

But you are involved, Bit. You carried a piece for us. You wouldn't want that shit to get out ... Would you?

Oh *crap*! A shiver went through me from the tips of my Afro curls to the nail of my baby toe. No, I wouldn't want any of that info to get out. After they jailed my ass the feds would fling away the key. Mum and Elaine would both maul me.

Gran would give me an uppercut and whatever chances I ever had with Venetia – or any chick for that matter – would trickle down the ghetto sewage drain. And doing shit for Manjaro is just … wrong. How many others did they roll to his yard so Manjaro could maul them?

I tried to sleep but found it impossible. I felt the tears build up behind my eyes. I had no choice. How would Mum, Dad, Elaine and Gran feel to see my mangled ass in a hospital bed? Maybe … maybe I could say this was the last favour I was doing. Eventually, I replied to Lady P's message.

OK, I'll do the favour.

The reply came five minutes later.

Good, we'll give you a time to meet tomorrow.

20

Stepping on Bubbles

Mum cooked me a nice breakfast after I got up later that morning. I could barely open my eyes but I was sinking fried mushrooms along with eggs, bacon and beans. I was wondering what kinda favour Manjaro wanted from me as Mum sang in the kitchen. 'Oh, let it go, baby, it's just another love TKO ...' Then I heard Mum's mobile phone ringing. She answered it and moved into the lounge. I stood by the kitchen door and listened. 'Hello?' Mum said. 'After school tomorrow? You're gonna take the both of them bowling? Are you going to buy them something to eat? Of course I should ask ... No, I haven't told them yet – it's not my place to do so. I thought we settled this on the phone last night, or wasn't you listening? I'm not gonna change my mind on this ... You can tell them *yourself*. I am not doing your dirty work! How am I supposed to know how they'll take it!'

Mum killed the call and I quickly retreated back into the kitchen. She entered and turned to me as I was sinking my mango juice. 'Your father is taking you and Elaine out after you finish school tomorrow,' she said. 'He has something to tell you.'

'What's that?' I asked.

'You'll find out,' Mum replied, avoiding looking at me. 'Make sure he gets you something to eat.'

Jonah called for me again for school and he didn't make any remarks about my face. He didn't let up on the Venetia issue though. 'So you just finished the sketch and she went home, right?' he asked as we bounced down the steps.

'That's right, Jonah! That's all there is to it, bruv. Did I ever say she was my girl? No, I didn't. It was just a drawing thing.'

'Yeah, that makes sense,' Jonah said. 'I don't mean any offence, bruv, but Venetia King and you? You two don't exactly go together like rice and peas or butter on toast. She's going places, that chick – she's outta these ends.' I thought back to everything Venetia had said to me about getting off the estate. It made me feel uncomfortable to think that I didn't want to get off the estate. Was that wrong? It was all I knew.

Just like on the previous Monday morning, McKay was waiting at the bottom of our slab. He was sucking a lollipop but when he spotted us he pulled it out of his mouth and chatted in that fast style he used whenever he got excited. 'Tried to text you two last night but didn't have enough credit,' he started. 'Number nine Remington House has been raided.

There were untold feds there and they were taking out computers and shit. It all happened about nine last night. Some chick and a brother were arrested ...'

Oh God! I hoped they didn't have the yard under surveillance. If they did I was in it up to my eyebrows.

'How do you know?' asked Jonah. 'You're always exaggerating. Was you there?'

I tried desperately to control my breathing. I hoped Jonah and McKay hadn't noticed that I had my full panic on.

'My brother was there,' replied McKay. 'He was riding his bike last night and he saw all the flashing blue lights and shit. He said they were taking out things in black bags. I'm telling you, bruv, who knows what arms they carried out of that yard.'

'Maybe it's not arms,' I said in hope. 'Maybe ... maybe it was just an everyday search thing. The feds do that shit nuff times on this estate. Look how they tore up Mitchell Swaby's floorboards but found nothing.'

'My bruv said there was nuff feds there,' McKay answered. He gave me a long look. 'More than the usual amount of feds in a search raid. It seems like the feds wanna stop Manjaro warring with Major Worries.'

Shit! I don't wanna be part of this war. Don't wanna be on anyone's side. Maybe this is why Manjaro wants another favour. What is he gonna ask me to do?

All the way to school McKay didn't stop talking about a possible Crongton war and how we should all think about wearing bulletproof vests. He even wanted to suggest to the head teacher that students shouldn't have to attend school

197

cos the ends were getting too dangerous to step through. I thought about the text messages that I received last night from Lady P and my stomach was thinking about it too – I almost brought up my breakfast near the school gates.

My first lesson of the day was English and it was a relief to get away from McKay – I wasn't loving the way he looked at me when he was spilling the news about the raid. He *knew* I'd stepped into number nine Remington House.

The teacher gave us our instructions but as soon as my pen kissed the paper I felt a vibration in my pocket. I just knew it was another message from Lady P. Sweat rapidly bubbled on my forehead. My neck felt itchy. I loosened my tie and tried to relax myself by taking deep breaths. I wrote two sentences before taking my phone out of my pocket and reading my text.

Meet me in the supermarket car park at 5. Bring your schoolbag. P.

Maybe I should just step to the fed station and spill everything? No, can't do that. Mum doesn't need any more stress. And say I do 'fess up to the feds? They might wanna put us in some witness protection programme and move our asses to some small, messed-up country town that we've never heard of where the cows look weird. No bredrens, different school, probably no mobile connection and everyone back in South Crongton calling me a Judas. I might never see Dad or Steff again. I can't see Elaine agreeing to live like that with Jerome. She'll probably go her own way. She has a toxic temper but I can't imagine her not in my life … I'll miss everybody.

No, I'd better do what Lady P wants me to do. If I keep the shit to myself I should be OK.

I replied to Lady P's text.

OK, I'll be there.

'Lemar Jackson!' called Ms Birbalsingh, our English teacher. 'It would be nice for you to find something interesting to write on the page instead of on your phone. *Put it away!'*

I managed to get to lunch break without having a nervous breakdown. Lasagne was on the menu again. I had sunk half of it when I spotted Venetia King taking a seat opposite me. God! Could my day have got any worse? *If she mentions Sergio's name I swear I'll spew out my lunch on her school blazer. If I ever see his motorbike in the ends I'll run it over with a ten-ton truck with spiked tyres.*

New silver earrings were nicing up Venetia's face and she had trimmed her hair into a close crop. God! She looked as tasty as a chocolate flake sexing up one of Jonah's mum's butterfly cakes. Delicious. I tried to make it look like I didn't notice her but she caught me – and gave me one of them knowing stares from a girl where they seem to know exactly what you are thinking. And I was thinking, *Can't help loving her to the max but hate this Sergio guy.* I was sure she spotted the clues in my eyes. After an awkward two minutes, she spoke.

'How's tings, Lemar?'

I thought this was the first time ever she'd actually called me Lemar. Maybe she felt sorry for my sad ass.

'Could be better,' I replied, looking over her right shoulder.

'I should've … I should've told you about … about Sergio.'

'You could say that,' I replied.

'I didn't … believe me, Lemar, I didn't know you had a … serious ting for me … not until you spilled something on the stairs of your slab.'

What does she mean that she never knew I had a ting for her before we went down the steps of my slab? Every guy in my year and the next year has a ting for her. Guys who ride motorbikes have a ting for her. If the Pope saw her he'd have a ting for her. There are life-forms on undiscovered planets that would have a ting for her.

I shrugged. 'I'll get over it. It's not a biggie. I'm glad you both like the portrait.'

'We love it. Sergio said …'

A smiling Sergio bounced into my mind with his Hollywood teeth, his world of black leather and his revving motorbike. I couldn't take any more. I stood up, picked up my half-sunk dinner and put it in the slop rack. I had this serious urge to glance behind to see how Venetia reacted but I managed to check myself. The truth was it felt like some ugly insects with don't-mess-with-me pinchers were getting their munch on my heart.

21

Lady P

'I'm going to McKay's,' I told Gran.

I had completed my history homework about the First World War – from what I could make out, it was all about kings, queens, dukes and other rich people getting poor people to fight their battles. Maybe Manjaro and Major Worries were doing the same deal – getting brothers and sisters like me to do their shit for them. There was no way I would delete or wound anybody but I was *still* being used in their war. Like those First World War soldiers, I just didn't see any other choice. I didn't wanna stress out my family and I didn't want to be known as a snitch – snitches in Crongton had the same lifespan as a choc ice on a barbecue. Maybe if I did this last favour for them they wouldn't ask my ass to do anything else. I was clinging to that hope.

'Are you having your dinner there?' asked Gran.

'Er, no. We're just checking homework notes on history. I'll be back in about an hour.'

I set off for the supermarket with my rucksack slung over my left shoulder – it was about a twenty-five-minute walk from my slab, not too far from where my dad lived in Crongton Green. When I arrived, I parked myself on a bench just outside the entrance. I watched shoppers come and go, thinking that they had no freaking idea of why I was here. Again, I thought of going to the feds – those officers who came to my gates were proper serious but at least they wouldn't delete me – I remembered Elaine had left their card in the kitchen.

Five minutes past five. No sign of Lady P. My heart started another boxing round with my ribcage. I palmed away the sweat from my forehead. Should I roll home? I'd arrived here at the time Lady P told me to. What could they say? Then I thought of that poor brother who got a beat-down in Manjaro's hallway. Would they do the same shit to me, if Lady P turned up and I wasn't here? If it took days for my face to recover from Elaine's beat-down then this guy would probably look into his mirror weeks after his pounding from Pinchers and Manjaro and cry an ocean.

Don't bounce away yet, Lemar, I told myself. *Give it to quarter-past-five. If I step then they can have no arguments.*

'Hello, Lemar. Waiting for your mum?'

I jolted and spun around. It was Jonah's mum, Mrs Hani. She was pulling a shopping trolley – there seemed to be a world of cake ingredients inside.

My heart and my ribcage were swapping some mad blows.

'Er, no, Mrs Hani. Just waiting for a bredren.'

'Waiting for a friend,' corrected Mrs Hani. 'Jonah just called me. He's at home with McKay playing games. I thought you'd be there with them?'

'Er, um, no, Mrs Hani. I'm ... I'm just doing a favour for a bredren.'

She squinted like one of those secret-service agents on TV when they interviewed a suspect.

'A favour for a friend,' she corrected me again. 'OK, nice to see you. Say hello to your mum for me.'

'Nice to meet you too and I'll say hello.'

Mrs Hani clip-clopped away. I let out a monster sigh. As soon as my heart returned to its normal beat I spotted Lady P standing in the walkway that led to the entrance of the store. Her arms were folded and she looked like she had lost her wallet which had a nice picture of her niece or somebody inside it.

I slowly approached her, and when I got within ten metres, she veered off into the car park. I followed her. There was no hello. She didn't even look at me. *Better not ask her about the raid on Remington House,* I thought. When we reached her car she opened the front passenger-side door. 'Get in,' she ordered.

I did what I was told. R & B music was playing on a low volume from the car stereo. There was a minty smell inside. From her reflection in the rear-view mirror I could see her opening the boot, taking out a black plastic bag and placing it on the back seat. I took in a deep breath and swabbed my forehead again. Once again I recalled the yelps and cries of pain from Manjaro's hallway. Once more, I wondered who that brother was.

She joined me in the front, picked up her handbag that was resting by the foot pedals and took out an envelope.

'Phone,' she demanded, reaching out her hand.

I gave her my mobile. I was going to tell her how to switch it on but she knew what she was doing. She deleted all my text messages before handing my phone back to me.

'We want you to look after something for us,' she said. She was gazing through the windscreen. 'Just keep it safe. *Don't* open it. It'll just be for a few days until tings calm down, you receiving?'

I nodded.

'You're not going away or anywhere different in the next few days, are you?'

'No,' I replied.

'Good. Just do what you normally do, go school and shit, you get me? Don't get your liccle ass into any kinda trouble. And when we come for it we'll give you another touch.'

'What … what is it?'

She still didn't look at me. Through the windscreen, she was watching this mum yank the hand of her straying little boy. 'Ask me no questions and I cannot tell you any lies,' she said. 'I want you to go to the back seat, close the door and put the bag in your school bag, right?'

I nodded again. 'When are you gonna come and get it back?'

'As I said, when things have cooled down. I reckon no more than a week.'

'A week!'

'Keep your voice down. There should be no worries cos you've never been in trouble with the feds before, have you?'

I thought of the fed visit to my yard. Maybe someone from Manjaro's crew had seen them enter my gates. But I didn't spill anything and I wasn't under suspicion. 'No,' I finally answered.

'You haven't even jacked a chocolate bar from a shop have you or thrown a stone through one of the windows in the old factories?'

'No,' I repeated.

'So we thought. So stop sweating – everything will be cool. The feds won't trouble you. Just go to school as usual, do what your mum says as normal and keep it on the down-low.'

'All right.' I couldn't believe this shit. So this was why Manjaro was interested in my ass. My gold medal for being a decent boy most of my life was to become a runaround for him and his crew. My good behaviour was their shield. *Is this what their programme is all about? Be bad, and get caught up in gangs. Stay decent, and still get caught in crews?*

'When you get home, put it in the bottom of your wardrobe or something, you receiving? Put it in a place where your family doesn't normally go.'

'No worries.'

Lady P checked the rear mirror and then glanced each side of her. '*Make* sure it's zipped in your bag before you get out of the car.'

'OK.'

'All right, go to the back seat.'

I climbed out of the car, closed the door gently and stepped into the back. Lady P's eyes were on me, through the rear-view mirror, all the way. I picked up the black plastic bag without even pausing to see what was inside and put it in my rucksack. When I secured the zip, Lady P passed me a white envelope. 'OK,' she said. 'It's all wrapped up like a birthday present. *Leave* it that way. As I said, just carry on as normal, *don't* ask for us, *don't try to call us* and don't step to our place in Crongton Heath, you receiving?'

'I get it,' I said.

'Cool.' She nodded. 'The man hopes that you can spend some of the money on Jerome. You shouldn't forget that he's Jerome's dad and he wants to do right by him. Think about that. Anyway, time for you to fly.'

'OK.'

She was still studying me via the rear-view mirror.

'Don't look so worried,' she said. 'It's not loaded.'

The whole of my insides trembled. I opened the car door with two hands just to stop one of them shaking. I stumbled as I climbed out of the car. Lady P started the engine, indicated and drove away. I watched her disappear before I started stepping. I had this mad urge to look in the black plastic bag and rip off the brown paper and masking tape that covered the gun. Maybe it *was* loaded but Lady P didn't want to freak me out by telling me. I resisted the temptation. I put the envelope inside my rucksack.

Spend some of the money on Jerome? *No!* If I spent any notes on him, Elaine would ask me where I got the money from – and that would spill nuff maggots into the shit and piss pot. Plus, I didn't want Manjaro's money messing up Jerome's life.

I arrived home twenty-five minutes later. I could smell snapper fish from the kitchen. 'Home, Gran,' I called out. 'Just gonna change.'

'Lemar,' Gran called me. 'Come here!'

I stepped to the kitchen and I found Gran washing rice. 'What did me tell you about greeting me when you reach home?'

'To … to greet you properly and don't just call your name?'

'So why you just holler my name and head straight to your room?'

'Sorry, Gran.'

'Come here!'

I still had my rucksack strapped to my shoulders but Gran gave me one of her bear hugs. 'I'm glad that you're beginning to take your history homework seriously, Lemar. Your art is wonderful but one tasty spice is never enough for a good fish. You understand?'

'I understand, Gran. I know other subjects are important. Dad goes on about it all the time.'

'And make sure you *try* harder at your maths. If you don't then how are you going to count all the money you receive when you're a world-famous artist?'

Gran's embrace tightened as she squashed her cheek against mine. Her right arm was pressing against my ruck-sack. I took a short step back. 'Not sure about that, Gran. Anyway, gotta do some more homework.'

Finally, she let me go. 'You're a good boy.' She turned back to the cooker. 'Me just going to boil some rice and dinner will be done.'

'OK, Gran, thanks.'

I went to my room and closed the door behind me. For a few minutes I just parked on my bed, staring at my rucksack. Then I took out the black plastic bag. There was a brown package in it crossed with masking tape and string. I took it out. It was heavy. I closed my eyes and my mind was filled with all the action films and games I had seen and played where a gun had been used. There were so many. Now I had a real one in my hands wrapped in brown paper and tied with yellowy-white string. This was no film. No game. Lady P said it wasn't loaded. Maybe she was saying that just to scare me. It might have been something else. I had to check it out for myself. Using my thumbnail I tore off a tiny bit of brown paper. Something shiny and black stared back at me. I touched it and it was cold and metallic. *God save my ass.* I put it back in the plastic bag and let out a long breath. There was a knock on my door. I quickly placed the plastic bag in my rucksack.

'Come in, Gran,' I said, trying to keep my breathing steady.

'Your clean clothes,' Gran said, handing them over. She looked at my floor and tutted as she picked up a rubber and a couple of pencils. She placed them on my desk. '*Don't* leave your clothes on the bottom of your bed like you usually do, Lemar. Put them in your wardrobe.'

'OK, Gran, thanks.'

'Dinner will be ready in about twenty minutes. Me just waiting for the rice to cook.'

'OK, Gran. Thanks.'

Gran left. I looked at the top of my wardrobe where there were two suitcases. *No,* I thought. *Can't put it up there. Say Mum comes in my room and needs a suitcase. Drop that.* I glanced at my small chest of drawers. *No, drop that too – Mum or Gran are always putting my underwear in there.*

I opened my wardrobe door. There were games I didn't play any more resting on top of old trainers and spare blankets. *No, can't put it in there either.* Now and again Gran came into my room and cleaned out my wardrobe. She was always cussing me about the state I left it in. *Damn! Where am I gonna put the gun? I should've given this more thought before I agreed to do this shit. I don't have anywhere my family don't get their sniff on.* Lady P overestimated my levels of privacy. I was a fourteen-year-old bruv, for God's sake! Didn't she know that privacy was virtually outlawed in my family? *Maybe I should just leave it in my school bag. Yeah, slap it down to the bottom and put my books and stuff on top of it.*

I emptied out my rucksack, placed the package at the bottom then put everything else on top. *This is the one place no one goes,* I reasoned. And at least I won't have to arrive home one afternoon and find Mum or Gran holding up the gun and asking me, 'Where did you get this from?' *Shit! They might use it on me! Yeah, let me stick to this programme until I can think of a better one,* I thought.

Opening the envelope Lady P had given me, I counted a hundred pounds. Manjaro's money. All in twenties. *I'm gonna have to hide this too. No way can I spend any of it, but I can't just fling it away.* I placed the notes in one of my old trainers in the back of my wardrobe, pushing them right down into the toe part.

I was just closing the wardrobe door when Elaine bounced into my room. 'All right, bro,' she greeted.

Doesn't she ever knock? I raged inside my head. *All right, bro? Man! Her manners and character have been under some serious surgery.*

I picked up my rucksack, zipped it up and put it in a corner of my room before joining my sister on the bed. 'All right, sis. What's up?'

'Just wondering what Dad's gonna tell us tomorrow. Has he called you or said anything?'

'Nope,' I replied. 'He's probably gonna lecture us about the other night and tell us that we're brother and sister and that we shouldn't be fighting and shit.'

'Yeah, it could be that.' Elaine nodded. 'But he's already cussed me out for beating you down when I went to see Steff yesterday.'

'How is she?'

'She's coming out of hospital in a couple of days so Dad and Shirley are well happy.'

'That's all good,' I said. 'Maybe Dad's got me in line for a cuss attack. That's the problem of having two parents who don't live together – if you do a wrong you get your ears slapped by one and then you have to wait a few days to get your ears boxed by another.'

'Yeah, that's for real,' Elaine agreed. 'But I think Steff's illness is really getting to him. He wasn't his usual self.'

'Maybe he's feeling the stress,' I suggested.

'You're right, Lemar. With Mum's issues and Dad's worries I don't wanna stress out the situation even more, you hearing me?'

'I'm hearing you, sis.'

'*Good.*'

She left as abruptly as she arrived. *God! If she knew about* my *issues she'd flip.*

22

Bowling in the Gutter

McKay, Jonah and I were walking home after school the next day and as usual we were arguing about something. I kinda liked the banter cos it stopped me stressing out about the gun in my rucksack – I hadn't taken it off my back all day. I didn't dare leave the gun in my bedroom. If someone ever found it ... But neither did I want to risk putting it in my locker – the teachers had started random checks on students' lockers, trying to find knives, pills and other illegal drugs. I wasn't sure what I was gonna do with my bag when I had a PE lesson. Anyway, I got through the day OK without getting interrogated, strip-searched, mauled and bounced to the fed station – I knew they don't do that shit to kids at school but I couldn't help fretting about it.

'I'm telling you,' insisted McKay. 'When the prime minister gets an invite to visit the ends, he sends a clone or a robot of himself.'

'Wouldn't the people know that it's a robot?' replied Jonah.

'Yeah,' I said. 'People aren't dumb you know. When they hear the whirring and bleeping and shit, people will find out.'

'You two are soooo gullible,' accused McKay, raising his voice. 'You're soooo easily fooled. Do you really think that when they invite the prime minister to the bad ends of a place like Ashburton, like they did today, he's gonna go himself? Do you really think he's gonna waste his time with the ghetto people from Ashburton or Crongton where the most inter-esting building is a phone shop? I mean, Ashburton's a dump – not even refugees and homeless people wanna step there.'

'They've got the art college,' I mentioned.

'They've got a really good kebab shop,' said Jonah. 'Just around the corner from the High Street.'

'That hardly sexes up the place,' remarked McKay. 'And as for Crongton, the tallest building is Bit's slab. *No*, bruv! The prime minister ain't gonna waste his time. He's gonna send a mother-freaking clone. This clone is taught to speak, walk and shit like the prime minister, I'm telling you. It's so real the prime minis-ter's wife can't tell them apart – she don't know who to go to bed with when the ten o'clock news ends. She probably wants her own clone so she can send it to bed with him.'

'McKay, you have come up with some real crap since I've known you,' laughed Jonah. 'Some of it made us get our giggle on, some of it didn't make sense. But this one? Has your hard drive malfunctioned, bruv? It's a conspiracy theory too far, bredren. You better seal your mouth about your crazy theories before they take you away to a madhouse, bruv. Keep spilling your shit about clones and robots and your new best bredren will be a straitjacket, believe it! And anyway, when he was in Ashburton today visiting the ghetto ends and they give him something to sink, what does he do?'

'*The clone is trained to eat,*' stressed McKay. 'And drink. It can probably bust a fart too and flick a bogey. They can get robots to do any shit now. I'm telling you these clones are *seriously* lifelike.'

'Whether it's a robot or the real prime minister, any prime minister visit *isn't* gonna stop the war between North and South Crong,' said Jonah. 'My dad showed me the local paper this morning. The feds found untold knives and shit at Remington House. Four people were arrested.'

McKay shot me a quick glance, as if I knew more about this raid than what the papers were reporting. I carried on stepping.

'I wonder where the feds are gonna raid next,' added Jonah.

Maybe my *yard*, my inner voice said.

'They're probably raiding the yards of Major Worries and his North Crong crew,' replied McKay. 'The feds know that this war is getting serious.'

We neared my slab and McKay rolled away to his block. I was just about to bounce up the steps when McKay called me. 'Bit, Bit! Come here for a sec.'

'I haven't got any time, bruv. My dad is taking me and my sis out.'

'Just get your liccle ass here,' McKay demanded. 'It'll only take a sec. I wanna ask you something about history.'

History? McKay had never asked me anything about history in his life. I jogged up to him thinking he wanted to borrow some money – maybe he was getting embarrassed in asking Jonah all the time. 'What is it?' I asked.

'Why are you so quiet today?' he asked, his tone serious.

'What do you mean so quiet?'

'You have hardly said diddly all day,' accused McKay. 'On the way to school you were quiet like a female teacher's fart, at lunchtime you only opened your mouth when you sank something and even on the way home you weren't chirping and arguing like you usually do. What's up, bruv?'

'There's nothing up,' I lied.

'You sure? Nothing stressing you out? Manjaro been asking you to do favours and shit? He asked you to carry a gun to Remington House.'

'I don't know what it was I carried to Remington House,' I said. 'I didn't peel off the wrapping.'

'What else could it have been, Bit? Come on! Use your hard drive! Has he asked you again to carry a piece to somewhere else?'

'*No, no!* Manjaro hasn't asked me to do anything. I haven't seen him.'

'Then what bitch of a slab is breaking your back?' McKay pressed. 'I know something's misfiring in your hard drive.'

'OK, OK,' I relented. '*Don't* say diddly to Jonah, you know what his mouth's like ... things didn't work out with Venetia.' I reckoned I could take a slap to my ego, sharing this shame, if it stopped McKay asking too many damn questions about Manjaro. I did not need my bredrens to find out I was carrying a piece.

'Things didn't work out with Venetia?' McKay repeated. 'Did

you *really* expect them to? Bruv, you wanna fling away your high hopes. Venetia's the fittest chick in our year. She wants to step up to places. You'll probably never have someone as sweet as her step through your drawbridge. You gotta let it go, bruv, otherwise you'll be crying lakes for the rest of your days. You know what you should do? Get over Venetia with an ugly girl, have a one-week thing with her just to get your bounce back. Trust me, it works. When it comes to getting your kiss on with the ugly girl, dodge the lips and just kiss her on the cheek and say that you're the kinda brother that respects girls. After you get your confidence back, sack the ugly girl and move on.'

McKay needed to step away from ever thinking about being a marriage counsellor. But at least he seemed to have accepted my reason for being so quiet. Truth of the matter was I had been fretting all day about what I was carrying in my bag.

When I arrived home, I found Dad sitting in an armchair in the front room. He was wearing his work uniform, sipping a hot drink. There was a plate of custard creams on the table and Gran was nibbling one. From the look on their faces it seemed my entrance had deleted a serious conversation. I guessed that Mum wasn't home – there was no way Mum would serve Dad a cup of tea or biscuits.

'Hi, Lemar,' he greeted. 'How was school today?'

'Hi, Dad, hi, Gran. Same as usual.'

'Get yourself in gear,' he said. 'We're going bowling. They've got a pizza kitchen and a burger bar inside the place so we can eat there.'

I hoped Dad didn't ask to look at any of my schoolwork. I

didn't want to take anything out of my rucksack or even open it. And *damn!* Bowling wasn't on my weekly agenda. Lady P told my ass to keep my movements on the low-profile tip. But I couldn't get out of bowling. I'd have to take my rucksack along but where would I put it? *Shit!*

'Elaine coming?' I asked, trying to keep calm.

'Yes she is,' replied Dad. 'She's getting ready.'

'OK,' I said. 'Gonna nice up my armpits and put something on.'

'Congratulations about the gallery thing,' he said. 'Maybe one day you can sketch Shirley, Steff and me.'

'Yeah – one day.' If I wasn't serving a life sentence.

I went to my bedroom and closed the door. I dropped on my bed. In my head I saw a sentence with letters the size of tower blocks. *HOW AM I GONNA KEEP THE RUCKSACK SAFE WHILE I'M BOWLING?*

Elaine, who had left Jerome with Gran, and I rode in Dad's van. He seemed to be in a good vibe – the news about Steff soon leaving hospital seemed to have slapped a smile on his face.

'Real glad that Steff is getting better,' I said. 'When can I see her?'

'She needs rest but you can see her in a few days or so,' answered Dad. 'She'd love that.'

'What has she got exactly?' asked Elaine.

Dad stared straight ahead before answering. 'It's called acute lymphoblastic leukaemia.'

Elaine covered her mouth with both hands. I didn't have any idea what acute leukaemia something was but going by Elaine's reaction it was proper serious. Dad took one hand off the wheel and squeezed my shoulder. 'It's treatable,' he said. 'She'll be all right. At first doctors thought her flu symptoms, tiredness and illnesses were down to just having a weak immune system ... At least now we know.'

Elaine and I swapped worried glances.

There was silence for a few minutes until Dad told us stories about his workmates and how rude people can get when he delivers something for them. I think he wanted to change the subject from Steff. The three of us very rarely spent time together so I laughed at Dad's tales and almost forgot there was a gun in my rucksack that was strapped to my shoulders.

We were about two or three streets away from the bowling alley when Dad turned to me. 'Lemar, why didn't you leave your schoolbag behind? We're bowling! Not going there to do homework. Give yourself the night off.'

'Er ... you and Elaine are always better than me at bowling so when you're getting your battle on I might just catch up on stuff.'

'Thought you'd be glad to go out,' Dad said. 'You two should do more stuff together just like you used to – it might stop the stupid fighting.'

'Dad!' Elaine protested. 'I'm nineteen with a baby and Lemar's fourteen. We're not gonna be interested in the same sh— things.'

We reached the Crongton Mega Bowl, hired our bowls and got our roll on. There were lockers where you could put your shoes, possessions and stuff but I decided to keep my rucksack strapped to my back – I was sure those people behind the counter had master keys and shit.

Dad and Elaine were crashing eight or nine skittles with one shot and I was only managing four or five with two shots. Many of my efforts ended up in the gutter – Elaine found it all hilarious, especially when I messed up a shot and Dad called out, 'Good try!'

'I told you I'm not good at this, Dad.'

'Then take off your bag!' he said. 'You can't bowl with that thing weighing you down.'

'I'm all right, dad,' I lied. 'It doesn't bother me.'

'Stop being ridiculous!' Dad replied as Elaine was taking aim. 'Take it off!'

I loosened the straps and eased off the rucksack. I placed it under the table where we were sitting. After that, I marched back to sit beside my bag following every roll I had. Meanwhile, some brother in the next lane was trying to impress Elaine. When one of his bowls bounced into the gutter, Elaine laughed out loud. 'You're bowling in Crongton but it looks like you're aiming for Ashburton,' my sis called out.

'Let me buy you a drink and a burger and I'll show you how good my aim is!' the brother replied.

'You sure you can afford it?' Elaine teased.

'I can afford that and a link up afterwards,' bragged the brother.

Elaine got her giggle on but Dad shook his head.

'*Your* turn, Elaine!' Dad raised his voice. It was good to see her smiling for once and kinda funny that Dad was playing the hardback daddy even though Elaine was a mum herself.

*

At the end of our game, Elaine won. She jumped up, punching the air with her right fist, then performed a victory dance before bouncing in front of Dad, chanting, 'Who's the mummy? Who's the mummy?'

Dad could only shake his head. Elaine was still grinning as we rolled to the cafeteria.

We sat down and ordered a pizza. I placed the rucksack awkwardly between my feet. Elaine swapped a glance with Dad and she suggested, 'Why don't you just put it in a locker?'

'Things go missing from the lockers,' I said. 'Can't trust the people who work here.'

Elaine looked at Dad again and shrugged. *God! The way I'm going on I'm gonna have a nervous breakdown.*

'You got lucky,' said Dad to Elaine. 'Enjoy your win now cos it won't happen again!'

'You're getting ancient, old man,' laughed Elaine. 'You better see a doctor about the arthritis in your fingers. It must be traumatic to realise you're never gonna beat your daughter again. Accept it and deal with it, Dad.'

'You win once and you're getting so damn cocky with it. I don't think I'll let you win again.'

'Like you had a choice who was gonna win.'

Dad and sis tried to get the better of each other by swapping insults until our pizza turned up and they got their munch on. Elaine was sinking the last slice of pineapple and ham when she asked Dad, 'So what do you wanna tell us, Dad? That you're gonna quit playing me at anything cos you know you're gonna lose? Wouldn't blame you if you did. Maybe we should switch to Connect Four.'

Dad looked at both of us and I knew that what he had to spill was something serious. He took in a short breath.

'Shirley, Steff and I have to move,' he said. 'There's a really good children's hospital in East Wickham and we'll be moving close to it. It has all the facilities that Steff needs ...'

Elaine crossed her arms. Her expression switched. She started chewing the inside of her cheek. '*Never* heard of East Wickham,' she said.

'Nor have I,' I added.

Man! Venetia's been forever chatting about rolling off our estate and now Dad's spilled the breaking news that he's doing it for real.

'As ... as I said,' Dad resumed. 'It'll be really good for Steff cos it'll mean we don't have to do so much travelling for her to get the treatment she needs ...'

'*Where* is East Wickham, Dad?' Elaine urged, her tone becoming angry. I looked at Dad and then at Elaine. Dad nervously fingered some crumbs on his plate.

'It's ... it's ...'

'It's far, innit, Dad,' Elaine raised her voice. '*How* freaking far?'

'About ... about a four-hour drive.'

The look Elaine gave Dad was brutal. It could've knocked out a stampeding rhino. For a second I thought she was gonna jump on Dad and maul him.

'You'll see me every other weekend,' Dad promised, chatting quickly. 'And you can come up and stay with us. We're gonna get more space up there. We're doing an exchange with the local—'

'*Four hours!*' Elaine shouted. 'What's that? Two hundred

miles? How are we gonna afford the train fares if we wanna see you on the odd day? You know the train companies are too freaking t'ief! Are you sure there isn't somewhere nearer? Have you checked? Steff will wanna see us too! What's the name of this freaking place again?'

'East Wickham,' I put in.

'You're going to East Wickham!' Elaine repeated. 'I understand that Steff needs nuff help, but ...' She paused. When she looked up her eyes were framed with tears. For a second, I remembered that Elaine was still a teenager, even if she had a child of her own. 'Aren't you our dad too?' she asked quietly. 'Doesn't Jerome deserve a granddad? He hasn't got any other male role model in his life ...' She dropped her glance to her lap and stopped talking. Tears splashed into her open palms.

Other diners started to notice our conversation. Elaine didn't care, and neither did I. Our dad had hardly been around over the past few years, and now it looked as though he was never going to be around. And it wasn't too long ago since we'd lost Granddad.

'Elaine, please,' Dad said. 'All because we're moving away it doesn't mean—'

'Yes it does!' Elaine snapped, looking back up. 'What are you gonna say? That you're gonna drive up every other weekend? Maybe you will at first but after a few months of that you're gonna come up with excuses about being tired from work, something wrong with the van and Shirley needs you at home or some shit like that—'

'It *won't* be like that,' Dad interrupted. 'I promise. I'll drive up every other—'

'Yes it *will*,' said Elaine. 'It's happened to some of my mates when their parents separated and their dads moved away. Nicole used to see her dad every Sunday but now she's lucky if she sees him once a year. She and her younger half-brother hardly recognise each other.' She turned to me, wiping her tears. 'How often do you see Dad, Lemar? Every two weeks?'

'About that,' I answered.

'It's gonna get a *lot* worse,' said Elaine, switching her glare to Dad once more. 'Steff will forget she's got an older sis and a big bruv.'

'I won't let that happen, Elaine,' replied Dad. 'I'll come up here on a Friday night and stay in a cheap hotel over a weekend if I have to. If Steff is OK I'll bring her with me.'

'Lemar *needs* a dad twenty-four-seven,' said Elaine. 'He might not think so but he does. Jerome's gonna need a male role model in his life. Did you think about that, Dad? Did you? Or don't you give a damn? Maybe Mum's right about you. We're *not* your priority any more.'

'I have no choice,' Dad said quietly, staring at the leftovers on his dinner plate. 'I'm really sorry but I don't know what else to do. I will try to see you guys as much as I can—'

'Oh! So already you've dropped the every other weekend shit,' charged Elaine, getting angrier. 'Now it's you'll see us when you can! How much is *when you can*? Every freaking six months? Or is that pushing it? I guess we'll be lucky if we have the pleasure of your company once a year! Let's have a carnival when you turn up!'

More heads turned. I started to sink lower into my seat.

'*Please* try and understand,' pleaded Dad.

Elaine stood up, threw her napkin on the table and hot-stepped out.

Dad was still staring into his plate. 'You understand, don't you, Lemar?' he asked.

I checked to see if Elaine was around before nodding. 'She'll ... she'll come around when she calms down. She's ... she's been through a lot.'

'Steff— Steff needs chemotherapy and all sorts,' Dad stuttered.

There was an awkward silence of a couple of minutes before Elaine returned. '*Lemar!* Come on! We're taking the bus home.'

Dad didn't look up as I stood up, grabbed my rucksack and joined Elaine. She started jogging and I had to hot-step after her. By the time I caught up with her I noticed tears in her eyes again. We walked on in silence until we reached a bus stop. We sat down on the bench.

'That was kinda harsh,' I said. 'He's only moving for Steff. You know she's really sick. I have to say it – you're being a bit selfish, sis, and you did say you were gonna try to control your temper. Dad don't need your drama, sis!'

'I know,' Elaine admitted after a while. 'I'm not really mad at him. I'm mad at the stressed-up situation. I'm ... I'm just so vexed with the world right now. And I haven't had too much luck with *men*. Dad left home for another woman, Granddad died and Jerome's dad is a two-timing piece of shit. And now Dad's off to ...'

'East Wickham.'

'It's all mad,' said Elaine.

224

'I understand, sis ... I won't be able to hot-toe to Dad's yard every time you give me a beat-down now, will I?' I joked.

Elaine chuckled at first and then she laughed out loud. 'Sometimes, Lemar, you're hilarious, do you know that?'

'You wanna hear McKay,' I said. 'Shall we go back to the cafeteria?'

Elaine thought about it. 'No. Let it sink in. He's gotta realise that him moving away to ...'

'East Wickham.'

' ... is a big deal for us,' Elaine resumed. 'If he knows it's a big deal then he'll take coming to see us every other Sunday seriously. I love Steff to the max and everything but why should she and Shirley have *all* of Dad? That can't work.'

The bus screeched to a halt and Elaine and I climbed on, going to sit on the back seats. She said nothing on the journey home but I couldn't help thinking that what she said about Steff and Shirley made her sound just like Mum – proper bitter. So much for my hidden gun being the big danger alert of our outing. Elaine's toxic temper had even beat the shit out of that!

23

Usain Bolting

For the next week I must've produced oceans of sweat as I carried around my rucksack everywhere I went – every time I passed a teacher my heart would start quaking like a big drum being headbutted by King Kong. The same happened any time Gran, Mum or Elaine stepped into my room. 'Why are you so freaking jumpy?' Elaine had asked me more than once.

I heard nothing from Lady P or Manjaro. Lady P had told me that I'd keep the gun for a week! I was even thinking about getting rid of the damn thing – those big bins around the back of my slab were looking kinda tempting. Those thoughts didn't last long though, not with the beat-down of that mysterious brother still replaying in my memory.

We'd rolled into June and the sky was getting its sun on. McKay and Jonah were in our year's athletics team – Jonah in the sprints and McKay flinging the shot-put. There was a meet at Shrublands Rec, the small track and field venue not too far from Crongton Heath – Crongton's amateur football team played there but they were worse than crap. They played in a league where all the defenders had weight issues and where the strikers sank beers for their breakfast – well, wasn't sure if they did sink beers for breakfast but watching them play made me believe it. Anyway, we all did our PE in the summer there and we all hated the two-mile trek.

Our year was competing against Ruskin Hill boys, some posh school about ten miles away who had their own track and field next door to their school. We hated them for that. We heard that at the back of their school they looked after flamingos, storks and other big birds in some kind of little zoo. We didn't love them for that either.

McKay and Jonah wanted me to cheer them on at their meet.

'Why should I come and support your asses?' I protested. 'When I asked you to come and support me at the art gallery, you laughed in my face!'

'Come on, Bit!' persuaded Jonah. 'We were only joking.'

'You weren't joking, Jonah,' I replied. 'At the time you said you'd rather spend time watching a debate in Crong Town Hall than come to the gallery.'

'There's gonna be a world of snobby people there, bruv,' McKay said. 'Gonna feel out of place.'

'If you don't come then I'm not supporting your ass at Shrublands Rec,' I insisted. 'You ain't supporting me.'

'Venetia King's gonna be there,' Jonah said.

'*So!*' I raised my voice.

'Don't go there, Jonah,' McKay warned. 'Bit will start bawling oceans.'

'I don't give a shit,' I said. '*And I'm over her!*'

'I tell you what,' said McKay. 'You said the mayor and everyone will be getting their wine-sip on, right?'

'Er, yeah,' I said, not sure where the conversation was going.

'Make sure we get a glass of wine each,' said McKay. 'And we'll clap your ass the whole time you're at this gallery. Damn! We'll even promise not to jack the kids from rich schools.'

I thought about it. 'What do you mean clap my ass?'

'We'll clap at the right times and shout you on when the mayor and the posh people mention your name,' explained McKay. 'But get us some mother-freaking wine. The mayor's gonna be there so it should be better than the ghetto wine they serve at parents' evenings.'

'OK, I can work with that,' I agreed.

'Deal!' said McKay. 'Your gallery thing is two days after our meet, right?'

'Yes,' I said, having no idea how I would place glasses of wine in their grabilicious hands. And how would McKay tell the difference between cheapo wine and the expensive shit?

'It's not gonna last too long is it?' fretted Jonah. 'Not more than half an hour? I mean, what is there to do in a gallery?'

'Believe it or not,' said McKay, 'you get to look at paintings and shit and pretend how good they are even if they don't make any damn sense.'

'Just make sure the both of you come,' I insisted.

'Oh, by the way ...' McKay said.

'What?' I asked.

'You're *not* over Venetia King.'

Mr Smallwood, our rugby-loving mangle-eared PE teacher, drove us in a school van to the meet at Shrublands Rec. My rucksack was strapped to my back – it was now like a second vest. Ms Lane, the slab-thighed girls' PE teacher, sat with him in the front. Venetia parked behind me and tapped me on the shoulder. 'I'll be coming to your gallery exhibition,' she revealed.

In my head I heard the revving of a motorbike and saw a grinning Sergio. I didn't answer her. I didn't even turn around.

We arrived at Shrublands Rec and, while the others went to get changed, I parked on the seventh row of a small stand that was more like a shed. I was surrounded by the parents of Ruskin Hill boys and they were recording and taking pics of everything on their well-expensive cameras, smartphones and tablets. They clapped everything and said things like 'Keep going, Michael, proud of you!' I looked around and couldn't spot any mums and dads of our team.

Jonah could've won the hundred metres even if he'd stopped to sink one of his mum's butterfly cakes, ask the starter if he had any fit-looking daughters and performed a long jump before he finished his race. All the brothers from our school and even some from Ruskin Hill congratulated Venetia when she won her two-hundred-metre sprint. Shortly after I watched Venetia, I bounced into the field to watch McKay fling the shot-put – he won too, screaming a mad scream as he threw that heavy ball. He did his Incredible Hulk impersonation when he received his winning certificate.

By the time Mr Smallwood drove us home, he was well happy cos we had won a few events and no Ruskin Hill brother got jacked or suffered a beat-down. I was kinda glad that Jonah and McKay had invited my ass to the athletics meet. It had sort of relaxed me and to get my roar on for my schoolmates made me feel normal for the first time in weeks.

Ms Lane was encouraging Venetia to take the sprints seriously and run in the area trials. Meanwhile, McKay was trying to convince Jonah to let him be his manager. 'Listen to me, bruv, would you rather trust a bredren from school days or some prick in a suit who doesn't even know that your mum bakes wicked cakes?'

'Watch your mouth, McKay,' Mr Smallwood rebuked.

'McKay!' replied Jonah. 'If I ever get well famous for running you're *not* gonna be my freaking manager. I'm gonna get someone who knows what they're doing, someone professional.'

'So I can't be professional?' McKay argued. 'Trust me, Jonah, your maths ain't too good … in fact your maths is dia-freaking-bolical – even playing with an abacus gives you worries. So you're gonna need someone like me checking your sponsorship deals and shit, making sure you're getting paid right … and I *want* twenty-five per cent.'

'No, McKay,' Jonah resisted. 'You will probably get me paid in fried chicken and barbecue ribs.'

Everyone roared with laughter, even Mr Smallwood and Ms Lane.

We were just approaching Crongton High Street when we heard a siren. Everyone looked behind and we saw this ambulance weaving through the traffic at a mad speed. Mr Smallwood pulled over to let it pass. People were hot-stepping towards Footcave, a sportswear shop on the corner of the High Street. Someone ran across the front of our van in the opposite direction. When he reached the pavement, he knocked an elderly pedestrian over before he got up again and hot-toed away. Others stopped stepping and looked here and there, wondering what was going on. Motorists were climbing out of their rides to get a better view in front and behind us. Then we heard a woman screaming, 'Oh my God! Oh my God!'

'He's been shanked – stabbed!' yelled a different voice. 'He's just a young boy! He's been stabbed!'

Something thick and chilly rampaged through my chest. It felt a little bit like that cough medicine that Mum used to give me – but colder.

'Stay in the van until we can get through the traffic,' instructed Mr Smallwood.

Kiran Cassidy pulled open the van door and bounced out. McKay followed him.

'The rest of you stay in the van!' Mr Smallwood raised his voice.

'*Stay where you are!*' yelled Ms Lane, spotting the rest of us rising from our seats.

No one took any notice, except Venetia King. She sat there on her seat with her hands covering her face.

I'm not sure what moved my legs cos fear was jabbing me,

but I just had to see what had happened. It only took seconds to reach Footcave. We arrived just as the paramedics were stepping out of the ambulance.

A world of people were circled around this boy on the ground. His T-shirt was soaked in blood. His eyes were closed and his face was calm. He wasn't moving. A shop assistant dressed in a yellow and green striped shirt and a green baseball cap pressed a towel against the boy's chest. There was a hush within the circle but outside there was nuff shouting and shoving. More sirens echoed in the distance. The paramedics took over. '*Please* give us room.'

Someone was crying. Another person was yelling. The shop assistant's hands were covered in blood. Something messed up happened to his eyes. An older person put an arm around him and led him away. The paramedics went quickly about their work. But the boy on the ground still wasn't moving. His eyes remained closed and his face still looked calm. It seemed as if he was in a perfect sleep, like three on a Sunday morning. They were pushing his chest. They used a small torch to check his eyes. They fiddled about with his tongue. I didn't think he was breathing. McKay, Jonah, Kiran and everybody looked on. One paramedic kept on pressing his chest with one hand on top of the other and the other held a dressing against the wound. No response.

I thought of Venetia losing her cousin. I had to glance away. Blood had spotted the trainer display by the window. The blue flashing light of the ambulance forced me to squint. My stomach cramped up. I had to get out.

Just as I stepped into the street I heard a voice – it belonged

232

to Kiran Cassidy. 'That's Pinchers' little brother,' he said. 'Yeah, that's Nico D. He's only thirteen. It must've been a North Crong yout' who shanked him.'

I almost bumped into Mr Smallwood. 'Get in the van!' he shouted at me.

I did what I was told.

When I reached the van, Venetia was still holding her face in her hands. Ms Lane had her arm around her shoulders. Venetia lifted her head and offered me a look. I knew it was a question. 'Some ... some boy got shanked,' I revealed. 'Not ... not sure if he's gonna make it.'

'I *hate* this place,' Venetia replied before burying her face in her hands again.

Kiran, Jonah, McKay and the others returned to the van. Fed cars raced by. As Mr Smallwood started the engine, no one said a diddly. It was only when we pulled up outside our school that Kiran spoke. 'I think he's dead ... it was definitely Pinchers' brother, Nicholas Dyson – Nico D.'

'He was a quiet yout',' another said. 'He was in Year 8. He loved balling in the park. He wouldn't trouble an ant.'

By the time we bounced out of the van, Venetia was in tears. I told McKay and Jonah that I was gonna wait for her. They started rolling home and eventually Venetia climbed out of her seat. 'I'll walk you home if you want?'

She nodded.

We walked slowly. Both of us were staring at the ground. The straps of my rucksack were chomping into my shoulders. God! If she knew I was carrying a piece around she would maul me. She didn't say anything until we were within sight of her home slab – Somerleyton House. 'My cousin, Katrina, was only twelve when she died,' she said. 'A year older than me at the time. She was a better basketball player than me and a much better dancer. Faster than me too. Who had the freaking right to take her life? Who had the freaking right to shank this ...'

'Nicholas Dyson.'

'Why do they do it? It's messed up, Lemar.'

She'd called me Lemar again.

'Will you be all right?' I said.

'Yeah. Thanks for walking me back to my slab, Lemar.'

I watched her enter her block before rolling away. God! I didn't even know that Pinchers had a little brother who went to our school.

The gun in my rucksack felt heavy. Or maybe the seemingly extra weight in my bag was guilt. I had to fling the gun away. But I didn't know how to get my bravery on. It seemed so easy for the Batmans, Supermans and the Ironmans to do courageous shit. But what should you do in real life when you were a short-ass and up against brothers like Manjaro and Pinchers?

Mum got me up early the next morning. She was on an early shift and had made crumpets for my breakfast. 'You get your liccle backside straight home from school, right,' she ordered. 'They said on the news last night that they think it's all about a local gangland feud and Nicholas Dyson got caught up in it – God rest his soul. I can't believe one of these idiot gangsters have killed a *thirteen-year-old boy*! Don't these boys have

234

mums and dads to guide them? Don't they know they're carrying guns and knives? It makes me feel sick, Lemar. Get yourself home straight from school!'

'What about tomorrow, Mum?'

'Isn't the teacher driving you up to the gallery?'

'Yes, Ms Rees's giving me a ride. So it's OK if I go?'

'Make sure she drives you home. I don't want to fret about you when I'm at work.'

'I will, Mum.'

Mum left for work. My guilt wouldn't leave me alone. I only managed to sink one half of my first crumpet. I drank two glasses of orange juice. I went to the kitchen and washed up my plate and glass and then returned to my bedroom. I thought about Nicholas Dyson and couldn't imagine how his parents were feeling. What would his brother, Pinchers, do? How would Manjaro take it? They were bound to ask for the gun quick-time. Wasn't sure if it'd be a relief to get rid of it or not. I kept wondering how many more would get deleted in this mad North Crong–South Crong war.

My phone was blinking. I looked at it for five minutes before picking it up. Giant concrete fists started to beat the crap out of my heart again. An unknown number. I just knew it was Lady P. The half-crumpet I had just sunk was having issues with my bowels. I finally opened the text.

We need it. Be at the supermarket tomorrow at 5. P.

24

Deadline

I don't even remember the first school lesson I had that day. I do recall Year 8 kids crying in the playground and hugging each other. It didn't seem real.

I was thinking of Lady P's latest text and Nico D's lifeless body. I wanted to throw the gun away but Nightlife, Smolenko and Nicholas Dyson were all dead. Manjaro might delete me if I didn't turn up at the supermarket at five the next day. *But I wanna attend my gallery exhibition. People give Jonah nuff respect cos of his new phones and gadgets and cos he sprints like the wind. Even McKay gets his props for flinging the shot-put and being funny. But me? I'm not that funny and even though I like to get my bounce on at basketball, I'm too freaking short to impress anyone. If I attend the gallery event then I'll hear people clapping my ass cos they know I did something good. Why can't I have that too for once in my messed-up life?*

I replied to Lady P's text during second period.

Can I meet you at 8?

Lady P answered almost immediately.

No. We have plans for that evening – make sure you're there.

Shit!

What about earlier?

I replied.

No, we're on the road tomorrow afternoon – make sure your liccle ass is on time. 5!

For the rest of the school day I hardly said a word to anybody. I rolled around school in a daze. This time McKay didn't get suspicious cos everyone was in shock about Nico D. Even he was silent during lunchtime. We stepped home still not believing what had happened. We noticed fed patrols all over our estate – the teachers had told us that the feds were there to make us feel safer. All it did to me was cramp up my stomach, force me to look over my shoulder every ten paces and make my armpits leak.

I passed the two big grey bins behind my slab and I stopped walking.

'Why are you standing there?' asked Jonah. 'Let's step up. The bins stink, bruv. Brothers fling their dead dogs and shit in there.'

The gun felt weighty in my rucksack. It was as if I were carrying the shot-put that McKay flung a day ago. *Now's the time,* I tried to steel myself. *Fling the gun away into one of the bins and spill to the feds. It's easy. Just pick it out of your rucksack and throw it in the bin. No worries. No more slaps of guilt. The gun's wrapped up in masking tape and brown paper inside the black plastic bag so Jonah won't even know what it is. Just do it! Elaine will get it. Mum will understand. Gran might give me another uppercut but she'll understand too. You might have to spend some time at the fed station but at least they won't give you a beat-down. And you'll be safe there from Manjaro, Pinchers and the rest.*

'You all right, Bit?' Jonah queried.

'Yeah, I'm good,' I replied after a short while. 'Just got a bit of a headache.'

I wasn't lying. All this stress was making my head bang.

I followed Jonah up the stairs of our slab, cursing myself cos I wasn't brave enough to get rid of the gun.

My evening at home was like any other evening. Apart from the fact I had a gun in my rucksack and Manjaro probably wanted to blaze away someone with it. Whoever it might've been could well have a cousin like Venetia who would still be leaking eye-water years later. I had to somehow get my bravery on.

Gran cooked salmon fillets and twisted pasta. She sprinkled cheese over my plate. Mum was leafing through a furniture catalogue. Elaine was tending to Jerome who was getting his sneeze on. 'I don't want to take him out of the flat when he's sneezing like that,' she said. 'Not sure if I can make your gallery thing, Lemar.'

'Don't worry, Lemar,' Gran said. 'I'll be there to support you.'

My head was still banging. I sank a painkiller. Mum kissed me on the forehead before I went to bed. 'Proud of you, my beautiful boy! I've shown Gran how to use the camera on my phone. Enjoy the attention tomorrow – you deserve it.'

I went to bed at 8.45 p.m. I know exactly what time it was because I'd been obsessively checking the time on my phone. It was well early for me but I had to lie my ass down. I dimmed my light and stared at the ceiling. I couldn't find my courage. At 9.15 p.m. I texted Lady P.

OK, I'll see you at 5.

Lady P only took five minutes to reply.

Good! We've got a nice touch for you.

That night I wasn't sure if I slept or not. By the time Mum entered my room to wake me up, I had been staring at my ceiling for the longest time.

Mum had made me scrambled eggs on toast. She held my face within her hands and kissed me before she left for work – she was working a double shift. I didn't sink all of my breakfast. I washed up my plate before strapping on my ruck-sack. Gran was by the front door. She was sipping a mug of tea. She was smiling the way grandmothers do at their grandchildren. 'I'll see you at the gallery, Lemar. The 109 bus drops me right outside.'

'Thanks, Gran.'

'And me know how to use the camera on your mum's phone.'

'That's all good,' I replied.

Gran kissed me on the cheek before I opened the front door. 'If that headache is troubling you too much then come home.'

'I'll be all right, Gran.'

I stepped outside and saw Jonah peering over the balcony. 'Ready for your big day?' he asked.

'Yeah,' I answered.

We rolled to school silently. I guessed like me, Jonah didn't quite know what to say to express how he felt about looking at Nicholas Dyson's deleted body lying there on Footcave's floor. We'd seen that image so many times on film and in games. But seeing it in real life was messed up. Not even the slightest twitch. Not even a flicker of an eyelash. Just so *still*. How do you deal with that kinda shit if you're in a war? How are you supposed to carry on as normal? They don't teach you that at school.

My first lesson of the day was English. I didn't write a damn thing. All I could see or think about was Nicholas Dyson's red chest. I now understood why Venetia kept her ass in the van.

I had art before lunch. I just went through the motions and can't remember what Ms Rees asked me to do. I didn't even realise that I hadn't taken off my rucksack but still pulled on my apron.

Ms Rees walked over to me. Her hair had flicks of green and black paint in it. She smiled and then she tugged my rucksack. 'This must be awkward for you, Mr Jackson. Wouldn't you produce better work if you took it off?'

'*Leave it!*' I yelled.'*Don't* touch me!'

My classmates, including Jonah, all looked at me as if I had crapped on my desk. Ms Rees covered her mouth in shock. Her eyes widened. One eyebrow went higher than the other. She then rolled up to me and whispered into my ear.'I'll talk to you at the end of the lesson, Mr Jackson.'

The lunch buzzer sounded. Jonah looked at me and said he'd wait for me outside in the corridor. Ms Rees approached me. Her head was tilted at an angle. Her eyes were still on surprise mode.'I know that all of us are feeling a loss, but is something else the matter, Mr Jackson?'

I didn't answer.

'Since I've been teaching you, you have never raised your voice to me let alone been rude. Is anything wrong?'

'No, Ms Rees,'I mumbled.

'Is the event this evening making you nervous?'

My chance for an excuse.

'Yes,' I answered. 'I've been fretting about it, you know, talking in front of all those posh people and wondering if my stuff is good enough.'

'There's nothing to worry about,' Ms Rees assured me.

'You'll be fine. Your work deserves to sit alongside anybody else's, no matter what school they come from.'

'So I don't have to make a speech?'

'Of course not. It's just a celebration of the artistic talent in our local schools. I will introduce your work.'

'I . . . I didn't mean to shout at you, Ms Rees,' I apologised.

'I know, Mr Jackson. I expect it from a few of the others but not you. Next time if you're worried about something then come and see me.'

I thought about the gun in my rucksack. *No,* I said to myself. *You can't spill to her. Delete that mission from your mind.*

'Yes, Ms Rees,' I finally replied.

'OK, run along and go and get your lunch. Make sure you *never* talk to me like that again. *Oh,* Mr Jackson, be in my room as soon as the last buzzer sounds. Remember that I'm driving you to the gallery.'

'OK, Ms Rees.'

She sat down at her desk, shaking her head. I felt proper guilty. *God! How many other people am I gonna upset before all this is over?*

McKay had joined Jonah in the corridor. They were looking at me funny. 'What is it?' I asked.

'What's going on, Bit?' McKay asked. 'You've been acting weird for too long, bruv.'

'Yeah,' agreed Jonah. 'Seeing Nico D's body freaked us all out but you were acting all strange before that.'

'What's troubling you?' pressed McKay again.

'What's a matter with you two?' I raised my voice. 'There's nothing troubling me!'

'You're lying!' spat McKay. 'I can tell when you're off-key and you've been off-key for weeks – since you went around to number nine Remington House.'

'What's going on, bredren?' quizzed Jonah again. He narrowed his eyes. 'What's this all about?'

'I'm going to lunch,' I said, stepping off. 'You two are seeing shit that's not there. *Step* off out of my way!'

McKay and Jonah blocked my path. The gun felt heavy again in my rucksack. My forehead erupted in sweat. 'Get out of my way!'

McKay wasn't an easy person to walk around. 'Spill the shit, Bit!'

They seized me with their eyes. I glanced over my shoulder but I never would've out-sprinted Jonah. What was left of my conscience was telling me to spill to my bredrens.

'Has Manjaro got anything to do with it?' asked Jonah.

My heart was suddenly pumping. I stared at the floor. The river Nile was now falling down my temples, soaking my cheeks and drowning my lips. Some spike-footed little creature was beating the bull-crap out of my brain with a metal mallet. I couldn't keep the secret any more.

'You all right, Bit?' McKay asked.

'Yeah,' I lied.

'Then answer Jonah's question – has Manjaro got anything to do with it?'

In my inner vision I could see a close-up of Nico D's red chest. Then I saw his face. His eyes were shut. Not even the slightest movement. He would never browse in Footcave again. He would never go balling in the park again. If he had a gran she couldn't hug him any more. *Man!* I couldn't keep this shit to myself any longer.

'Yes ... he has,' I finally admitted.

In that school corridor, I told McKay and Jonah everything, apart from the fact that I had the gun in my rucksack. By the time I had finished, lunchtime was almost over. I had a sense of mad relief. I was still scared as anything but at least I'd shared it with my bredrens. I just hoped that by spilling to them they wouldn't be dropped into the stress pot with me.

'You're gonna have to go to the feds,' said McKay. 'And spill like a waterfall. You haven't got any choice.'

'No, bruv,' Jonah argued. 'Everyone in South Crong will know you're a snitch. Trust me, bruv, you don't want that on your CV. When you get home, take the piece and fling it away – throw it down the rubbish chute of our slab.'

'Bit, trust me,' McKay insisted. 'Take the piece to the feds. You might even get some reward money. They'll have to protect you. You might even get a better yard out of it, you know, bigger bedroom, back garden and shit. Your mum could start having barbecues. Jerome can get his crawl on in the grass.'

'What good is reward money and a better yard when Bit might have to move from the ends?' Jonah disagreed. 'He'll be a marked man. If he spills to the feds he might as well have a freaking bullseye on his back.'

'Whatever you do,' said McKay. '*Don't* step to the supermarket and give the piece back to this Lady ...'

'P,' I finished the sentence.

'Someone innocent might get blazed by that piece,' added McKay. 'And the feds might put your ass down as an accessory. You'll be looking at seventy years sinking porridge oats with plastic spoons, bruv.'

'As I said,' put in Jonah. 'Fling the gun away. After the gallery thing, take it from your wardrobe or wherever you've hid it and take it to the stream or something. We'll go with you.'

'Take it to the feds!' urged McKay.

The buzzer sounded. Ms Rees came out of her classroom. She stopped and looked at all three of us. 'Didn't you boys have any lunch?'

'We're ... we're not hungry, Ms Rees.'

'See you later, Mr Jackson. *Don't* be late.'

Ms Rees rolled away. Jonah and McKay looked at me. 'What you gonna do?' asked Jonah.

'I dunno,' I replied. 'But I'm not linking Lady P at the supermarket.'

I had maths and history in the afternoon. I kept on looking out of the window expecting Lady P, Pinchers and Manjaro to roll up. I got told off about three times for not paying attention but I didn't give a shit. Midway through history, I made up my mind. *I'm gonna attend the gallery exhibition and fling the gun away on the way home. I'll have to tell Lady P or Manjaro some mad excuse or something. Maybe I can say that they searched my rucksack at school and they took the gun. Yeah, I can say that. It's not like they're gonna bounce up to the school and ask for the gun back.*

From 3.15 p.m. it took about two hours for the time to reach 3.30 p.m. The buzzer sounded. I rolled slowly through the school corridors. I tried to breathe normally but found myself taking in long gulps of air. Ms Rees was tidying up her classroom. Specks of blue paint were added to her multi-coloured hair. 'Just sit down at my desk, Mr Jackson,' she said. 'I'll be with you in a minute.'

She didn't finish cleaning up until 3.50 p.m. She washed her hands in the sink and dried them on a paint-stained towel. We didn't leave her classroom until 4.05 p.m. *Lady P might be making her way to the supermarket by now. But my ass isn't gonna be there. Shit. Maybe I should leave Ms Rees and hot-toe it to the supermarket. No! I've made up my mind.* I knew that Jonah, McKay and Venetia were riding a bus to the gallery. Gran was also making her way there. What would it look like if my ass wasn't there to meet them?

Ms Rees led me to her car. It had a funky smell to it – I guessed it was a cat. She had a world of hats, scarves and sweaters on the back seats. She turned the ignition. The radio came on. Some guy was talking about some play he had seen – it sounded well boring. 'They picked up your collection yesterday, Mr Jackson,' Ms Rees informed me. 'I'm sure every-body's going to be impressed. To be honest, I'm glad for this gallery event – it's a distraction from the awful tragedy … Our headmistress is seeing Nicholas's parents this evening.'

4.15 p.m. We drove through the school gates. My heart and ribcage started round sixteen. It took us fifteen minutes to reach the gallery. It was a decent street. Four-wheel drives niced it up. Cars didn't have to park on the pavements like they did in most parts of South Crong. I climbed out of Ms Rees's car. I looked around for a moment. I spotted an antique dealers and a furniture shop where the two-seater sofa in the front window cost grands.

4.30 p.m. 'Come on, Mr Jackson. Don't just stand there admiring the scenery.'

We bounced into the gallery. My trainers squeaked on the polished wooden floor. Someone stuck a name badge on my chest. People were already there. Adults were sipping red and white wine. I could tell who the art teachers were cos they were the ones dressed in rainbow colours, skinny scarves and bangles. They all gave the impression that this opening was just as important as Michelangelo showing the Pope his new ceiling painting. Nervous-looking students were nibbling scotch eggs, cocktail sausages, crisps and chocolate mini rolls. I didn't feel like sinking any food.

The art was displayed on the gallery's white walls. I looked for my pieces and felt a proper surge of pride when I spotted some woman and a man studying my portrait of Gran. I wanted to hot-toe up to them and say that painting was *mine*. Gran herself was parked at the wine table. She had her best smile on and was sampling red wine. I went over to her. 'I have already taken a few pictures, Lemar! Me reach here about twenty minutes ago and when me mention that I'm the grandmother of Lemar Jackson they get me something to eat and something to drink. Me *well* proud!'

'I didn't realise there was gonna be so much people,' I remarked. 'The place is packed.'

'You have students from six schools here,' Gran said. 'And me don't care what anybody says, your works are the *best* of the whole damn lot of them!'

'You're biased, Gran.'

Ms Rees approached us and I introduced her to Gran. Gran glanced at her hair and started getting her giggle on. Ms Rees then led me away and introduced me to the mayor – she was quite ancient and the bright red lipstick she was wearing didn't go well with her powdered, pale face – she looked like a clown's grandmother. She read my name badge. 'Congratulations, Lemar! You must be so proud. Isn't this a great venue? We do our best to support the arts in schools.'

Ms Rees introduced me to other students who all looked as awkward as I was feeling. It was a relief when I parked next to Gran again. I checked the time. 4.55 p.m. *Shit!* Lady P would be finding a parking space. My armpits started to flood again. Then I spotted McKay, Jonah and Venetia. All three of them came over. I prayed that McKay and Jonah would behave themselves in front of Venetia and Gran.

'Bit, Bit!' said McKay. 'Need to chat to you about something.'

'Now?' I asked.

'Yes, *now!*' McKay said.

I glanced at Venetia. She looked proper baffled.

It was obvious what McKay wanted to discuss. If I didn't roll with him he'd only keep on about it. 'All right,' I said.

I stepped with McKay to a corner. Jonah followed us. 'What you gonna do?' McKay wanted to know.

'I dunno,' I answered.

'You better think quick, bruv,' said Jonah.

'I know one thing though,' I said.

'What's that?' asked McKay.

'I don't want you two bruvs involved in my drama,' I said. 'The pot smells bad enough with me in it – don't want you two swimming with me.'

'But ...' started Jonah. 'You're a bredren. We wanna help—'

'*No,*' I insisted. 'Stay *out* of it!'

'Venetia's coming over,' warned McKay.

'She *must* not know,' I said. 'If you two spill anything to her I'll blank you for the rest of my days.'

Venetia was still dressed in her school uniform but she was easily the prettiest girl in the room. She walked over to us. 'What are you guys whispering about?' she asked.

'Man business,' answered McKay.

'You shouldn't leave your gran on her own,' Venetia said to me.

'We're coming back now,' I replied.

We bounced back to Gran who was still enjoying her drink.

Without hesitation, McKay jacked two glasses of red wine and handed one over to Jonah.

'What about me?' complained Venetia.

I looked for Ms Rees but she was busy with another teacher. McKay handed Venetia her glass of red wine.

A few minutes later, some man in a bow tie was striking an empty glass with a little spoon. Everyone stopped talking and paid attention. I checked the time. 5 p.m. The owner of the gallery, some strange-looking guy in jeans, a white shirt and a tartan waistcoat, gave us some boring speech about how he wanted to promote art in the community and support students. By the time he'd finished, McKay and Jonah were on their second glass of wine and Venetia and I were still on our first. Gran asked me to pose by my paintings and she took more pics – it was a struggle to get my smile on.

5.36 p.m. People were sinking the food while walking around, appreciating the art. Gran, seemingly satisfied that she had taken enough pics, parked at the wine table. Jonah, taking pics with his phone, and McKay were chirpsing a couple of female chicks from another school. Venetia was admiring my 'concrete jungle' painting.

It was then that I sensed a vibration in my pocket. My heart accelerated like it came around the final bend of a mad race. I poured myself a half-glass of white wine. I had to sit down. My brain-ache returned with a vengeance. 'That's *enough* wine, Lemar,' Gran said quietly.

Not sure why I filled my glass cos I didn't even like the taste of wine. I placed the glass on the table and took out my phone. I opened the text.

If you don't reach within five minutes with my piece I'm gonna come to your gates, boot down your door and get the piece myself! Mjro

MJRO? That had to be Manjaro. My school shirt stuck to my back.

'Gran! Gran! We have to step!'

'Whatever for?' she asked. 'Your teacher hasn't introduced your work yet.'

'Trust me, Gran, we have to step. Elaine's in a whole heap of worries. I have to warn—'

'What worries?'

I yanked Gran's arm. '*Now*, Gran. We have to step home *now*.'

'OK, I'm coming!'

I led Gran out of the gallery. McKay spotted us and him and Jonah hot-toed after us. 'What's going on, bruv?' McKay asked. 'Why you stepping? Your name hasn't even been called yet.'

'I ... I have to get home,' I replied.

'We'll come with you,' said Jonah.

'*No!* As I said, I don't want you involved. Trust me on that.'

Behind McKay's shoulder, I saw Venetia bounce out of the building. 'Tell Venetia sorry for me, tell her ... something. Tell her I'll chat to her soon.'

'But!'

I didn't give Jonah time to finish his sentence. Gran and me hot-stepped to the bus stop. I glanced behind and saw Jonah and McKay explaining something to Venetia. I prayed they didn't spill anything about the gun.

I tried to call Elaine. *Shit!* Not enough credit. I tried to text. It didn't go through. 'Pass me Mum's phone, please, Gran.'

She handed it over. 'What is all this about?'

I called Elaine and just as she answered a bus arrived. We hopped on the bus and filled the nearest seats. '*Elaine!* Are you at home?'

'Yeah, Jerome is sick. Why?'

'Don't answer the door.'

'Why? Who's gonna knock down our gates? What's a

matter with you, Lemar? Ain't you supposed to be at your gallery thing?'

I took in a deep breath. 'Manjaro's coming for something I was holding for him.'

'What are you holding for him? Why are you even dealing with my ex, Lemar? What did I tell you?'

'Just *please* don't answer the door.'

'So what are you saying? You're chatting and dealing with my ex behind my freaking back? Didn't I tell you I wanted nothing to do with his two-timing ass? Didn't you hear what he *done* to me? Didn't I tell you to step away if he wanted to chat with you? *Don't* you freaking listen to a word I say? What's he coming for? When you get home I'm gonna—'

I deleted the call. If I didn't I think my hard drive would've exploded. I couldn't get home quickly enough.

I willed the bus to go quicker but it stopped at every damn stop! It seemed that every freaking passenger was searching in their pockets for change. One woman jumped on the bus and took seven hours asking for directions. If McKay had run home from the gallery with his salad-dodging bulk he would've reached our slab before us.

We rolled off the bus at 5.57 p.m. Gran struggled to keep up as I hot-stepped to our block. For some reason I thought of Venetia's cousin, Katrina, and how her life was blazed away. When I arrived at the back of our slab I emptied my rucksack, grabbed hold of the black plastic bag and threw it in the large grey bin.

'What are you doing?' asked Gran.

'Something I should've done from the start.'

I picked up all my books and put them back in my rucksack. I started bouncing up the stairs. 'Lemar!' Gran called.
'Hold on! Me legs can't spring up the stairs like yours.'

As I waited for Gran my mind was in a whirl trying to think
of my next step. *Elaine will launch a cuss attack but maybe when
she's done she can call the feds. Yeah, just be on the safe side. She
can use that card that the feds left. I might as well spill to the feds
now that I've thrown away the gun. Shit! Manjaro and his crew
are not gonna love me.*

We climbed up the last flight of stairs before we reached our
floor. I dug into my pocket for my front-door key. I was pushing
it into the lock when I heard heavy steps and felt a big hand grip
the back of my head and slam it into the door. My headache got
worse. Manjaro must've been waiting for my ass on the stairs
leading to the next floor. I just about managed to turn the key.
My front door opened and I stumbled into the hallway, falling to
my knees. *'Where is it?'* Manjaro screamed. *'Where's my piece?'*

As I struggled to my feet I saw Gran trying to reach me,
squeezing past Manjaro.

'Young man,' she was saying. 'This isn't—'

Manjaro's eyes widened, first with shock and then with
anger. 'Keep your beak out of this!' He shoved her towards the
front door, but she stumbled and I heard the crack of Gran's
head against the wall. She instantly slumped to the ground,
her legs splayed out.

'Gran!' I tried to move towards her but two punches
stunned me and everything became blurry. I felt myself being
dragged into my bedroom. *'Where's the piece, you little piece of
shit? Where is it?'*

Another punch to the side of my head rattled my brain. My legs went all weak and I fell against the wardrobe. *'Where is it?'* I heard Manjaro roar again. *'Where did you hide it? Show me, you liccle piece of shit!'*

He kicked and punched me again. I heard running feet from the lounge and then the hallway. A screaming voice blasted my room. It was Elaine. *'Get your freaking hands off my brother!'*

She was pulling him out of my room. Manjaro threw a mad punch in my direction, but lost his balance. God! I knew Elaine was strong but I had no idea where she found the strength to drag him like that. They both collapsed into a heap in the hallway. Now she was in nuff trouble. I frantically looked around my room to see if there was anything I could throw at him. He was getting to his feet. I had to help Elaine. My heart was pumping like the air in a mad bouncy castle. Fear filled my head. Manjaro was back on his feet. *God!* The veins were dancing in his neck. Had to somehow help sis. I just rushed at him. I had no clue what to do when I reached him. Pure terror was churning my stomach. He was distracted by something. I saw something moving out of the corner of my eye. Jerome had crawled out his room and was making his way through the lounge. *No! He shouldn't be here!* I was running too fast to stop my momentum and crashed into Manjaro. He swatted me away like I was a bird trying to peck King Kong. I fell to the floor, banging my shoulder against the wall.

Then Jerome made that gurgling sound when he calls for his mum. All of a sudden, Manjaro froze, turning to gaze at his son. He was still, like a DVD on pause. His eyes didn't blink.

Elaine didn't waste a moment. She struggled to her feet, flinging me a warning look. She raised her arms above her head, coming up behind Manjaro. Then there was a mad crashing sound. She'd licked him in the back of the head with a vase from the hallway, bits and pieces of terracotta rolling across the carpet as Manjaro slumped to my feet. He sort of did this fish-on-land dance on the floor and tried to get back up, stepping heavily on to one foot, but his eyes rolled back in his head as Elaine took another swing with the last piece of the vase.'*Leave my brother alone!*' Elaine screamed.

Unbelievably, Manjaro was rebooting. Slowly, he got back up to his feet. Elaine and I shared a glance and we knew it was all over. He did this messed-up walk to the door, and yanked it open. He stood, his shoulders almost as wide as the door frame, and shot a final glance back into the flat. Not at me or Elaine, but at Jerome who was still crawling towards my sister. I swear, I saw Manjaro's eyes swimming with tears.'I'm sorry,' he slurred at Jerome, who got his giggle on. Then Manjaro was gone, slamming the door behind him. Dropping what was left of the vase, Elaine rushed to Gran and cradled her head.'Call an ambulance!'

My fingers were trembling but I managed to call 999 using Elaine's mobile. Elaine sat on the floor, holding Gran's head and rocking to and fro.

'Can … can I call for … for an ambulance … please. It's … it's my gran … she's been knocked out … yes, she's breathing … the recovery position?'

On hearing my last two words Elaine heaved Gran over on to her side, placing her arms in front of her body so that she couldn't roll over. I managed to tell the operator our address. I deleted the call and then I glanced at Gran. I could barely see her cos of the tears filling my eyes. But I could make out that her chest was heaving up and down. Also, her head was twitching.

'Is she … Will she be OK?' I just managed to choke the words out. Elaine and I stared down at her, lying on the floor. She looked so helpless.

'I don't know,' Elaine said, lifting Jerome in her arms and holding him tightly to her.

25

Stapled Mouths

I sat beside Gran. She was moving her head from side to side. 'Keep still, Gran. An ambulance is on its way.'

She raised her arm and momentarily gripped my wrist before placing it back down again.

'What were you holding for Manjaro?' Elaine asked, her back to me. She'd gone to stand by a window, keeping an eye out for the ambulance.

For a moment I couldn't speak. I watched Jerome trying to tug one of Elaine's earrings. 'A ... a gun,' I finally revealed. I hoped Gran was too out of it to hear.

Elaine swivelled round and stared open-mouthed at me. She didn't seem to feel Jerome pulling her earring. She shook her head slowly in disbelief.'Sometimes ... sometimes ... you haven't got the freaking sense you were born ... *don't* you ever use your head, Lemar?' She tailed off from what I thought was gonna be a full-on cuss attack.

It was like the pain of the truth was too much for her. I felt as small and as helpless as one of those calves that are born in the wild with untold lions sniffing around for their dinner.

'We're gonna *have* to call the feds,' Elaine said, finding her voice again. 'When they reach our gates *don't* tell 'em shit about the gun, you hearing me? *He's not* getting away with this! I swear he's *not*. He could've killed you and Gran.'

I nodded and gazed at Gran. Her eyes were half-open.

'Where is it?' Elaine wanted to know.

'When I got back from the gallery, I . . . I threw it in the big bin downstairs.'

'At least you have *some* sense left in your dumb prick head! Why didn't you come to me when Manjaro was asking you to do something? Sometimes, Lemar, you just . . . give me the freaking phone!'

I passed on the mobile to Elaine. 'Let me think,' she said. She kissed Gran on the forehead as she thought things through. 'Better call Mum and Dad first,' she decided.

Her fingers worked fast. I glanced at Gran. Her eyes were open but I didn't think she knew where she was or what had happened to her.

'*Mum! Mum!*' Elaine called. 'Gran's been knocked out. She's coming out of it but she's well dazed. I've called for an ambulance and it's on its way. Meet me at the hospital.'

Elaine gripped the phone tighter as she listened to Mum. Jerome tried to wriggle free from her other arm. 'Mum!

Listen! The important thing is that Gran gets to the hospital ... yes, I'm going with her ... Manjaro ...' Elaine's eyes darted towards me. 'No, I don't know why he came round ... I think he wanted to see Jerome or something ... We've always had issues about that.' My sister was lying to cover my ass! 'Anyway, it doesn't matter why that so-called big G was coming to our gates and taking liberties – that's just what he does to try and be *the big shot*. He was trying to get in the flat and I think he hit her or pushed her aside or something ... Lemar's OK. He's a bit shaken up but he'll live ... I don't know why he turned up on this particular day ... you know I don't want him in Jerome's life ... I'm not a psychic, Mum, I don't know what he was thinking ... Look, I'll explain when I see you at the hospital ... Yes, I think she's gonna be all right ... her eyes are open ... I've already said the ambulance is on its way ... Yes, I'll see you there.'

Elaine deleted the call and breathed out a monster sigh. She let Jerome resume his crawl and she knelt to caress Gran's cheek before calling Dad. She gave Dad the same news she'd told Mum. She killed the call, looked at me and said, 'He's on his way. He's gonna stay with you and Jerome while we're at the hospital.'

I nodded. I could hardly speak. 'Tha-thanks for ... for covering for me, sis.'

'What do you expect?' Elaine said. 'You're still my liccle bro. I'm still mad with your ass though. *Believe it!*'

I was scared shitless by the thought that Manjaro might return, stressed out by Gran being sparked out and fretting sweat about anyone else discovering my shit about the gun. 'He's … he's not gonna bounce back? Is he?'

Jerome had picked up a small piece of vase and had decided to see what it tasted like before Elaine scooped him up and pulled the shard from his fingers. She hugged him tightly and kissed him on the back of his head. 'I don't think so,' she finally answered. 'Once he saw Jerome, he knew the wrong he was doing.'

'Are you definitely gonna call the feds, sis?'

Elaine thought about it. 'Don't go blaming your own ass for what happened to Gran,' she said. 'I mean … I was stupid enough to go out with him in the first place … but yes, Lemar. As I said, I'll have to call the feds. *He* has to know that he can't just bust into my yard and attack *my* fam. *Who* does he think he is? He has to know he just can't do that shit.'

'I'll … I'd better clean this up,' I said, pointing at the dirt on the hallway floor.

'*Don't* move her,' Elaine instructed. 'Clear up around her. And *don't* say shit to Dad about the gun or to anyone else, you hearing me? If anyone asks about why my ex was round at our gates tell 'em he wanted to see Jerome and reason with me, right. Are you with that programme?'

'I hear you, sis.'

'If it gets out that you were keeping a firearm in your yard they'll send your liccle ass to a youth detention centre for six months or longer. Believe me on that. They won't give a damn if you're a good artist there and they won't give a shit that Gran was hurt. You'll be spending some long bitch nights dreaming about Venetia King, carrot cakes and your own comfy bed.'

That icy feeling pin-balled through my veins again. 'I'll ... I'll get the dustpan and brush.'

About ten minutes later, the ambulance arrived. The paramedics checked that Gran was breathing OK before they put a brace around her neck. One of them looked into her eyes with this torch thing. 'Concussion,' she said. 'She'll need to have a scan and an X-ray.'

'She'll be all right?' asked Elaine.

'We'll find out at the hospital,' the paramedic said.

They placed her on a stretcher and before they took her away I kissed her on her forehead. 'You'll be all right, Gran.' I hoped I was telling her the truth.

She managed a smile, raised her left arm and squeezed my hand.

'*Don't* let anybody step into the yard apart from Dad, right, Lemar,' Elaine instructed as she placed Jerome into my arms. 'Even if it's your bredren standing outside in a mad rain, don't open the freaking door. Dad should be here any minute now. I'm gonna call the feds from the hospital.'

I locked the front door but Jerome wasn't too happy that his mum left him. He cried as I brought him into the kitchen. I patted his back as I tried to take in everything that had happened. I sat down at the small kitchen table with him and made funny faces. Jerome smiled his innocent smile and then tried to eat my fingers. Man! His cute face had saved my ass. *Thank God* Gran seemed to be all right.

About a minute later, I heard a loud knock on the door.

That must be Dad, I thought. Jerome was sticking his fingers into my left ear as I carried him to the front door. *Shit! It might not be Dad. Manjaro might have returned.* I stood still for a little while. My heart started to pound again. I took a backwards step. Someone banged the door again. To my ears it sounded like a tree trunk gatecrashing a doll's house. 'Who is it?' I asked.

'Ms Harrington. Is that you, Lemar? Is everything all right in there?'

My next-door neighbour. Relief. But I can't let her in. Elaine warned me. And Ms Harrington chats too much anyway.

'Gran ... Gran's being taken to the hospital,' I said. 'I'm ... I'm not allowed to let anybody in when I'm home alone.'

'I thought I heard some banging,' she said. 'I thought I'd better check.'

'Gran fell,' I revealed.

'Oh ... give her my best.'

'Thanks for checking,' I said.

'OK, I'm going back inside. I'll call in the morning to ask about your gran.'

'Thanks.'

I returned to the kitchen and sank two more glasses of water. Just as I put the tumbler in the sink, my phone rang. It made me jump up in the air and I caught the living fright. *God! Manjaro hasn't deleted me but stress might.* I prayed the call wasn't from Manjaro or Lady P or anybody else from his crew. I took the phone out of my pocket. I looked at its face. Relief again. 'DAD' lit up the screen.

'Hi, Dad ... Elaine told you to call me when you arrived? Good thinking ... so you're downstairs ... brilliant!'

Seconds later, Dad slapped the front door. I smiled at Jerome, made him a funny face and said, 'Granddad's here!'

Jerome found the inside of my left ear much more interesting than Dad's arrival.

'Are you all right?' Dad asked as soon as I'd let him in. 'Let's hope *he* doesn't come back!'

'A bit mashed but I'll live. I hope I never see him again.'

Dad followed me into the lounge and he took Jerome. 'Elaine said that your gran was talking in the ambulance. Hopefully she'll make a full recovery.'

'She was sparked out, Dad!' I said. 'Never been so scared in my life.'

'I don't know why Elaine ever got involved with Manjaro in the first place,' Dad said, shaking his head. Guilt kicked me in the chest. It wasn't all Elaine's fault. *God! What would Dad do to my ass if he knew the real deal?* 'At the time she just wouldn't listen to me,' Dad continued. 'I ... I feel guilty cos I wasn't around. Maybe if I was—'

'It wouldn't have made any damn difference,' I cut in. 'You think Elaine listened to Mum or Gran?'

'You're probably right.' Dad nodded. Jerome escaped Dad's arms and started crawling beneath the dining table. Dad followed him with his eyes.

'How's Steff doing?' I asked.

'A lot better,' Dad replied. 'She's taking to her new medication well. Just yesterday she was pulling my hand to take her into the garden.'

'That's good to hear,' I said. I half-smiled, trying to delete the shame I was feeling inside. *What kinda big brother am I, getting involved in gang madness? What would she think of me if she knew what I'd been up to?* 'Can't … can't wait till we can get some sketching on and maybe when she's up and about I can take her to the gallery where they're showing my art.'

'She'll love all that,' Dad said. His eyes started to dampen but he wiped them dry. 'We're leaving Sunday week. It'll mean a lot to all of us if you and Elaine can spend a day with us before we leave. You think Elaine will … will come?'

'She will, Dad. Don't fret about that. She will.'

In the next four hours or so I answered calls from McKay, Jonah and Venetia. It was kinda nice that they were worried about my ass. I kept to Elaine's line that Manjaro was kicking up a fuss outside our front door cos he wanted to see his son and that was why I had to step home quick. I wasn't sure if McKay and Jonah bought it but I couldn't say a diddly about the gun with Dad there. I think Venetia believed me though. *God! I hope she never finds out what really went down.*

Mum and Elaine returned. Dad was at the table sipping a coffee and I was watching TV parked in an armchair. Jerome was sleeping in his room. On seeing Dad, Mum stopped in her tracks in the hallway. They exchanged a wary nod and a glance before Mum resumed walking.

'How's Gran?' I asked.

'She's doing good,' Elaine replied. 'She's catching sleep now. She's had a scan and an X-ray but they haven't found

264

anything serious yet apart from some bruising and swelling ...'

'They're keeping her in for observation,' added Mum. She folded her arms and looked at Dad. 'Thanks for staying here with Lemar.'

'Not a problem,' said Dad. 'Just glad I could help.'

Mum took her jacket off and sat down opposite Dad at the table. Elaine and I swapped glances. It was kinda strange to watch my parents being forced to be polite to each other.

'Let's hope that damn boy doesn't trouble our doormat again,' said Mum. 'Him *too outta order*!'

Dad nodded. 'I hope the police find him.'

'Have you two had anything to eat?' Mum asked.

I think Dad was too stunned to answer. 'No,' I said. 'I'm well peckish.'

'I'm not cooking now but I could order a pizza or something,' suggested Mum.

'I'll go halves,' offered Dad.

'Deal,' said Mum.

It didn't seem real. Elaine and I swapped an are-you-seeing-what-I'm-seeing look. 'I'm gonna check on Jerome. Lemar, come with me.'

I followed Elaine into her bedroom. Jerome had his full snooze on. She kissed him on his head and asked, 'How's he been?'

'He only fell asleep an hour ago,' I said. 'Dad was trying to rock him but he wasn't having it.'

'He's not used to him,' she said.

'Did ... did you call the feds?' I asked.

'Yes. They came to the hospital and interviewed me there. I gave 'em a statement ... Close the door, Lemar.'

I did what I was told and then parked on my sister's bed. She dropped her voice to a whisper. 'They're gonna wanna interview you too in the next day or so. You better be on point or otherwise we're all prison bait. And believe me on this. If I ever find my ass in a cell again I'll kill myself! Just tell 'em that Manjaro forced his way in and pushed Gran into the wall. I said to the feds that he was well desperate to see Jerome.'

I nodded.

'So you tell 'em the same deal, you hearing me? *Don't* tell 'em any shit about the gun.'

'Do I have to go to the fed station?'

'No,' my sister said, pulling the covers up to Jerome's neck. 'They have to interview you with an adult present, so they'll come here. I'll be with you. Maybe Mum too if she's not at work.'

I breathed out my relief.

'You done the right thing by flinging the gun in the bin, but it can't stay there,' Elaine said. 'I'm gonna have to move it and fling it somewhere it can't be found.'

'Where?'

'In the Crongton stream. There's a deep part beneath that little walk-bridge up by the flats on Dumbarton Way. You catch a world of diseases even if you dip your baby toe in that stream so I'll drop it in there.'

My head started to feel hot again. 'I'll offer to get the take-away,' Elaine said. 'And I'll jump in the freaking bin myself to get the piece. Is it in a bag or something?'

'Yeah, a black plastic bag. It was taped up in masking tape and brown paper.'

'All right, let me get changed into my sweats and when I come out I'll say I need a walk to clear my head, right?'

'Right.' I nodded.

I returned to the lounge. Dad was lipping a fresh mug of coffee. He was drumming his fingers on the dining table and kept on glancing at his watch. Mum had crashed on the sofa. She was flicking through the TV channels. 'What do you fancy?' she asked me.

'Er, I think Elaine's getting herself ready to step out and buy something.'

'It's nearly midnight,' said Dad.

Elaine emerged from her room a moment later. 'I'll get the pizza myself,' she said. 'I could do with the fresh air after spending all that time in the hospital. That sterilised smell is messing up my nostrils.'

'You're not going anywhere,' said Dad, standing up.

'I need to stretch my legs and clear my head,' argued Elaine.

'*He* could still be out there,' warned Dad.

'Trust me, he's *not* gonna trouble me now.'

'How do you know?' Dad pressed.

Elaine started to chew the inside of her cheek. She looked at Mum.

'I'm with your dad on this one,' Mum said. 'Keep your backside in the yard tonight.'

Elaine put her hands on her hips and I wondered if she was gonna launch a cuss attack. But she didn't. She chewed her cheek a little more. She stared at the armchair where Gran usually sat and said, 'I'm ... I'm sorry I ever linked up with Manjaro. Sorry ... sorry for everything.'

Her eyes started to flood. I wanted to step up to her and hug her – she had saved my ass and now she was stressed out to the max. Mum sat up but before she could say anything Elaine turned and marched back to her room. Dad went to follow her.

'Leave her for a bit,' Mum advised. 'Give her half an hour or so. Remember, she has just seen her ex-boyfriend attack her own grandmother and brother.'

Elaine had composed herself by the time the pizza arrived. Everyone was silent as they sank their meat feasts and garlic bread. Guilt was still punching my ribs and I wondered how I never spilled out the ugly truth. Mum was the first to finish and she suddenly announced, 'We might have to think about leaving this place and getting out of Crongton.'

I could see Dad wanted to reply but he sealed his beak. *God! Move? If we have to step I hope it's not too far. Don't wanna live in a wilderness.* Elaine had stopped mauling her garlic bread. She looked at Mum. 'We don't have to move,' she said. 'He's not gonna trouble us any more. I *know* him.'

'Your grandmother's in the hospital!' Mum raised her voice. 'I could put in for a transfer.'

I couldn't help but think it was my stupidness that put Gran in the hospital. I couldn't look anyone in the eye.

'The feds are gonna be hunting for him,' said Elaine. 'Trust me, he's probably miles from Crongton. And what about your job?'

But if they do catch him will he spill about my part in hiding the gun? I thought.

'Lemar and your grandmother could've been killed tonight!' spat Mum. 'And I'm not the most unemployable person in the world – I'll get another job.'

'I think we've all taken an emotional lick tonight,' said Dad. 'The main thing is that Gran is on the mend and the police know who to look for. You guys can talk about moving and everything else in the morning or when your heads are clearer. Let's get through the night.'

Emotional lick! Dad didn't know the quarter of it. If he did he'd probably lick me over the balcony.

Elaine resumed sinking her garlic bread. 'Dad's right,' she said after a while. 'This has all been traumatic.'

Our Cokes and orange juices were sunk in silence. Dad was the first to break it. 'I've gotta head out,' he said. 'Get back ... you know get back to my ...'

'Thanks again for coming around,' said Mum, staring at her plate. 'I understand that you have to get back to Stefanie.'

Everyone took a pause. Dad looked at me and then at Elaine. 'Will you spend a day with us before we leave?'

'Yes,' I said.

Elaine thought about it. 'Of course,' she finally replied, nodding. 'I wanna see my liccle sis and tell her not to forget me. Really glad that she's up and about.'

'Me too,' I added.

'It'll make Steff happy.' Dad smiled. 'And I'll do my best for Steff to see you as much as possible ... wherever you are.'

I glanced at Mum and she sort of half-smiled.

'Call me if you need anything,' offered Dad. 'Even if it's a ride to the hospital.'

'We will,' said Elaine. 'I'll hold you to that.'

I finally crashed after something past two. I laid flat on my back and stared at the ceiling. So much drama was rushing through my hard drive. The beat-down of that poor brother at Manjaro's yard, Steff being carried by Dad into his van on the way to the hospital, Nico D's red chest, Venetia crying in the school van, the gun in the black plastic bag and Manjaro cramped and paralysed by the sight of Jerome getting his crawl on in the front room.

I must've dozed off cos something woke me up in the night. My bedroom door was slowly opening. I shot up in bed. My stomach went all tight. I groped for my lamp switch. '*Who is it?*' I called out. I switched on my lamp.

'Lock down your tongue,' whispered Elaine. She had her black headscarf, tracksuit and trainers on. She didn't smell too fresh. She carefully closed the door and sat at the foot of my bed. 'Got rid of it!'

'Got rid of what?' I asked.

'The *piece*. What do you think? Had to dig it out though. You wouldn't believe what people fling in that damn bin! Had to use my phone for a light.'

'Thanks,' I said.

'I kinda owe you,' Elaine said. 'For giving you that beat-down. Anyway, I dropped it into the stream. You don't have to stress about it any more.'

'Manjaro might still wanna know where it is.'

'I don't think so.' Elaine shook her head. 'Go back to sleep. It's just gone five. I hope my brutal stench doesn't wake up Jerome.'

'It probably will,' I said. 'It woke me up.'

'Remember, now you owe me one, Lemar. And if you ever tell anyone that I once dived into a block bin your life is *over*.'

She left my room and shut the door silently behind her. I didn't hear her footsteps along the hallway.

26

A Traumatic Experience

I was on lockdown. Mum didn't let me out of the flat for two days. She took a day off from work on the first day and used most of it discussing with Elaine whether we should move out of the ends. I didn't want to go. All my bredrens were in South Crongton and I didn't wanna step into a new school and new ends and take all the hobbit and short-ass jokes. I imagined Venetia telling me to go for it but I wondered how she would really feel if she had to step out of the ends and never return.

Elaine told me that the feds were coming around to interview my ass at ten in the morning. She had cooked me a fried breakfast and while I was sinking my eggs and bacon she reminded me not to spill any shit about the gun. 'Forget about ever seeing that damn gun and having it in your possession,' she said. 'Delete that from your head. Remember, you were coming home with Gran and he was waiting for our front door to open cos he wanted to see Jerome but I wouldn't let him in.'

'I got it.'

'They interviewed Gran yesterday – she hardly remembers anything. Only Manjaro shouting at you and being slammed against the wall.'

'We're kinda lucky there,' I said.

'You ain't wrong,' said Elaine. 'So *don't mess it up!*'

The feds slapped on the door at ten on the dot. Elaine let them in. She showed them into the kitchen where I was sipping my mango juice. One was male and the other female. 'So you're Lemar?' said the female fed.

I nodded and took another sip.

'How are you feeling, Lemar? It must have been a traumatic experience.'

'You could say that,' I replied. I glanced at Elaine. She was watching me like I was stepping along a tightrope between two high slabs.

'It did shake me up,' I admitted.

'Do you think you're ready to answer just a few questions on what happened to you on the day of the incident?'

'Yes,' I said, locking my fingers together.

The male fed had already taken out his notebook. Elaine nodded slightly. I readied myself for the next question. 'Can you tell us what happened when you arrived home in the late afternoon on the twenty-seventh?'

'I ... I put my key in the door and felt someone pushing me into the door. It ... it was Manjaro. I fell over in the hallway. Gran tried to help me but he pushed her into the wall. Gran—'

'Can you slow down a bit, please, Lemar,' the officer asked.

I took in a breath. I glanced at Elaine and she nodded once more. My stomach tightened. 'Manjaro pushed Gran into the wall,' I continued. 'Gran was knocked out. He was shouting out for Elaine and Jerome. I got up but he punched me.'

'Manjaro punched you?' The female fed wanted confirmation. 'And shoved your grandmother into the wall?'

'Yes,' I said. 'He punched me twice and kicked me. It made me all dizzy.'

'What happened after that?' the officer wanted to know.

'I don't remember much. My head was spinning. I just heard him shouting and Elaine screaming, "Leave him alone! Leave him alone!" Then Elaine hit him with the vase.'

'And then?' the officer pressed.

'He got to his feet and ran out of the flat,' I answered.

'No one else was with him?'

'No,' I said.

The male fed scribbled down more notes. He swapped glances with his colleague. I wondered if they knew Manjaro was Jerome's dad.

'Is that all?' I asked, wanting the ordeal to be over.

'Yes,' the female fed replied. 'For now. Once Manjaro has been found – and that won't be easy because no one's talking – we'll arrest him and prepare a case for the CPS. We may require a fuller statement. We'll let you know of any developments.'

'What's the CPS?' I asked.

'The Crown Prosecution Service,' the fed answered. 'We have to convince them that the case is worth pursuing.'

I nodded even though I didn't fully understand.

'He's not showing it,' Elaine said. 'But my liccle bro has been proper stressed out by all this.'

'I understand, Ms Jackson.' The female fed nodded. 'Manjaro is known to us and we're doing all we can to apprehend him.'

'*Good!*' said Elaine.

'There are already extra patrols around the estate because of other incidents, and officers have been alerted to be on the lookout for Manjaro.'

'I hope you catch his ass!' Elaine spilled her anger.

She showed the feds to the door while I sank another glass of mango juice. A mad tiredness suddenly came over me and I wanted to get my snooze on. I hadn't slept properly for God knows how long.

Elaine returned to the kitchen. 'You done good, bro,' she said. 'You look like you need to go back to your bed.'

'I do,' I agreed.

'Remember Dad's taking you to the hospital later on.'

'Yeah, I asked him if I could bring McKay, Jonah and Venetia with me. They've been ringing off my phone asking if I'm all right and they wanna see Gran too.'

'That's good, bro.' Elaine smiled. 'You've got some good bredrens. Hang on to them.'

Wasn't sure my sis would've said that if she had heard McKay farting up the classroom in IT or Jonah taking pics of the fit girls during basketball practice with his damn phone. But yeah, they were good bredrens.

'Go to your bed, Lemar,' Elaine ordered. 'I've gotta wake up Jerome and give him his breakfast. You wanna look your best for when your girlfriend bounces in.'

'Venetia is *not* my girlfriend!'

'What is that thing that Gran says? Yeah ... she could be your girl if you play your dominoes right.'

Dad dropped Venetia, McKay, Jonah and me outside the hospital entrance. 'I'll be about an hour,' he said. 'I might as well make a few deliveries while you're visiting your gran – don't wanna pay the rip-off parking fees in the hospital car park. Make sure you're standing here when I return.'

'Thanks, Dad.'

'Give my best to your gran!'

Dad indicated and pulled away. My bredrens had been quiet in the van and I could see McKay was bursting to say something. 'You sketched a portrait of Venetia, right, Bit—'

'It was brilliant,' interrupted Venetia. She was sniffing the flowers she had bought for Gran and Jonah was carrying a large slice of rum cake wrapped in foil that his mum had baked.

'So I hear,' said McKay. 'And I give you ratings for that. Can you do a sketch of me flinging the shot-put? I wanna nice up my hallway with it.'

'And I want a sketch of me running on the track and leaving nuff brothers behind,' added Jonah. 'And can you draw steam coming off my spikes? *Don't* make me ugly, Bit!'

A Traumatic Experience

Venetia got her chuckle on as we entered the hospital. I read the scrap of paper that told me what ward Gran was on. 'That'll be ten pounds each,' I said.

'Ten notes!' McKay raised his voice. He looked proper scandalised. 'How many times have you parked in my yard and sampled my dad's fried chicken wings, breasts and legs? Let's not even talk about the fries! About a million times, bruv! Did I ever charge you for one skinny liccle wing? Or one chip? *No!* Liberties!'

'I paid him ten pounds,' said Venetia. 'It was worth it. Sergio loves it to the max.'

'Who's Sergio?' wondered McKay.

'Yeah, who's Sergio?' repeated Jonah.

'Er ... just a guy I know,' answered Venetia.

I tried not to let the mention of *that* name spoil my vibe. If he loved the portrait that much he should've been forced to eat the damn thing – with a side of glass!

'I haven't known you for too long,' said McKay to Venetia, 'so don't be offended. But are you freaking nuts? Trust me, Bit would've paid *you* ten pounds to park yourself in his yard and to let him get his sketch on. In fact you could've charged twenty pounds just to say hi to him.'

God! I thought. *She must never find out about the money Manjaro gave me for hiding the gun. She'd never chat to me again and she'll be forever riding on that damn Sergio's motorbike.*

'And you're not getting ten pounds from me!' said Jonah. 'You must've sunk a thousand of my mum's chocolate butterfly cakes and did I charge you? No! And don't think I never realised that you jacked biscuits and shit when I wasn't looking! And I have to pay ten pounds for you to do a sketch of me? You're taking the living piss. I should sue your liccle ass. If you were a true bredren you'd offer to do portraits of all my family ... and my cousins, aunts and uncles too.'

We stepped into a lift and I could see Venetia trying to delete her giggles. There was a doctor reading a chart with us and a guy wearing a dressing gown with his foot in plaster. Thankfully, by the time we stepped out of the lift my bredrens had calmed down a bit.

'Lemar wants to be an artist but what do you guys wanna be when you finish school?' Venetia asked.

McKay didn't have to think about it. 'Own a world of fried chicken takeaway shops. Yeah, man! But I wouldn't have one in Crongton though.'

'Why not?' I asked.

'Cos bruvs like you will be begging for discount,' answered McKay. 'Nah, bruv, I can't be bothered to deal with that. I don't care *who* you are, you have to pay for my shit. No one's getting any freeness. Not even fit girls. No offence, Venetia.'

'What about you, Jonah?' asked Venetia, still trying hard not to laugh.

'Olympic one-hundred-metre champion,' he replied. 'Yes, bredren. And I'll make sure they pay me a million a year just to advertise a smartphone or something. If my agent can't get me that then his ass is sacked.'

'What if you get an injury?' wondered Venetia.

'Then I'll be the Paralympic wheelchair champion,' laughed Jonah. 'Legs, wheels or blades, no one's getting past me.'

I looked at the scrap of paper again but I wasn't sure if we were on the right floor. I rolled in front of a nurse to get her attention. 'Excuse me, can you show me the way to St Saviour's ward please?'

'Keep on going, take the right at the end of the corridor and it's the third ward on the left.'

'Thanks.'

Gran was resting against a family of pillows. She was wearing Granddad's tatty dressing gown and a black, green and yellow headscarf – the Jamaican colours. She spotted me and my bredrens and her face lit up.

Venetia presented the flowers. 'We hope you're feeling better,' she said awkwardly.

Jonah gave Gran the slice of rum cake. 'Look forward to seeing you back on the block,' he said. 'Mum says that when you're up for it to come on down and help sample her rum.'

'Thank you so much,' Gran said, her voice cracking. I could hardly bear to see her propped up in a hospital bed. For the first time in my life, she actually looked ancient – and it was all my fault. 'You're very kind taking time out to see this old woman.' She turned her gaze on me. I forced myself not to look away.

'No worries,' I said, trying to smile. 'Can't wait to have you back home.' It felt as though Gran had CCTV to see into my soul. Man! I hoped I was wrong. *She wouldn't love what she'd find there, I told myself. No cute liccle grandson who likes to watch her bake cakes but a guy who hides guns for Gs.* My bredrens were watching me closely. Jonah and McKay knew the deal with Manjaro. Had they guessed what part I'd had to

play in Gran's injuries? Did they think I was a living, breathing hypocrite?

'You haven't got long to wait,' Gran interrupted my
thoughts and smiled. 'The doctor will check on me in the
morning and if he thinks it's all right then I can go home.'

'That's all good,' said McKay. 'And sorry I didn't bring you
any chocolates or fruit or something. My budget's a bit low
and my dad has got my pocket money on lockdown – he says
I buy too many sweets.'

'Don't worry about not bringing anything,' said Gran. 'Just
pay attention and do well in school and I'll take that as a gift.
And *that* goes for all of you!'

'We will,' said Venetia. 'You have to study hard if you wanna
get out of Crongton.'

'No matter how hard I study I still don't get maths,' joked
Jonah.

Only Gran didn't get her giggle on. 'Listen me,' she said,
searching all of our eyes. Her hand reached for mine and I let
her take it. I wasn't going to fret about anyone laughing at me
now. 'You're all good at someting. *Everyone* is blessed with
some kind of talent.'

We all nodded. I was lucky – I had my art. Was that my road
out of this mess? Had Venetia been right all along? Should I
think about stepping away from Crongton, too? I might not
have a choice. After all, Manjaro's bad ass was still out there
somewhere, and I wasn't gonna hold my breath waiting for
the feds to slap handcuffs around his wrists.

'Now come here and give your grandmother a hug.' Gran
smiled and pulled me weakly towards her.

'Here?' I said. Now embarrassment really was hotting up my cheeks.

'Yes – right here!' she cried. Venetia gave me a gentle shove and my bredrens hid their mouths behind their hands.

I leaned towards Gran and she gave me one of her tightest bear hugs. I could hear Jonah and McKay giggle behind me but I didn't care. Despite the mistakes I'd made – and I'd made some big ones – Gran was coming home. Elaine had saved my ass like the good big sis she used to be and Mum seemed to be back on point to some kind of happiness. I'd even get to see Dad and Steff, despite them moving.

As I pulled away from Gran, my phone vibrated in my back pocket.

'Lemar!' Gran chided. 'You shouldn't even have your phone switched on in a hospital.'

'You gonna get that?' Jonah asked darkly.

'No,' I said, pulling out my phone and switching it off. I refused to even look at the screen. 'Not now.' Whoever it was could wait.

About the Author

Born in 1963 to Jamaican parents living in Brixton, ALEX WHEATLE spent most of his childhood in a Surrey children's home. As a teenager he was a founder member of the Crucial Rocker sound system, writing lyrics about everyday Brixton life and performing under the DJ name Yardman Irie. He spent a short stint in prison following the Brixton uprising of 1981; following his release from prison he continued to write poems and lyrics and became known as the Brixton Bard.

Alex teaches in various places including Lambeth College, holds workshops in prisons and is frequently invited to schools to speak to students, inspiring in them a passion for literature with his own story. He was awarded an MBE in the Queen's Birthday Honours list for services to literature in 2008. Alex's first novel, *Brixton Rock*, was published to critical acclaim in 1999, with six more following. *Liccle Bit* is his first Young Adult novel.